"One of these days you'll take me seriously," Jaimie warned.

Matthew looked at her. Her soft hands were folded primly in her lap, that outrageous, citified diamond bracelet of hers twinkling in the sunlight.

She was a walking, talking temptation for him to forget the reasons he shouldn't get involved with her.

For one thing, she was an employee. A temporary one at that.

More important, she would get hurt, sure as God made little green apples. Because Matthew had no intention of getting serious about anyone, much less a city girl so obviously unsuited to life at the Double-C.

They were fine reasons, Matthew told himself.

But they didn't keep his hand from lifting and skimming down Jaimie's oh, so tempting velvety cheek.

"Oh, sweetheart, I take you seriously," he growled. "Don't you ever doubt it."

MARRY ME,
Cowboy

THE RANCHER
AND THE REDHEAD
Allison Leigh

RAWHIDE
& Lace

Silhouette Books

Published by Silhouette Books
America's Publisher of Contemporary Romance

For Austin
Always

 SILHOUETTE BOOKS

ISBN 0-373-65335-2

THE RANCHER AND THE REDHEAD

Copyright © 1998 by Allison Lee Kinnaird

Visit Silhouette Books at www.eHarlequin.com

Printed in U.S.A.

ALLISON LEIGH

Allison Leigh started writing early by penning a Halloween play that her grade-school class performed. Since then, though her tastes have changed, her love for reading has not. And her writing appetite simply grows more voracious by the day.

She has been a finalist in the RITA® Award and the Holt Medallion contests. But the true highlights of her day as a writer occur when she receives word from a reader that they laughed, cried or lost a night of sleep while reading one of her books.

Born in Southern California, Allison has lived in several different cities in four different states. She has been, at one time or another, a cosmetologist, a computer programmer and a secretary. She has recently begun writing full-time after spending nearly a decade as an administrative assistant for a busy neighborhood church, and currently makes her home in Arizona with her family. She loves to hear from her readers, who can write to her at P.O. Box 40772, Mesa, AZ 85274-0772.

Please address questions and book requests to:
Silhouette Reader Service
U.S.: 3010 Walden Ave., P.O. Box 1325, Buffalo, NY 14269
Canadian: P.O. Box 609, Fort Erie, Ont. L2A 5X3

Prologue

The ranch is no place for a soft man. How many times had his dad drilled that fact into his head?

He might only be nine years old, but Matt considered himself a man. He wasn't as old as Sawyer, true, but he was big and strong enough to pull his weight at the ranch. To handle a man's responsibilities.

But standing behind his father, looking at the empty hospital bed, he felt the sick lump in his throat grow and grow until he thought he'd puke. Or start bawling like a baby. The way his little brother, Daniel, had cried all last night in bed, scared when their dad had carted her off in the truck to the hospital, bleeding and far, far too still. The fact that it was near blizzarding outside had only made things worse. He had stood in the too-quiet, too-empty front room of the big house and stared through the window at the dark, not needing to see the wall of snow that fell to know that it was still coming down, wet and heavy and blowing.

Finally Matthew had gone into Daniel's room and held

him on his lap until the kid had stopped crying and fallen asleep. Even Jefferson, seven and stoic, had joined him in Danny's room, climbing onto the top bunk before going to sleep. Eventually Sawyer had joined them, throwing himself on the floor, covering his eyes with a bent arm. He didn't have anything to say and had looked like he would hit anyone who was dumb enough to speak to *him*. Not that anyone had felt like talking. Except Danny, who now and then had mumbled in his sleep.

Matthew hadn't slept at all. Every time he'd closed his eyes, all he'd seen was the way she'd looked when he'd found her, crumpled in the white snow outside the old barn, blood pooling around her legs, soaking through her thick coat and the bright red dress she'd been wearing for Christmas Eve. Soaking into the white, white snow.

Gritting his teeth, he swiped a hand across his nose and banished the visions from his head. From down the hallway, he could hear the nurses singing "Silent Night." For a second he wished that he'd stayed with his brothers and not wangled that ride with a trucker here to the hospital. "What about the…you know…the baby."

His father, strong and proud and never given to obvious emotion, turned toward him. Grief etched hard lines in an already hard face. His jaw worked, though no tears softened the man's stark, ice-blue eyes. "He's fine. We'll name him Tristan. Like she wanted." He cleared his throat. "The doctor said he'll be ready to leave the hospital in a day or two."

They would all go home to the ranch. Everyone but *her*.

His mother.

"Dad?"

His father looked at him. He hadn't called him Dad for more than a year now. "What is it, boy?"

It took a minute for Matthew to get the words out, steady and strong, the way a Clay was expected to be. "What are we gonna do without her?"

Squire Clay turned back to look at the neatly made bed. His shoulders seemed to sag for a moment. "I don't know, son. I don't know."

Chapter One

Thirty years later

She was going to fall.

His heart lodged painfully in his throat as Matthew Clay looked up into the barn rafters and watched red-stockinged feet slowly inch along the rough beam high above his head. His fingers curled. The crazy woman was going to have splinters in her feet from now until spring. If she lived that long.

"Here kitty, kitty."

Her soft voice floated down, and he closed his eyes for a moment. But he couldn't *not* watch and he looked up again, fully expecting to see her tumble from the beam at any moment, plunging forty feet to the unforgiving ground.

She was down on her knees now, nearing the cross beam. One slender hand reached out toward the gray ball of fur huddling a few feet from her fingertips, and the other hand was braced on the beam. Dark hair fell past her elbows as she inched forward, and even in the subdued light of the barn he could see glints of red fire shimmer in the luxurious auburn waves.

She was going to fall.

He wanted to yell at her. Call her a fool. But she didn't know he was standing here, below her. If he made a sound, he would startle her. And she would fall for sure.

He wondered what he'd done wrong in his life to deserve this.

"Come on, kitty, kitty," she sang softly, encouragingly. The cat's only response was to meow once, then leisurely begin bathing herself.

He saw her shoulders sag for a moment, then she was inching forward again.

"Here kitty, kitty. Come here you ornery cat." Her voice never lost that soothing lilt. "Come on." She stopped abruptly, lifted her hand and looked at it.

Splinters, he thought.

"Come here, kitty. If you ever want me to sneak you another can of tuna, you'd better come here. Kitty, kitty." She inched forward again.

Matthew picked up the sound of boots crunching in the snow and he turned to the yawning entrance of the barn just as his father appeared. He lifted his hand in warning. Squire Clay frowned, then looked up in the direction of Matthew's lifted thumb. To Matthew's disgust his father seemed to find the sight of that redhead's death wish utterly amusing. Even Sandy, the golden retriever, who sat next to Matthew's leg, wagged her tail with enthusiasm.

Suddenly the woman snatched up the cat and cradled her in one arm while she maneuvered herself around to straddle the rafter. Her legs dangled on either side of the beam and she sat for a moment, cuddling the cat. Then she looked down. "Hi, Squire," she called. "How're you feeling this morning?"

Squire scratched his chin. "Fair as the weather."

Matthew muttered darkly. Several feet of snow covered the ground outside the barn.

The woman's eyes shifted his direction. "Morning, Matthew. Happy Valentine's Day." Her smile was bright and vivid. Just a little bit crooked. Just a lot sexy.

She wasn't going to fall...he was going to climb up there after her and push her off. Matthew drew in a slow breath. Exhaled it even slower. "Get. Down. Now."

Her smile dimmed several watts. Then she shrugged. "Sure." Still holding the cat, she swung her legs up onto the rafter and rose. Without a wobble, she walked across it, as surely as a practiced gymnast on a balance beam.

He could feel the gray hairs sprouting all over his head.

"I remember you boys climbing around up there like that," Squire commented.

Matthew snorted as he moved across to the ladder built against the wall. "Kids." He looked up to watch that crazy female, still cradling the cat, curl her feet over the rungs as she began her descent. He watched her to make sure she didn't fall, he told himself. Not because of those ridiculously snug jeans she wore. "We were kids," he reiterated. The slender curves descending toward him were anything but childlike. "Adults oughta know better."

She suddenly jumped lightly to the ground, skipping the last several rungs, and he didn't move fast enough. Her pointed elbow glanced off his chest and the crown of her head bumped his jaw.

He swore inwardly and hoped he hadn't bitten off a chunk of tongue.

Jaimie Greene shook her head to clear the hair from her eyes. "Sorry," she said breathlessly. D.C. purred contentedly beneath her arm, and she focused her attention for a moment on the pregnant cat. It was better than looking into the icy blue eyes of the irritated man glaring down at her.

It was just her luck that he'd come upon her while she'd

been rafter walking. "It didn't take me long," she started to explain. "Just a few minutes. Up and down."

"I don't care if it took you all day," he said. "Stay off the rafters. I want your word," he added, inflexible as always.

"Fine. But really, I was perfectly safe—" He cut her off with one look. Matthew Clay had that look perfected. The first time she'd been on the receiving end of it had been a year and a half ago. It had been her first of many visits to the Double-C, and she'd accidentally backed one of his pickup trucks into a fence post. Half a dozen of his precious calves had gotten loose. It had *not* been one of her finer moments. She patted D.C. again and gently placed her on the ground. Sandy padded over and leaned heavily against her leg and she scratched the dog's head. "I had to get her down," she began again, reasonably. "She was stuck up there."

"That stupid cat got *up* there all on her own. She'd have come down when she was ready." Matthew glared at her. "Don't go up there again."

Mentally Jaimie clicked her heels and snapped off a smart salute. Physically, however, she controlled the urge, instead pointing at the animal in question. "She's pregnant. Her balance might be off. What if she fell?"

"What if *you* fell?"

"Don't be silly. I taught gymnastics at a children's activity center for a while. I was perfectly steady up there." She looked hopefully at Squire for support.

As usual, he didn't fail her. "Leave the girl be, Matt," Squire said. "Everybody's got their feet on the ground again."

Matthew, fists propped on narrow hips below the sheepskin jacket he wore, looked from his father to her. He huffed, clearly annoyed, then stomped out of the barn. Sandy, faithful dog that she was, followed. Even D.C. sprang after him.

"Traitor," Jaimie muttered after the departing feline.

Squire looked over at Jaimie, and she had to smile. His eyes were exactly the same translucent hue as his son's, but Squire's contained a decided twinkle. Something that Matthew's definitely lacked. And that was a pity indeed.

She gingerly brushed her palms together, wondering how on earth she would get out all the splinters. "See my shoes anywhere?"

"Over there." Squire pointed toward the bedraggled pair she'd left lying beside a stack of feed sacks.

"Right. Thanks." They once had been a pristine white. But the past seven weeks working around the Double-C ranch had taken their toll. She stuck her feet into them, grimacing at the cold, wet feel of the canvas. Joining Squire by the barn door, she shivered as the cold air penetrated the heavy, knit sweater she wore over a thermal undershirt. She would hesitate to say the barn's interior was toasty, but it was considerably warmer than it was outside.

"Where's your coat, girl?"

"I forgot it. I was trying to feed D.C. It was only going to take a minute."

"Hell's bells," Squire muttered. "There's three feet of snow out there." Even as he spoke, he was shrugging out of his own dark blue parka and tossing it around her shoulders. "How can a person forget their coat?"

Jaimie just shrugged. She knew he didn't really expect an answer. Still, she didn't need to take the man's coat. He'd barely been out of the hospital six months since his heart attack and surgery.

He waved off her protest before she could voice it. "How's Maggie feeling this morning?"

Her sister-in-law had been up pacing half the night. "She was sleeping when I left their house this morning," she told Squire. They stepped out from the shelter of the barn, and the new day's sunshine reflecting off the white snow nearly blinded her. Their breath created rings of white clouds about their heads as they tromped across the snow-plowed road toward the big house. She wasn't sure she would ever get used to a Wyoming winter. It was about as foreign to her Southern Arizona-bred nature as it could get.

"I remember when my Sarah was pregnant with Matthew. She couldn't keep a thing down, either. Not for the first five months or so, as I recall. Lost weight she couldn't afford to lose." He dropped his arm over Jaimie's shoulder and led her up the back steps of the main house, which he occupied with two of his sons, Matthew and Daniel. "Everything turned out okay in the end, though." He stomped his boots on the linoleum floor, leaving a trail of dirt and melting snow. "Maggie'll be okay, too. Mark my words."

Jaimie sighed and slipped out of the parka. "I hope so," she murmured. She loved Maggie as much as she would a real sister. Was, in fact, closer to Maggie than she was to her brother, Joe. "She still has two months to go before she's due." She slipped off her own shoes and eyed the muddy floor. It was her job to clean up that mess.

For the briefest of moments she thought longingly of the clerical job in nearby Weaver that she'd given up in December when she'd taken over here at the ranch for Maggie. She hadn't had to mop a single floor in that office. Of course, she'd been busy avoiding the roving hands of Bennett Ludlow, her boss.

Now that she thought about it, muddy floors were preferable.

"Ignore that." Squire took her elbow and led her through the inner door into the warmth of the big kitchen. "Sit and have some coffee with me first."

"You're tempting me again," Jaimie protested halfheartedly. "You know Matthew told me to get that mudroom cleaned up today."

"Oh, forget Matthew for a few minutes. That mess ain't going nowhere. Besides, there's no point in having a pretty girl around, if ya can't tempt her." He grinned slyly.

"You are a bad influence," she accused tartly. A bad influence, a man whose stubbornness was legendary in these parts—or so she'd heard—and in the past several weeks, one of her favorite people. Oh, he was gruff and pretended to be hard-bitten. But she knew better.

He was like a beautifully grilled steak. Singed and crispy on the outside, perhaps. But inside he was as soft and tender as butter. Look at the way he often checked in on Maggie, or the way he tossed Jaimie a droll smile whenever Matthew was taking her to task for some foolish thing or other. Like in the barn just now.

Yes, she was fond of Squire Clay. And bad influence or not, she pushed him toward his favorite chair at the oblong table that occupied the center of the spacious kitchen, then took down two mugs and filled them with the steaming brew from the pot that was always kept full and hot. She handed one of the mugs to Squire, along with a saucer from the cupboard, before sitting down at the table across from him.

She just loved sitting with the man over coffee. Delighted in the way he would pour his hot coffee from the mug into that delicate saucer, then proceed to drink his coffee from it. She understood why he did it. She was still gingerly sipping her own blindingly hot coffee when he'd finished drinking two full mugs' worth.

"I don't see how you never spill," she said as he poured more coffee into the saucer.

Squire got up and retrieved another saucer. He plunked it down beside her. "Try it yourself."

She looked from her full mug to the saucer. "Don't you have one that's not so flat? Where's the coffee supposed to stay on that thing?"

He chuckled. "Chicken."

"You don't fight fair," Jaimie muttered. She rolled her eyes, then carefully poured a small measure of coffee onto the saucer. She managed to lift it up and place it in her hand, balanced lightly on the tips of her fingers, just the way Squire did it, without spilling. She even managed to gingerly swallow the first sip or two.

Until she noticed the man silently standing in the doorway leading to the dining room, and she spilled the entire saucer down her ivory sweater. "Don't you laugh," she warned him, hastily whipping the sweater over her head. She quickly took it to the faucet and stuck it under running water.

Matthew couldn't have laughed if his life depended on it. Not when his tongue was stuck to the roof of his mouth at the sight of her smooth curves lovingly outlined by that pink undershirt. He wondered vaguely when long johns started coming in pink with little red hearts on them, then caught the knowing glint in his father's eyes.

Perfect. Just perfect.

He almost turned around and headed back to his office and those invoices that were giving him fits. It was bad enough that he couldn't turn around these days without finding *her* underfoot. But he would be hanged if he would let that redhead run him out of his own kitchen.

He'd come for coffee. And that's what he would get.

He had to reach past her for a mug, and as he did so, he could smell the lemony scent of the shampoo she used. She slid him a look from those dark green eyes. His "What?" was more of a growl than a question.

She raised an eyebrow. "Grumpy today, aren't you? Didn't you eat your prunes for breakfast?"

Sass. That's what she'd been giving him from the day she stepped onto the Double-C. Sass. "Haven't *had* breakfast yet," he reminded her pointedly. "The cook was crawling around on the barn rafters."

At least she had the grace to lower those slanting green eyes.

"Well, fine then." She left the sweater in the sink under a steady trickle of water. "What would you like this morning? Pancakes? Waffles?'' Already she was opening cupboards. Her lilting voice dripped with meekness. ''Eggs Benedict? Crepes Suzette?''

Sass. ''Forget it.'' He reached for the coffee and splashed it into his mug. Ignoring the smirk on his father's face, he headed back to those invoices.

Closed in the sanctuary of his office, Matt leaned back in his chair and scrubbed his hands over his face. She was driving him nuts. Right up the proverbial wall. If it weren't for the fact that she was here purely to help out Maggie right now, he would tell Jaimie to go. The woman had no business being on a ranch. She was a city girl, and she needed to go back where she belonged. He would pay for the plane ticket himself, as long as she got out of his hair.

But she *was* here to help her sister-in-law. Maggie was the Double-C's cook-housekeeper and the wife of Matthew's foreman, Joe Greene. And Maggie was pregnant and sicker than any person deserved. Nearly seven months along, she'd already been hospitalized three times with complications. So when Maggie was ordered off her feet for the remainder of her pregnancy by her obstetrician, it had seemed natural that Jaimie step in to pick up the slack.

The Double-C needed a housekeeper and a cook, if they weren't all going to starve to death. Matt could cook enough to keep himself alive, but Squire's diet was more exacting since his heart attack and surgery last year. He couldn't live on bacon and eggs. The prospects for hiring someone to temporarily fill Maggie's duties hovered somewhere between slim and none. Not many folks were willing to move out to their remote corner of the world in the summer, much less the dead of winter.

Which left Matt stuck with Jaimie. She'd quit her job in town, and instead of spending the odd weekend here and there visiting her brother and sister-in-law, she'd left behind the room she'd rented and moved, lock, stock and barrel, to Joe's house at the Double-C. Until Maggie was able to resume her regular duties, Matt couldn't see any way of telling Jaimie to go. It was that simple.

And that impossible.

At least she could cook, he thought. He rubbed the crick in his neck and sipped at the hot coffee. Turning in his chair, he looked out the wide, uncurtained window. Sandy padded over from her usual spot behind the desk where she often slept. He absently rubbed the silky head she propped on his knee.

He waited for the sight of the neatly snowplowed road, solidly built outbuildings and snow-covered fields beyond to soothe him as it usually did.

He was a man born and bred to run this place. The Double-C. Oh, he and his four brothers knew that they all shared equally in the ownership, profits and losses included, of the ranch. But they all knew, just as well, that it was Matt's at heart. He loved it the most. The only one who willingly gave it his life. His love. Just as Squire had, before he'd turned the reins over to him several years ago.

Matthew had known as a child that he never wanted to leave this particular stretch of seemingly endless land. And since the day his father had placed the Double-C in his hands, he hadn't wanted for another thing. His days were consumed with the 1001 details of running their prosperous holdings. His nights were spent sleeping the sleep of a satisfied man.

Until lately. Until that...*redhead*...came to stay.

He muttered an oath, not the least bit soothed. Sandy looked up at him with a little bark, and he grimaced. He gave the dog a final scratch, then raked his fingers through his own hair and resolutely turned his attention back to the stack of invoices sitting on his desk. His computer hadn't been any help at all, and he was doing things the old-fashioned way. He picked up his pencil and started running the totals. Again.

When the soft knock sounded on the door, he was no

closer to putting his finger on the gnawing problem than he had been a week ago, when he'd first noticed the discrepancy. "Yeah!" He jabbed the Clear button on the adding machine and began again.

The door opened and a tray appeared, followed closely by Jaimie. Sandy's nails clicked softly as she slipped out, but Matthew barely noticed. Surprise held him still as Jaimie nudged aside a stack of newspapers and set the tray on the corner of his wide desk.

He looked at the fluffy omelet accompanied by bacon— brown and crispy just the way he liked—and a mound of country-style hash browns. Not the grated up, sissy kind, but chunks of potatoes, liberally spiced with tomatoes, onions and lots of pepper. There was at least one good thing he could say about Jaimie, he acknowledged. She cooked a heck of a breakfast.

He could've done without the heart-shaped paper sticking out of the side of the hash browns. But by now he was almost getting used to it. There had been Christmas tree cutouts over the holidays. Now hearts for Valentine's Day. No doubt she had a stash of green paper somewhere, just waiting to cut out shamrocks for St. Patrick's.

Hallmark probably loved her.

"Breakfast," she announced, looking down her straight little nose at him.

"So I see." He thought it was mighty nice of him not to mention that the meal was more than a few hours late.

She gave a haughty little sniff and swiveled on her heel. But the effect was ruined when she abruptly lifted her foot, teetering awkwardly for a moment. She shot him a defiant look over her shoulder and straightened, walking across the oak-planked floor with a stiff gait.

Matthew cast a swift, longing glance at the hot food. He tossed down his pencil and caught her before she could sashay out the door. "Hold it, Red. What's wrong with your foot? A splinter, I'll bet." He took one look at her mutinous

expression. "But you'd rather eat cow pies than admit it."
He shook his head and steered her toward the desk. "Sit,"
he ordered, nudging the newspapers over even further to
make room for her. *"Sit."*

"I'll bet you don't order Maggie around like this," she
said, finally perching on the edge.

Matthew's laugh was short on humor. "Maggie doesn't
crawl around on barn rafters." He pulled the white first aid
kit off the top of the filing cabinet and flipped it open. "She
has more sense." He pushed through the contents until he
found the tweezers. "Okay, let's have it."

He saw the way she looked at her foot. And the exact
spot on him that she would have liked to plant it. "It's
Valentine's Day," he warned softly, then gestured. "Be
nice. Now give me your foot."

Her lips twitched. She sighed, then lifted her foot. "The
splinter is in my heel."

Matthew took her foot in his hand and started pulling off
the bright red sock. "This is damp." He peeled it off and
dropped it on the floor. "You're gonna get sick walking
around with wet feet. What were you doing? Finally mopping the floors?" He held on to her heel when she huffed
and started pulling it out of his hand. "Well?"

"Well what?"

Lord, give him patience. "Why are your socks wet?"

"Why do you care?" Jaimie flushed and wanted to re-
tract the words, but they were already out there. And she'd
earned herself another one of the "looks."

She braced her weight on her hands and leaned back
slightly while he studied the heel of her chilled foot. She
closed her eyes, thinking that she wouldn't mind having
Matthew Clay bending her over his sturdy wooden desk,
for a reason entirely other than splinter removal. Her eyes
flew open as she banished *that* thought. Lately it seemed
like thoughts of that nature had been springing into her
mind with far too much ease.

"Hold still," he murmured.

"I am."

He merely arched an eyebrow and took a firmer grasp on her wriggling foot.

"That hurts," she complained.

"Sue me." Her foot felt ridiculously small and cold, as his hand, usually as steady as steel, hovered over the minuscule edge of the splinter. Her toes curled and he found himself studying the bright red polish on her toenails, vaguely surprised that she hadn't somehow figured a way to paint hearts on them.

"Can't you see it?"

"Yeah, I see it."

"Then what's taking you so long?"

"Would you quit wiggling?"

She pushed herself up. "Look, it's somewhere on the heel. Just right th—"

Matthew's head lifted and she went silent. Six inches, maybe, separated their noses. Fascinated, he watched her wide eyes. They were as green as the moss that grew on the rocks down by the swimming hole in the springtime. The pupils dilated. The tip of her tongue slipped over her lips, and his attention zeroed in on the glisten of her lower lip.

"Matthew?"

He blinked and cleared his throat, staring stupidly at the tweezers in his hand as if he'd never seen them before. "Hold still, I said." He bent over and quickly worked the splinter from her heel.

He heard her sigh faintly as he turned to flick the splinter into the trash can beside his desk. She muttered her thanks in a begrudging tone that made him want to smile.

"Any more?" He took her hand before she could tuck it in her back pocket. "Jaimie," he asked, when her fingers curled protectively into her palm. "Let me see." He nudged her palm flat. Sure enough he found three splinters on the tips of her index and middle fingers. In seconds he had them removed. "The other one?"

He knew she didn't want to give him her other hand. He could tell by the way she gave that little shake of her head. The one that cleared the bangs from her eyes. She always did that when she didn't want to do something.

She did that little shake a lot whenever he was around.

He waited patiently, confident that he could outwait her. He waited, and watched how the sunshine filling his office struck her vibrant hair. Finally she grimaced and pulled her hand out of her pocket, holding it up for him to see. A glittering strand of diamonds winked up at him from her wrist. He'd told her more than once that she was going to lose that bracelet, working around the ranch.

"Thought you said your bracelet was your good-luck charm," he said smoothly. Every time he saw the wink of those diamonds, he wanted to shuffle her back to the city where she so obviously belonged. "Guess that luck doesn't extend to warding off splinters."

"I didn't fall off the rafters though, did I?" She smiled, challenge written clearly in her emerald eyes.

True. When he found himself studying her eyelashes, so thick and brown, he dragged his attention back where it belonged—to the splinter dug into the underside of her thumb. "That's gotta hurt." He could see the shard of wood angling beneath the pale skin. It was three times the size of the other splinters.

She shrugged. "I can get it," she said. "Your breakfast is getting cold."

"Breakfast'll keep." With the tip of the tweezers, he tested the edge of the splinter. "It's in there good, isn't it." He turned around slightly, lifting her palm to the bright light streaming in the window. "Almost…got it…there." He held the ragged wood splinter up for their inspection. "Nasty." He wiped it onto the edge of the trash can and tossed the tweezers back into the first aid kit, then swabbed the area with an antiseptic pad and covered it with a bandage strip. "That'll teach you to rafter walk."

She abruptly pulled her hand away, smoothing down the bandage herself. "I suppose *you've* never climbed up in the rafters. I climbed up there to get D.C. and I'd do it again."

She tossed her head back to glare up at him, and her hair, unruly and glorious, fell past her shoulders, almost to the small of her back. It occurred to him that she really was magnificent when annoyed.

"I'd have thought you would care a little more about the cat you named after the Double-C. And I know she's your cat, 'cause Squire told me," she finished with a "so there" look.

"There's always been a cat or two around this place." He wasn't taking ownership of that animal. "You think I named that flea-bitten mothball after the Double-C?"

She rolled her eyes. "D.C. Double-C. It doesn't take a rocket scientist."

His hands were at her throat before he knew what had happened. They wrapped around the smooth creaminess, his thumbs pushing her impudent chin up until she looked him in the face. He liked seeing her green eyes widen between those lush eyelashes. He really liked surprise finally silencing her. He lowered his head toward hers until he could feel her breath, soft and unsteady, on his lips. "Damn cat," he said softly.

Her hands were on his wrists. "'Scuse me?"

"*Damn* cat. Not Double-C."

Her lashes lowered. "Oh."

He looked at her lips. At the high color of her cheeks. A portion of his mind wondered whether she would taste like the dark, rich coffee she made every morning.

A saner part of his mind demanded to know what the heck he was doing thinking such things.

Jaimie swayed when he dropped his hands suddenly as if she'd grown horns. She watched him round his desk and sit down, pulling the breakfast tray toward him as if nothing at all had just happened. As if the air hadn't been snapping and sizzling between them.

She huffed and bent to pick up her sock.

"You didn't tell me why your socks are wet."

She nodded, marveling. "You know, you're right."

"Jaimie—"

"They're wet because my shoes were wet. Okay?"

"And your shoes are wet because…?"

"Snow does that when it melts." She flipped the sock and started putting her foot inside. Then decided against it at the cold, clammy feel of it.

His lips tightened. "Didn't you get boots yet?"

"No."

"Why not? I told you that you needed to get some boots. This is a ranch. Not some vacation resort in Arizona."

"And when the great Matthew speaks we jump," she muttered, bending over to remove the second sock.

"You do, if you want to work here. I told you a long time ago that those canvas tennis shoes were little better than nothing. If you can't be bothered to get some in town, why haven't you borrowed a pair of Maggie's? Or there's probably a pair in Emily's room, still. She always kept extra boots here for when she visited."

Jaimie thought of her petite, blond sister-in-law. And of Emily, Matthew's even more petite, delicate, brunette sister-in-law. "Well, that would be fine," she said with exaggerated patience, feeling like an Amazon for even having to point out the fact to him. "Except their feet are about two sizes smaller than mine."

He shrugged. "So get your own pair. Like I told you to."

She propped her fists on her hips. "And how do I do that? Hmm? You told me never to get behind the wheel of one of your precious vehicles again. That I was to keep myself in the house where I couldn't do any serious damage. Remember?''

Actually, he had forgotten he'd told her that. His temper had gotten away from him when she'd managed, yet again, to back one of the pickup trucks into a fence post. The woman was truly a menace behind the wheel of a truck. In the year and a half since her first visit to the ranch, she'd managed to back three different trucks into three different fences. And that was during the time when she'd spent only weekends with her brother and Maggie.

He wondered if she had better luck in Drive than Reverse. It was probably just as well that the woman didn't own her own vehicle now.

Still, he couldn't have her going around the place without suitable boots. She would probably end up with pneumonia or something. He didn't need that on his conscience, too.

''I have to go to Gillette this afternoon.'' He picked up his fork. ''We'll get what you need then.''

She was silent for so long that he looked up from his food.

''Is that an invitation?'' Her voice was all silky and smooth, and if he'd been a fearful man, he would have ducked at the knives shooting from her bright eyes.

''Call it what you want.'' He forked a bite of fluffy omelet into his mouth. It practically melted on his tongue. ''Two o'clock. Make a list and be ready. We're not going to spend the afternoon browsing the malls.''

Jamie's eyes narrowed as he bent his attention back to his breakfast. She hoped he choked on it. ''Fine,'' she snapped. But he never even looked back up at her. His attention was already divided between the invoices he'd been studying when she came in and his meal.

She glared at his head. The fact that it was an exceptionally nice head did nothing to soothe her mood. Nor did it help that her mouth fairly watered simply by looking at him. He was the Marlboro Man, come to life. Better really, because Matthew didn't smoke. But he came complete with well-worn denim jeans that only accentuated his long, muscled thighs, and soft flannel shirts that seemed to stretch for miles across his broad shoulders. He was as large as a towering oak tree. And as solid. He had to be a walking, talking temptation to half the women in Wyoming, Colorado and Utah combined. Unfortunately, around her he had the temperament of a grizzly awakened from his winter's sleep.

So why on earth did she find him so darn appealing?

Chapter Two

After leaving Matthew in his office, she returned to the kitchen and cleaned it up, then ran back to the foreman's house where she was staying with Joe and Maggie. The cozy brick cottage was beyond several barns, about a half mile from the big house.

She found Maggie, shaky and wan, fixing herself a cup of soup, and Jaimie shooed her sister-in-law back into bed. It was proof that Maggie felt really crummy when she didn't put up much of a fight. Jaimie prepared a light meal for her, then hastily scribbled the list of supplies that Maggie suggested.

She quickly tidied up the cozy two-bedroom home, then hurried back to the big house to prepare Squire's lunch. As she passed the large, empty bunkhouse on her way, she felt inordinately grateful that the only people working the ranch at the moment were Matthew and his younger brother Daniel, Joe and herself. She wasn't sure what she would have done if she'd have had to cook for a dozen men in addition to her other chores.

It was a wonder to her how Maggie had managed. But then, Maggie had been raised on a dairy farm in Wisconsin. She had grown up feeding farm hands, cows and horses alike. The closest Jaimie had ever gotten to a horse was when she took riding lessons at the YMCA in Phoenix when she'd been in high school. She'd never seen a cow up close until she'd come to visit Joe and Maggie shortly after they'd moved to the Double-C.

Eventually Jaimie managed to swab down the mudroom. She bent over to wring out the cotton mop head, grunting slightly at the effort it took. Straightening, she heaved a sigh and arched her back. Looking about her, she felt ridiculously satisfied at the shining linoleum. In addition to the mudroom, she'd even mopped the kitchen floor. See if Mr. Blond-and-Beautiful could complain about that.

Huffing her hair out of her eyes, she folded her arms over the mop handle and looked out the window of the storm door, seeing the now-familiar gravel road, the snowy fields that seemed to stretch on forever. Who would have thought she would ever end up on a remote Wyoming cattle ranch, pinch-hitting for Maggie while she was supposed to be taking it easy with her pregnancy? But then, if it weren't for her brother, Joe, being here, Jamie would probably still be in Arizona or California, trying to figure out what to do with her life. Maggie had known how disconnected Jaimie had been and had encouraged her to move closer to them in Wyoming. They were family.

The only thing keeping Jaimie in the Southwest had been habit. She'd already visited the Double-C and her brother and sister-in-law. Knew that the wild, rugged landscape and the warm-hearted people there offered more than her current existence.

So she'd packed up and moved to Wyoming, landing the job at Bennett Ludlow's office—not that he'd been overrun with job candidates. But Bennett and her brother had become friends when Joe and Maggie first moved to the Double-C a few years back, and it had seemed ideal for Jaimie to take the job with Bennett.

She'd happily given it—and his roving hands—up, though, when Maggie needed her support.

Heaven knew that Maggie didn't appear to be getting much support from Joe these days.

At thirty-five, Joe was eight years older than Jaimie. Somehow or other, over the years, he'd ended up in Wisconsin, marrying Maggie when the ink on her high school diploma had still been wet. That had been ten years ago. Jaimie and her mother had flown to Las Vegas where Maggie and Joe had eloped, and she'd been a bridesmaid in the wedding. Still in her last year of high school, it had all seemed terribly romantic to Jaimie.

She rubbed her forehead. It had seemed romantic to her then, but the cool distance between her brother and his wife these days was anything but.

She sighed as she returned the mop to the cupboard. Hefting up the bucket, she dumped it in the oversize sink that was positioned on the far side of the washer and dryer.

She'd just finished rinsing out the sink when she heard the clomp of boots on the steps outside, and the door flew open, bringing with it a shivering draft of cold air. "Take off your—" she stared in frustration at the fresh trail of muddy snow "—boots."

Squire looked down. "Give it up, girl. This is what a mudroom is for."

Jaimie yanked off several paper towels from the holder affixed above the utility sink. "Then why does *he* keep harping at me to clean it up?" She glared at the *he* in question and crouched down to wipe up the footprints.

The door slammed shut behind him, and Matthew shrugged out of his jacket. "It's two. Aren't you ready to go yet?"

"Does it look like I'm ready?" She pushed at his boot. "Lift."

He frowned at her, but he lifted his foot and she slid a cotton rug under.

"You're not gonna traipse those muddy, gritty wet boots all over my clean floor," she muttered, situating the rug under his other boot.

"*My* floor?"

Squire chuckled and patted her shoulder as he stepped around them. "You still going in to Gillette?"

"Yeah." Matt bent and snatched the paper towels from her hand before she could start wiping off his boots. "Leave it," he said brusquely. "If you need anything, add it to the list on the counter." He raised his voice so Squire could hear.

Jaimie popped up and stood in his way when he would have followed Squire into the kitchen. "Wipe off your boots."

Matthew was tall enough to look right over the top of her auburn head. But there she stood, clearly planning to bar him if he should step off the dinky rug without tending to his boots first. He could simply pick her up and place her out of his way. In fact, the idea of closing his hands over her arms had a decided appeal. He crumpled the paper towel in his fist. And wiped his boots.

"We're leaving in ten minutes," he growled when she cleared the path to the kitchen. "Be ready."

Jaimie peered around the door, watching him stride through the kitchen. Lordy hallelujah, the man had an attitude. And the most incredible backside...

"You gonna stand there all afternoon?" Squire inquired.

She realized he was standing at the kitchen door, waiting to close it, keeping the heat in the kitchen. "I was thinking about it."

He closed the door behind her when she passed into the

kitchen. "You'd best be getting ready, girl. He'll leave without you."

"And I'd be stuck with whatever he decided I needed. He'd probably buy boots two sizes too small," Jaimie finished. "Don't forget to take your medicine," she reminded as she sat down and began pushing her feet into the tennis shoes. "You need to eat first—"

Squire snorted. "I'm old, missy, not senile."

She straightened and grinned. She wasn't sure exactly how old Squire was, but knowing he'd married before he'd been twenty, she guessed his early sixties. He stood tall and straight. Almost as tall as his son, and his silver-gray hair was thick and brushed back from a striking face, carved with years of experience. His ice blue eyes were startling against his tanned face. Just looking at him told her what Matthew would look like in another twenty years or so. "You're a sexy coot," she teased. "I know Gloria Day thinks so."

He grunted at the mention of the other woman's name. One of his nurses when he'd been hospitalized several months ago, they'd been more or less dating since Squire's return home. "Your time's ticking away," he reminded, rather than comment on Gloria.

"I should run back and check on Maggie." She glanced at the clock on the microwave. "If we're late—"

"Don't worry. Joe'll be back in by suppertime. I'll even check on her myself," Squire assured. "You got about six minutes."

She was already out the door. Her shoes slipped and slid over the snow and gravel as she jogged back to check on Maggie who was now soundly sleeping. She grabbed her coat, mittens and purse, and slip-slided her way back in just enough time to climb breathlessly into Matt's Blazer as it idled alongside the big house.

His arms were folded over the top of the steering wheel, and his dark brown cowboy hat was pulled low over his forehead as he watched her settle into her seat. "You're late."

The interior of the truck was nice and warm, but she still huddled into the depths of her coat. "Not by much." She set her purse on the floor by her feet then stuck her fingers in front of the heater vents. "Or you wouldn't have waited. Oh, that feels good." She drew in a long breath and wiggled her fingers in the stream of heat.

He tipped his hat up a notch with a gloved hand. "Try wearing gloves. Or is that somethin' else you don't have?"

She pulled the mittens out of her pocket and waved them in front of his nose.

"They'd do more good on your hands," he suggested drily.

She made a face at him, but pulled on the brightly knitted mittens. She looked out the window as he worked the truck around on the circular, gravel drive that fronted the big house. At least it had once been gravel. Now, except for deep wheel ruts, the gravel was covered with a thick coat of dirty, crusty snow.

She couldn't help the twinge of excitement she felt. Whether it was from the prospect of being in Matthew's company for the next few hours, or the idea of going to town, she couldn't tell. Probably a healthy dose of both. Jaimie hadn't seen another face, aside from Joe and Maggie, Matthew, Squire and Daniel, for nearly three weeks. Not even Jefferson, another one of Matthew's brothers, and his new wife, Emily, had been by the Double-C during that time. They were the Double-C's closest neighbors, owning the spread directly east. More than ten miles away.

This place was a far cry from Phoenix, Arizona.

It was painfully silent in the truck as Matthew drove toward the main gate of the Double-C. The only sounds were those made by the gravel and slush beneath the big tires, and the steady throb of the engine. Both of which seemed to underscore that looming silence.

Never in her life had she been tongue-tied, she thought, sliding a look his way. Not until she'd met Matthew Clay.

She sighed faintly and looked back out the side window. Her goose bumps finally died, and she unzipped her coat, settling more comfortably against the seat. As they approached the junction where the Double-C joined a paved road, he pulled over to the side and, reaching through the open window, retrieved the bundle of mail stuffed in the mailbox and dumped it on the seat between them.

From the corner of his vision, Matthew watched her slip off her mittens, which she'd been fiddling with for the past five minutes. He reached over and flipped on the radio. His fingers drummed on the steering wheel. What on earth had possessed him to bring her with him to town? He could've had her write down what size boots she wore. Then she wouldn't be sitting beside him, filling the truck with the lemony scent of her hair.

He glanced her way, but she was looking out the side window. Her hair streamed over the shoulders of her bright purple coat. Her toes, in those ridiculously inadequate shoes, tapped in time to the soft music from the radio.

He cast about in his mind for something to say, then felt like an idiot. So what if it was Valentine's Day? She wasn't a date, for cripe's sake. He didn't need to make small talk.

They backtracked to stop at his brother's place, but didn't stay to visit as Emily was elbow deep in bread dough and Jefferson—well Jefferson, as usual, was trying to distract his wife. And doing a decent job of it, if the glob of bread dough on the front of his sweater was anything to go by. Jefferson was clearly recuperating well from the surgery he'd had less than two months earlier. Matt added Emily's items to his list for town since he knew she didn't want to leave Jefferson any more than necessary. He could have called her on the phone, but hadn't. He wanted to see with his own eyes how his brother was doing. Stopping gave him the excuse. Unfortunately the stop seemed all too brief when Matthew contemplated the long drive yet ahead of them.

He was far too aware of the way Jaimie tucked her chin into the raised collar of her coat and hurried after him as they left Jefferson's house.

"Doesn't it *ever* stop blowing?"

He held open the door for her as she clambered up into the truck. "Nope." He rounded the Blazer and climbed in.

In just the few minutes it had taken to walk from the protection of the house to the vehicle, her nose had turned pink with cold. She jiggled on the seat, her hands tucked between her thighs.

"Cold?" Now there was a brilliant observation.

"I never thought I'd have fantasies about a Phoenix summer," she muttered. "But right now, 112 degrees sounds pretty good."

Then why don't you go back there where you belong and leave a man in peace? He started the engine, then reached behind the seat for a folded blanket he kept sitting on the back seat. He tossed it on her lap. "Here."

Her hands hurriedly spread the red-and-black-checked wool over her legs. "I like Emily and your brother. They're very happy, aren't they?"

"Yeah. Finally." He wheeled the truck around and headed for the main road. In minutes they whizzed past the Double-C's main gate toward the state highway.

"Emily is about five months along now, isn't she?"

He shrugged. "About that."

"Why is Jefferson the only one of you guys who's married?"

Jaimie's nose was still pink and he upped the heater a notch. "'Cause he's the only one of us who has found the right woman," he said, feeling impatience curl through him. Why couldn't he get the dozens of ways *he* could warm her up out of his head? He turned the heater full blast this time and pushed all the vents in her direction.

"Surely there's—"

"There's not a lot of women in these parts," he said abruptly.

"Maybe not, but this isn't some isolated island, either."

"No. It's Wyoming. Where the winters can last for eight months of the year."

"So?"

He shrugged, wondering why he felt so edgy. "There aren't many women I've known who're willing to put up with it." The understatement was so huge, he wondered why he didn't choke on it.

"Emily 'puts up' with it. She loves it here. So does Maggie."

"They're exceptions."

She gave a snooty little sniff. "Spoken like a man."

"What's that supposed to mean?"

"Nothing." She adjusted the blanket. "Don't you want a wife? Children?"

What he wanted was sex. With her. And that was completely out of the question. Irritation skittered down his spine and he dragged his thoughts from tiny red hearts decorating thermal shirts. He checked the highway and smoothly passed a slower-moving Jeep. "What for?"

"What for?" She flopped her hands. "What do you think, what for? For love. For someone to hold at night when it's below zero outside and the snow is piling up in six-foot drifts. For a child to pass the Double-C on to. To teach your kids how to care for the land. To share your love for it—how it's the only thing in the world that lasts." She looked out the window. "What for," she muttered, shaking her head.

Matthew's fingers tightened around the steering wheel. "The Double-C's not mine alone. It belongs to all of us. Whatever kids we have will all inherit the land."

"Oh, I know that. Maggie told me all about it. But *you're*

the one who lives for the Double-C. It's only natural that
your children would feel the same."

"Maggie tell you that, too?"

He felt the warmth of her gaze, but kept his own strictly
on the road. "No," she finally said. "I can figure some
things out myself."

A faint buzzing sounded in his head. A warning. "Not
everybody's cut out for ranching. Sawyer couldn't wait to
leave," Matthew told her, speaking of his older brother.
Since when had that *redhead* tuned in to him this way?
"As soon as he was old enough, he enlisted in the Navy.
Jefferson was outta here by his eighteenth birthday. And
Tristan—" He shook his head, thinking of his youngest
brother, who made no secret of his preference for the ocean
over the ranch. "Tristan's busy designing computer pro-
grams, or whatever, raking in the dough down in California."

Only Dan, five years younger than Matthew, had stayed
on at the Double-C. He would have been the perfect foreman, if he'd only agreed to it. But Dan hadn't wanted to
be that tied down. Not even to the Double-C. Instead, Matthew had ended up hiring Joe Greene a few years back. Joe
did his job capably enough. But he wasn't as good as Daniel
would've been.

"What's your point?"

"Only that you can't assume that because *I'm* a rancher
down to my soul, my kids—which I don't plan to have,
anyway—would feel the same way."

"Jefferson came back to it." She leaned her head against
the seat. "Maybe your other brothers will, too."

"I don't think I'll hold my breath." Sawyer would rather
swallow nails than consign himself to life as a rancher.
Tristan felt the same. But that didn't mean his oldest and
his youngest brothers weren't closely tied to the family's
home. They were. They had both come the minute Matthew
had gotten word to them last year when Squire had had his

heart attack. They'd dropped whatever they'd been doing and had come. Pure and simple. That's the way it was with family.

"What about you?" He decided it was time to turn the tables. "I don't see you with a passel of kids hanging on your skirts."

"And go through the kind of misery Maggie's going through? No, thanks." She shook her head, but her eyes didn't meet his, and he knew with a start of certainty that she was lying right through her lovely teeth.

He didn't know what disturbed him more. The fact that he read her so easily, or that she felt some need to hide whatever maternal urges she had.

She suddenly straightened. "Look."

He followed her pointed finger and saw nothing unusual. No downed fence. No cattle loose. Just billowy snow, covering the fields and drifting across the road on the constant breeze. Another thirty minutes or so and they would leave Double-C land behind.

"The antelope," she prompted.

He barely gave the trio of animals nuzzling a split bale of hay half a glance. "What about 'em?"

She pushed his arm. "They're pretty."

"They're eating *my* hay."

"Well, they have to eat."

"So do my cattle."

Her lips twitched and she craned around in her seat to watch the animals as they left them behind. "It's really beautiful here," she mused. "No wonder Joe and Maggie came and stayed."

Matthew ignored the note of...of what...in her voice. Longing? "How's Maggie feeling, anyway?" he asked. The sooner Maggie safely had her baby and things got back to normal, the better.

Jaimie scooted around until she was facing forward again, and her faint smile faded. "Miserable. She has another doctor's appointment on Friday afternoon. She says that everything is going fine. But she's hardly eating. And what she does eat, ends up, well, coming up. I thought morning sickness was supposed to end after the first three months or so. Hers just seems to get worse.''

Had Jaimie's face always been so expressive? He shifted in the seat. ''Maggie's strong,'' he told her quietly. ''She'll be okay.''

''She'll need someone to drive her to town.''

''Joe—''

''He's not comfortable at the obstetrician's office.''

Matthew frowned, glancing her way. She looked like she'd just swallowed a mouthful of prune juice.

Her fingers pleated the edge of the blanket and she looked out the side window. ''His pickup is one of those dinky kinds, you know that. Maggie would be uncomfortable the entire drive and she shouldn't drive herself. You know how she gets dizzy and light-headed.'' She glanced his way, a glint of challenge in her eyes. ''I thought I'd better, um, you know...drive her.''

His thumb slowly tapped the steering wheel. He had an appointment on Friday that couldn't be rescheduled, with the owner of a bull he'd been wanting for more than a year, or he would simply offer to take Maggie himself. Save himself some downed fence, no doubt. ''You have a lot of experience driving in ice and snow?'' He smiled faintly. ''Doubt you had much of that in Phoenix.''

''No. But we had dust storms and rain.''

Big deal. Matthew held the thought.

''Look,'' she offered calmly. ''I'm a perfectly capable driver. I even drove a cab for a while.''

His eyebrows shot up.

''I did.''

He could just envision her behind the wheel of a big yellow taxi cab. ''For how long? One day? Two? Until you ran over a stop sign or something?''

"For six months." Her dark green eyes snapped at him. "And I never hit anything."

"You saved that up for me, did you? Thanks. I'm touched. So what other talents are you hiding?"

"One of these days you'll take me seriously," she warned.

He looked at her. Her hands were folded primly in her lap, that outrageous, citified bracelet of hers twinkling in the sunlight.

She was a walking, talking temptation for him to forget all the reasons why he shouldn't get involved with her. For one thing she was a good ten years, and then some, younger than he. For another, she was Joe's sister. She was an employee. And last, most important, she would get hurt, sure as God made little green apples.

All of which were fine reasons, he told himself as the list raced through his head. And none of which kept his hand from lifting and skimming down her oh, so tempting velvety cheek.

"Oh, sweetheart, I take you seriously. Don't you ever doubt that."

Chapter Three

Three hours later, Jaimie was still breathless.

It wasn't fair that he could simply level her with a single touch to her cheek. She hadn't been able to think straight since then—not while he'd rapped out a confusing array of orders at the feed and supply store, not while they'd swung through the supermarket where he purchased an enormous amount of staples considering how brief the list was, and certainly not while he'd been busily choosing clothing for her at the Western-wear store.

He'd pointed her toward the boots he considered appropriate. He'd insisted on finding her a suitable pair of work gloves. He'd even talked her into choosing a cap and a wonderfully soft, warm scarf. But when he'd headed for the thermal underwear, she'd put her foot down. If she ever wanted to sleep again at night, she knew she couldn't do it while wearing long johns that *he'd* chosen.

Then they'd almost had another set-to when it came time to pay the bill. But Matthew, in his usual high-handed manner, had simply told the clerk to charge it to the Double-C. That had been that. The clerk had ignored the cash clenched in Jaimie's fist and had cheerfully handed over the purchases.

And now, here they were. Sitting in an unpretentious café colorfully decorated with a multitude of big red hearts, while love songs streamed continuously from the jukebox in the corner, and she *still* couldn't think straight. She wondered what kind of mush she would be reduced to if she ever managed to get him to kiss her.

She caught him looking at her over the top of his red, laminated menu, and hastily looked down at the matching one she held in her own hands. What on earth was she dreaming about? If there was a man on earth immune to "female managing," Matthew Clay was it. He would act purely on his own decisions. And nothing else. Matthew considered her a nuisance. An absolute hazard on the ranch. No matter how hard she tried, no matter what she did, the only thing she usually earned from him was "The Look."

She shifted on the unyielding seat and folded the menu. Her eyes automatically veered toward Matthew, and she determinedly looked out the window beside them instead. She touched her finger to the cold glass. It was dark outside now. Other than the stop light at the corner and the occasional passing vehicle, mostly all she could see were their own reflections.

His hat sat on the table where it joined the wall right beneath the window. She wanted to pick it up, run her fingers around the dark brown brim. She wanted to put it on her own head and kiss him. Because it seemed safer, she stared back at the window and clasped her hands in her lap. Just in case they got any crazy ideas. She saw him raise his long, blunt-tipped fingers and rake them through his dark blond hair with the distinctive hat-band mark, riffling the thick strands.

The waitress, a young woman in jeans and a bright yellow sweatshirt shouting Explore Yellowstone! approached and filled Matthew's coffee mug, then waited, her order pad and pencil poised.

Jaimie turned in time to see Matthew's eyes skim up the waitress's shapely hips. "I'll have the special," she announced brightly, completely unaware of what the special was. As long as it drew the woman's eyes toward her and away from positively ogling Matthew, she didn't care.

Matthew's eyes swiveled to Jaimie. She could have kicked him for the faint smile playing at the corners of his lips, as if he could read her like a book. The waitress snapped her gum and turned her attention back to Matthew.

"With a baked potato on the side," Jaimie added.

The waitress glanced at her, uninterested. "The special comes with a baked potato," she said, extremely polite. "You want two?"

Jaimie could've sworn she heard Matthew snicker. "Yes." She shook the bangs out of her eyes. "I want two."

Raising her penciled brows slightly, the waitress made a production over writing that down. "Anything else?"

"Iced tea."

The waitress had already turned her attention to Matthew.

"With lemon." Jaimie looked at the container of sugar sitting between the salt and pepper shakers on the other side of Matthew's hat. "Fresh lemon. And artificial sweetener," she added.

"Want to order dessert now, too?"

Jaimie looked the waitress right in the face. "No, thanks." She smiled deliberately.

The waitress eyed her. Blew a bubble. Dismissed her. "What'll you have, honey?" she asked Matthew.

Honey. Jaimie rolled her eyes and looked back at the window, only to catch Matthew watching her. The amusement in his eyes was clearly reflected in the window. His dimple flashed briefly and then he was quietly giving the waitress his order.

"I'm surprised you went for the special," he said when the waitress had plunked a glass of iced tea next to Jaimie's flatware. "I never figured you for the chicken-fried steak type."

Chicken-fried steak. Well, at least it wasn't something she detested. Like liver and onions. "Really. And just what type did you figure me for? Oh, wait. Sushi probably."

He leaned back against the booth, stretching his arm along the back and his legs beneath the table. "Probably."

"Sure, I *love* my fish raw." She gave a mock shudder. "Give me a break."

"Hey, I don't have anything against sushi," he said. "Of course, we don't have too many restaurants 'round here that cater to it."

"So what's your favorite food? Steak, I'll bet."

"It'd be blasphemous if I didn't like steak." The corner of his lips lifted. "But my all-time favorite is liver and onions. Lots of onions. You might remember that, the next time you want to drive somewhere."

Jaimie barely contained a shudder. A real one. Wouldn't you know it. But if it put a smile on Matthew's face, she figured she'd better bone up on the fine art of cooking liver.

The waitress reappeared with salads and a sashay for Matthew that a blind person could've noticed.

Matthew bit back a chuckle at the darts shooting from Jaimie's eyes. "Some reason you don't like the waitress?"

She lifted her shoulder. "Don't be silly." She stabbed the cherry tomato dead-on with her fork and juice squirted.

"Bull's-eye," Matthew murmured, turning his attention firmly to his own plate. He would do well to concentrate on his meal instead of the way her eyes seemed to deepen or lighten depending on what emotion she felt at any given moment.

For a moment she was blessedly silent while she attacked the lettuce on her plate. "How long have you been in charge of the Double-C," she asked a few minutes later.

He stifled a sigh. She was the talkingest woman he'd ever met. But it wouldn't kill him to have a civil conversation with her. If only to remind himself that he knew how to exchange small talk with a beautiful woman. Small talk was harmless enough, after all. And maybe it would keep his thoughts off other things. Like the way her throat rose, creamy and long, from the neck of her shirt.

"Officially I was the foreman for eight years," he said. "Then one day Squire up and said he'd had enough. Turned it over to me. Lock, stock and barrel."

"How long ago was that?"

"Five years." There was nothing interesting to talk about down that road. "What about your parents?" he asked.

"My father died several years ago. He was only fifty-seven," she said after a moment. "Mom followed a few years later."

He hadn't known. Joe never discussed his family. Not even Jaimie until the first time she had arrived for a visit. "How old were you?"

He found he really wanted to know, and it had nothing to do with passing the time until they could get out of this café that looked like a mad Cupid had struck it.

Her shoulders shifted restlessly. As if she wished she'd never said anything. "Twenty."

"In college?"

She nodded. Poked at her salad some more.

"What were you studying?"

Her mobile lips stretched into that slightly crooked, impish smile. The one that drove a jangling dart through his gut every time he saw it. "Sure you want to know?"

"I asked, didn't I?"

"Men." She glanced at him as if to gauge his reaction. "Just kidding. Actually, it was…ah, business administration. But only because I couldn't decide *what* I wanted to study." She set her fork down and returned his look with a tart one of her own. "I suppose when *you* were twenty, you had your entire life mapped out. Planned to the last detail.''

''When I was twenty,'' he responded smoothly, ''and in college, my plans were to graduate, marry BethAnn Watson and double the Double-C.'' He loved that surprised look on her sassy face. Loved it so much that he didn't even wonder over his bringing up BethAnn.

''What happened?''

''I graduated and, in time, doubled the Double-C.''

''To the marriage bit.''

''Oh, that.'' He realized he had finished his salad somewhere along the line. ''She had her sights set elsewhere,'' he said shortly. *Elsewhere* being his neighbor, good old Bill Pickett. Apparently the weeks and months of isolation on a ranch in the middle of Wyoming, which she'd whined and complained about with Matthew, had become more attractive when they'd been attached to Bill.

''You must be joking!'' Jaimie said, then colored.

''No joke.'' He watched her, entranced by the way her pink cheeks made her eyes seem even brighter. ''She said no, and expected me to chase after her.'' He realized what he'd just admitted and sat back in his seat.

''Obviously you didn't go after her.''

Obviously he was losing his mind to be discussing this. Next thing he knew, he would be telling her about the way BethAnn had wrapped her truck around a tree two winters after marrying Bill. ''Why do you say that?''

''Because you're...alone.''

God, he really didn't like the direction of this conversation. And he really only had himself to blame. ''Being single and being alone ain't exactly the same thing,'' he drawled slowly.

Her eyes widened a fraction. But before she could comment, the waitress arrived to place a huge array of food before her.

The baked potato sitting alongside the generous chicken-fried steak covered nearly half of Jaimie's plate. The potato sitting alone on a side plate was even larger. He bit back a smile. "So what happened to the business administration," he asked, drawing her somewhat shell-shocked eyes back to him.

Her fork and steak knife were poised over the steak. "Hmm?"

"Business admin," he prompted. "You going to eat that second potato? I could use it."

She blinked. Looked from his lone bowl of chili to her own laden plate. Relief brightened her eyes and she slid the side plate his way. "Please. Help yourself."

He busied himself with removing the foil from the hot potato. "Now, what happened with college?"

Her lively expression stilled. "I dropped out," she said flatly. She waved her fork and a chunk of potato flew off, landing on the floor. "Add it to the list of things I've never finished," she muttered.

Matthew casually leaned over and scooped up the potato in his napkin before somebody slipped and fell. He straightened to see her viciously slicing through the steak. "Money?"

"What?"

"Was money the problem?"

"Money's *always* a problem."

The tide of red flowing up her neck told him she probably hadn't meant to say that. Well, he knew how she felt, since for some reason he said things around her that *he* didn't mean to say. He chopped up the baked potato and added it to the chili, searching for a safe topic. "Did you grow up in Phoenix?"

"Yeah." After a moment her shoulders relaxed. The knife stopped sawing its way through the plate. "Ever been there?"

"A few times on business. Was pretty congested."

"It's been growing a lot. I never much liked the heat

during the summer.'' She nibbled at the steak. ''My dad was a city engineer. As soon as he could, he took an early retirement, and he and Mom moved to Florida. They liked the weather.''

''Why not California? It would've been closer. To hear my little brother talk, San Diego must be the closest place to heaven on earth.''

''Mom had an old friend who lived in Florida. She and Dad had always talked about one day going there, too.''

Once they did, they weren't alive long enough to enjoy it, Matthew deduced. Finally he set down his fork. ''I don't think it matters how old you are when you lose your parents. It's still hard. I was nine when my mother died.'' He remembered the day like it was yesterday. And he wondered why on earth he was even bringing it up, skirting close to areas that he never wanted to think about, much less speak of. Wasn't it bad enough that he'd opened his mouth about BethAnn?

''Squire told me that your mother's grave is on the far side of the swimming hole.''

Matthew went still in surprise. Squire never mentioned the grave. In fact, he rarely even spoke of his deceased wife. As for Matthew, he'd stood at the gravesite only once. When she was put there. And though he'd been back to the swimming hole often enough over the years, he'd never traipsed around to where that marble headstone was located.

''What was she like?''

Jaimie's voice drew his thoughts. He paused, waiting until the waitress finished refilling his coffee mug and pouring Jaimie more tea. ''Happy. She was always singing around the house.''

''And Squire? He never remarried.''

Matthew shook his head. ''Until he brought Emily to live with us…she was, oh, seven, I guess…we never had another female on the Double-C.'' He cocked his eyebrow.

"Seems like we're overrun with women these days," he murmured. Mostly to see her hackles rise.

She didn't disappoint him. She slanted her head, peering at him through those wispy bangs that waved in her startlingly green eyes. "Gloria Day is probably going to land your father, you know. How do you feel about that?"

He shrugged, leaning back again as he sipped his coffee. "If she's up to the task of handling Squire, more power to her."

The diamonds at her wrist glittered as she slowly revolved her iced tea glass. "Squire." She sounded the name. "Why do you all call him by his name?"

That amused him. "Does Squire look like 'Daddy' to you?"

"Well, no," she admitted wryly. "But—"

"Actually, Jefferson is the one who started it. He called Squire 'Old Man' so often to his face, that Squire finally exploded. Told him to call him Dad, Pops, Father or whatever. But 'Old Man' was out. Naturally, Jefferson, who's as stubborn as Squire, wouldn't comply. But he also was only about six. 'Squire' was the result. We all started calling him that, just to keep him off of Jefferson's butt."

"Six," she echoed.

Matthew smiled, remembering. "Jefferson started early. He and Squire were butting heads before Jefferson was out of diapers. Of all of us, his coloring is the most like my mother's, but his attitude is all Squire. Not that he'd agree, of course. And, he still calls Squire 'Old Man.'" He took a glance at his watch and lifted his finger to the waitress. She immediately brought the check and he pulled out his wallet, peering out the window. "Is it snowing again?"

"I think so." Her auburn head leaned closer to the window. "Yup."

Matthew flipped some bills onto the table and stood up, settling his hat on his head.

Jaimie quickly gathered her belongings. "I'm just, uh, going to—"

She would sass him about his love life, but blush over visiting the ladies' room. Women. Go figure. He lifted his chin toward the rear of the restaurant. "Back there."

He was waiting by the door, watching the snow drift down, when she emerged. Her new scarf was draped over her head and twisted around her neck, looking graceful and elegant. Something he'd never expected when he'd shoved the sturdy knit into her hands at the store. The black color sharply accentuated her ivory skin and lush green eyes. She had one arm in her coat, and as she twisted trying to find the other armhole, he had to close his eyes against the sight of her curves thrusting against that heart-scattered thermal shirt.

Disgusted with himself, he yanked open the door, feeling the rush of frigid air. It did little to cool the heat pooling in his gut.

He stifled an oath.

Jaimie had to rush to keep up with his long legs as he strode across the small parking lot toward his Blazer. And she wasn't too short-legged herself. But her new boots were stiff, and she felt like an elephant in the side show. She brushed a snowflake off her nose. "Where's the fire?" she asked breathlessly when she finally caught up with him at the truck. Here they'd just shared a meal together; they'd carried on an adult, civilized, conversation. What had happened? What had she done this time?

He yanked open the door and turned to her. Towered over her. His hat, pulled low over his forehead as usual, blocked out the pale illumination from the parking lot light behind him. She felt engulfed by his warmth. And he wasn't even touching her.

She peered up at him, but couldn't see his eyes. The night was too dark and the Blazer's interior light too dim. "Matthew?"

His shoulders, even wider than usual beneath the thick layer of coat, moved with his sigh. He shook his head slightly, then tucked the edge of her scarf against her throat. She trembled, and his lips tightened. "Let's go," he said curtly.

But she hesitated. "What's wrong?"

"Get in."

"But—"

"Woman, get in the truck."

She crossed her arms at the autocratic order. "Ex*cuse* me?"

He gave that mighty sigh again. "You would try the patience of a saint," he said, clearly aggravated.

That stung more than she wanted to admit. "Well, pardon the hell out of me."

"Don't swear."

"You're not my father," she retorted. "I'll swear anytime I please!"

His gloved hands suddenly closed over her arms, and she gasped, fearing he would bodily deposit her in the truck. But he lifted her onto the toes of her stiff new boots and pulled her against his chest. "You're right. I am *not* your father," he gritted, then closed his mouth over hers.

Stunned, off balance, Jaimie caught hold of his shoulders. His lips were cool from the wintry air. But they burned right down to her bone marrow. Then coherent thought vanished when his tongue traced the seam of her lips.

Her lips parted, and her knees turned to jelly. A soft sound rose in her throat and she softened against him. If it weren't for his arm, an iron band about her waist, she suspected she would have just oozed into a puddle on the snowy ground. When he finally lifted his head, she was plastered against him, her gloved fingers twisted in his short hair. She had no idea what had happened to his hat.

All she knew was that she didn't want him to let go.

Even with the snow whirling about their heads and her nose growing numb with cold.

"Get in," he ordered, pulling her arms down from his neck.

She had no choice. It was either tumble into the truck or slide to the ground like a limp noodle. He scooped up his hat, dusted off the snow and jammed it back onto his head, striding around to the driver's side. He'd climbed in and started the engine before she'd barely closed her own door. "Matthew—"

He lifted his hand. "No. Not one word." He shook his head, peering out the windshield. "Bloody weather," he growled, turning on the radio and flipping through channels until he found a news station.

This time Jaimie decided not to press his edict. She didn't know what she would say, anyway. *Please kiss me again,* didn't seem to be something he would want to hear, even if it was a chant going round and round inside *her* head. Her hands shook as she fastened the seat belt around herself. The window was cold, and she pressed her forehead to it, willing her heart to slow.

Before it had a chance to, though, he'd opened his door again and climbed out. She leaned over to his side and looked out at him. He was pacing back and forth, a steady stream of soft oaths accompanying the wisps of his visible breath.

"Matthew? What's wrong?"

He went silent. His head lifted. He removed his hat, wiped his forehead as if he'd just endured a hot summer day, then jammed his hat back on his head. He shook his head once, then walked back to the door, pointing inside. "Weren't you listening?"

Sure. To my heart pounding in my ears. "The news?" she ventured.

"The weather." He lifted his arms to the sky. *"The*

weather.'' His teeth practically snapped between words as she received the mother of all looks.

She swallowed. It was snowing, true. But it had been snowing off and on since the beginning of November. What was so different now? She would have asked him, but he'd resumed his stomping up and down in the parking lot. Rubbing her forehead, she adjusted the scarf more securely around her neck and wiped the blowing snow off his seat, paying closer attention to the news broadcast. And then she wished she hadn't.

Matthew reappeared at the door. He climbed inside and pulled the door shut. Snow drifted from his hat, melting into nothing as it hit the seat between them. "They're closing the highway," he said grimly.

"I, um, just heard."

He pinched the bridge of his nose. "I don't need this," he muttered. "I really don't."

"We'll just have to stay here tonight," Jaimie offered. Sensibly, she thought. "There's a motel right across the road." She pointed through the windshield. "A couple of rooms and we'll be all fixed up. Surely the snow will be through by morning." Frankly, when she thought about it, she grew a bit miffed at his attitude. It wasn't as if he'd be cooped up with Medusa, after all. Or maybe he was afraid that she would try compromising his virtue. That, after that display of mind-blowing kisses, she would throw herself at him at the earliest possible opportunity.

"Not with my luck," he said under his breath, clearly thinking about the possibilities of the snow ceasing.

She huffed and crossed her arms. He snapped off the radio and drove across to the motel.

"You might as well come in, too," he said when he pulled up outside the office. "It'll be warmer inside than waiting in the truck."

She would have liked to argue. It wasn't as if his invitation had been particularly gracious. But common sense said that he was right. Through the window she could see a small line of people waiting at the registration desk. More people stuck by the storm, no doubt.

She followed him inside. Peals of childish laughter filled the small registration area, and, leaving Matthew standing in line, she headed around the corner to the lobby area. Half a dozen children sat around a big, square coffee table, their young heads bent over the brightly colored papers littering the table.

They were chattering away a mile a minute, and Jaimie found her feet carrying her over to one of the couches beside the table. She sat on the arm, looking over the heads of the children.

"They're making Valentines," the woman who sat on the other couch said, looking over at her.

Jaimie could see that. "You must carry a well-stocked purse," she observed. On the table, the children had red, white and pink papers. Pipe cleaners and white lace paper doilies. Safety scissors and glue sticks rounded out the art supplies.

The other woman held up a voluminous bag that was on the floor beside her. "We're moving to California to be closer to my family," she explained, glancing at her children. "It's a *long* trip."

One of the little girls turned to Jaimie, and gave her a gap-toothed smile. "Wanna help?"

Charmed by that sweet smile, Jaimie glanced over her shoulder. The line at the registration desk hadn't moved. Matthew was still acting like he'd been sentenced to torture. "Sure, why not?" She shrugged out of her coat and scarf and tucked her gloves in her pocket. Then she scooted forward to the edge of the couch. "What do you think I should make?"

The little girl giggled. "Hearts, of course."

"Of course. But just one, I think. That way you won't

run out of paper.'' Besides, Jaimie had made her share of hearts back at the Double-C in the past few weeks.

Finally finished with registering for a room that cost three times as much as it should have, Matthew followed the sound of Jaimie's laughter. He walked into the lobby and stopped short. There she sat, cross-legged on the floor, looking as innocent and carefree as the passel of children surrounding her.

She looked up then, noticing him. Her smile widened and something curled in his gut. He thumped his hat against his thigh and headed toward the couch. ''You 'bout done there?''

She nodded. ''Just let me finish this one part.'' She finished cutting the paper, then unfolded it. The littlest girl gave a heartfelt *ooh* when Jaimie held it up and handed it to her.

''It's like a snowflake,'' the child said, peering through the delicate lacy cutouts of the pink heart. ''You better keep it,'' she said shyly, handing it back to Jaimie.

''But I made it for you,'' Jaimie said softly. ''Have a good trip to California,'' she said to the mother, pushing to her feet.

''Izzat your husband?''

Matthew suddenly found himself the object of several curious eyes.

''Ah, no,'' Jaimie said hurriedly. ''We're...he's my bo—''

''We're friends,'' Matthew said calmly, earning himself a quick look from Jaimie.

''Okay, honey. We're all set.'' A harried young man rushed into the lobby, brushing snow from his coat. ''The room's ready now.''

Jaimie scooted out of the way as the kids suddenly flew into motion, hastily shoving hearts and scraps back into their mother's bag. Matthew took her arm. ''I need to move the truck," he said. She nodded and followed him back outside, donning her coat once more. Even in the protected overhang of the registration parking, the wind blew harshly.

He hustled her into the truck and then he drove around to the parking lot, finally finding an empty spot at the far end. He pulled in and shut off the engine. The thought of the motel room nagged at him, making his tone short. "You want any of that stuff brought in?"

In answer, she reached over the seat and took hold of the shopping bag that contained the rest of her new clothing, then pushed open her door.

The snow blew hard, stinging Jaimie's cheeks. She tilted her head against it, watching Matthew round the Blazer, then he was taking her arm and heading her toward the glass doors leading into the motel. His size took the brunt of the wind, for which Jaimie was grateful, though she would rather choke than admit it. He was still so obviously annoyed at this turn of events.

Inside, he glanced at the key in his hand and pointed at the stairway. "Upstairs."

Jaimie led the way, unwinding her scarf as she went. At the top of the stairs she paused and nearly jumped out of her skin when the ice machine next to her chugged into life, dumping a load of ice into its big bin. "Which way?"

He joined her, his fingers automatically flipping open the buttons of his coat. "Down there," he said after looking at the numbers on the wall.

She should have been warned. Should have expected it. But she chalked it up to that befuddled thinking thing that always happened to her when he was near. He stopped in front of room number 216 and inserted the key. The door swung open. "After you," he said.

Jaimie, mindless fool that she was, walked into the room. It was clean. Wonderfully warm. And looked like other motel rooms she'd stayed in. She saw that a large bed dominated the center of the room, and there was a television bolted to the wall, which hung above a dresser-desk combination. The bathroom was directly to her left. She dumped her sack, purse and scarf on the dresser. "Where are you?"

He closed the door and tossed his hat onto the dresser, where it settled atop her scarf. "Here."

Her finger paused on her coat zipper. "Excuse me?"

He shrugged out of his coat and shook it. Snow drifted to the tan carpet and melted. He hooked the coat over the chair tucked beneath the desktop. "One room."

Heat rushed into her cheeks. "No way."

Matthew brushed his hands through his hair, determined not to dwell on that one wide bed. He knew his expression couldn't be any happier than hers. "Sweetheart, if you want to sleep in the truck tonight and freeze, have at it. I'm sleeping on that bed there. What you do is up to you." He gestured politely to the door. "They've got one room. This is it." He didn't bother to mention that he'd had to pay the night clerk nearly three times the regular rate just to get it. Naturally it had been his luck to get stuck in town the same night every motel room in town had been booked. The people after him in line had not been pleased that he'd gotten the last room. "The bathtub is available if you're so inclined," he added.

"But—" She whirled to face the bed, color coming and going in her face. "But…we…this…" She turned to him again, then buried her chin in the collar of her coat.

"Relax, Red. I can control myself if you can," he snapped, more angry with himself than anything. If he hadn't been so bloody crazy and kissed her like he had, maybe this wouldn't be so blasted awkward. Maybe his nerves wouldn't feel like they were ready to jump out from beneath his skin.

Her color had risen again, and she shrugged out of her coat, hanging it up with jerky movements. Her eyes, wide and dark, met his for a fraction of a second before she soundlessly sailed past him, purse and shopping bag clutched to her chest. The bathroom door slammed shut, three inches from his nose.

He glared at the bed. At the closed door. He raked his fingers through his hair and swore beneath his breath.

He pulled out the chair and sat down, then reached for the telephone. He hoped like fury that Squire answered the phone. He didn't want to put up with Daniel's snickering, if Matthew had to explain the situation to *him*. Daniel had been egging Matthew to, well, a polite man wouldn't think too hard on what his younger brother had been yammering at him to do with Jaimie.

Pinching the bridge of his nose, Matthew was too honest not to admit, to himself at least, that lately his own thoughts had been leaning in that direction even *without* his brother goading him. His fingers jabbed the buttons on the phone so hard that number eight stuck, and he spent another minute prying it loose. By the time the line was ringing, his mood had settled even lower.

Joe answered the phone. Matthew nearly groaned with relief. Briefly he told his foreman where they were and why. He didn't expect much of a response from Joe. The man wasn't known for his conversation. But his foreman did confirm that it was snowing heavily at the ranch. Thankfully, Joe didn't see fit to comment on the fact that it was his *sister* who was holed up with the boss in a motel.

Five minutes later Matthew hung up. The bathroom door was still firmly shut. He wondered briefly, fruitlessly, what she was doing in there. Probably standing there, making faces at him from behind the safety of the closed door.

He rotated his shoulders restlessly and unbuttoned his shirt as he went over to study the controls on the heating unit built into the wall beneath the lone window in the room. He turned down the thermostat and flicked open the tan drapes. Snow, illuminated by the bright globes of the parking lot lights, still fell in a steady cloud of white.

Why hadn't he double checked the weather before leaving the ranch? Why had he brought her with him? *Why on earth had he kissed her?*

He was crazy, that was why. And she'd driven him there.

He breathed impatiently and yanked the tails of his shirt out of his jeans, his eyes on the closed bathroom door. Then, realizing what he was doing, he scrubbed his hands down his face and tried concentrating on something else. Anything else.

He flipped on the television. Sat in one of the rickety chairs next to the table. Stood up again and prowled around the room for a few minutes. Finally he yanked back the burnt orange bedspread and propped both pillows against the headboard, then sat back, trying not to think about the fact that unless that sassy redhead *did* sleep in the bathtub, she was going to climb into this very bed sometime before morning.

There was a remote control attached to the nightstand next to the bed and, for lack of anything better to do, he reached over for it. Ten channel-surfing minutes later, he turned off the television and tossed down the remote control. It had been a long time since he'd been in a motel, sure. But when had they started showing X-rated movies? His mind was already active enough without *them.*

He got up and rapped his knuckles on the bathroom door. "You planning to sleep in the tub after all?"

The door jerked open, and Jaimie stood there, staring up at him, her eyes stormy. Damp tendrils of hair clung to her freshly washed face. She was wearing a loose white T-shirt and the same jeans she'd been wearing earlier. "Maybe."

He shrugged, trying to ignore the unwanted shaft of desire that blasted through him. "Hey, sweetheart, it's fine with me. But if you don't mind, I'd kinda like to use the facilities—"

Sure enough, pink color rose right up her neck, and though a good five or six inches shorter than he, she managed to look down her nose at him. "By all means." She swept past him.

Before he went into the bathroom, he saw her slap her purse onto the dresser, followed by the rustle of the paper bag. She was muttering beneath her breath as she leaned down to pull off her brand-new boots.

Oh, yeah, he thought grimly, dragging his eyes from the way her jeans tightened over her rear. This was going to be a lot of fun. A real hoot. He slammed into the bathroom, yanked off his T-shirt and turned on the shower.

Cold.

Chapter Four

As soon as she heard the rush of water, Jaimie sagged. She pulled out the straight-backed desk chair and sat down. The narrow mirror on the wall beside the television reflected her image.

"What have you done wrong lately to deserve this?" Her reflection just looked back at her. Uneasy.

Okay, so maybe she'd had a fantasy or two strongly featuring Matthew. Everybody had a fantasy or two. Right? It wasn't as if she really intended…

For heaven's sake. It was Valentine's Day. For a few more hours, anyway.

She brushed a lock of hair away from her cheek and turned to look at the bed. The dated bedspread was heaped at the foot of it, the pillows bunched against the headboard.

The shower stopped, and through the closed door she could hear the metallic clink of the shower curtain rings. Too easily, her mind pictured Matthew whipping back that heavy white vinyl curtain, water sluicing from his powerful shoulders as he reached for the white towel hanging above the—

"Oh, Lord." Her heart started pounding all over again. She quickly bent and tugged off her other boot and shimmied out of her jeans. The doorknob rattled, and she dived for the bed, swiping a pillow and pulling up the covers. She would have pretended to be asleep, but she wasn't that good at pretending. It was enough that she didn't succumb to her cowardly urge to make herself a bed on the floor. She'd been engaged to be married. But she'd never been in a motel room with a man before. The etiquette of it all—if there was such a thing—was simply beyond her.

When Matthew stepped into view, she was holding the remote. It was an effort, but she managed to keep her eyes on the television. More or less. He crossed in front of the bed and sat on the chair by the window. His white T-shirt, sticking damply in spots, stretched snugly across his shoulders before it disappeared into the waist of his faded jeans.

She shifted uneasily against the pillow and pressed the channel button.

"I called the Double-C. Let them know we're waiting out the snow here."

His voice drew her eyes. His hair was darkly wet and slicked back from his face, making his eyes even more piercing. She looked back at the television, nodding.

"How's your hand? The splinters."

"Fine."

He leaned back in the chair, which gave an ominous creak. "We'll be able to get back as soon as it's light."

His voice was calm with no trace of his earlier frustration. Its deep tone set shivers scurrying across her shoulders. Again she nodded. Dropping the remote onto the mattress, she turned on her side, away from him, and closed her eyes. It didn't help. His image was printed firmly on the inside of her eyelids. Until now she'd never seen his feet bare before. It seemed distressingly intimate.

Matthew studied her back. Her hair streamed across the white pillowcase like strands of fire-licked mahogany. It was also all he could see of her, considering the way she was buried beneath the covers. She was nervous, he realized with a start. Otherwise she would be giving him a full measure of sass and vinegar.

"Sleepy?"

"Yes."

His lips twitched. Little liar, he thought silently. He watched her for a long while, knowing that she wasn't getting any closer to falling asleep. Raking his fingers through his hair, he rose and walked back to the bathroom, feeling her eyes on him as soon as he passed the foot of the bed. When he came out with his boots on, she had pushed herself up on one elbow.

"Where are you going?"

He pulled on his coat. "To the truck." Her eyes rounded. "I'll be back," he assured. He wasn't at all sure that his promise calmed her nerves any. He pocketed the key and left her staring after him.

Once outside he found the wind had calmed a fraction. At least he could see further than ten feet in front of him. He turned up the collar of his coat and strode over to his Blazer where he opened the back gate. The boxes from the grocery were lined up neatly, and he wasted no time reaching for two six-packs—one soda, one beer. His ears were burning with the cold but he took enough time to pull a deck of cards out of the glove box.

It was for a good cause, he told himself as he stuffed the deck in his coat pocket and strode back to the motel. She would relax, and maybe he could get his mind off of…well just *off*.

At the top of the stairs, he dropped some coins into the vending machine, adding to his small load. When he let himself back into their room, Jaimie popped up on her elbow. Her eyes took in his small burden as she slowly set aside the television control.

"Planning to drink yourself to sleep?"

That was more like the sassy woman he knew. He set the six-packs on the table. "Maybe. Here." He handed her a diet cola and the box of Cracker Jacks he'd gotten from the vending machine. "Happy Valentine's Day," he added gruffly.

Her eyes widened and color touched her cheeks as her long, slender fingers wrapped around the box. Then he felt stupid and wished he'd just kept his mouth shut. He yanked off his coat and tossed it aside. "Come over here."

She eyed him over the box of carmel popcorn. "What for?"

So I can have my way with you, he almost growled. If only to see her reaction, he assured himself. He gestured to the table, feeling absurdly warm again. "I don't have any construction paper and glue so playing cards'll have to do. Unless you're fascinated with some program on the idiot box there." He glanced at the television and did a double take. "I see you found the cable channel."

Her eyes flew to the television and her jaw dropped. "I didn't... Oh, Lord..." She turned bright red and scrambled for the remote. The screen went blank and she tossed back the blanket, giving him an eyeful of long, *long,* legs and a flash of black-and-white striped socks. "I wasn't watching that." She carefully set the Cracker Jacks on the nightstand.

He shrugged, reaching for a bottle of beer and checking the thermostat again. But it was set as low as it could be set. Maybe it was just him roasting from the inside out. "Suit yourself."

"I wasn't. You must have left it on that channel."

"Now, Red, why would I do that, when I've got live entertainment right here?" He said it lightly, but as he took a long pull of beer, his eyes followed the way she tugged the hem of her T-shirt an inch further down her thighs. He simply couldn't help it. No wonder he was feeling hot under the collar.

She gaped at him wordlessly, then tugged at her T-shirt again. She snatched up her jeans and dashed into the bathroom. When she returned, her regular color as well as her composure had returned. Mebbe she'd given herself a pep talk in the bathroom mirror. How to put up with a man when stuck in a motel room in three easy steps.

She took an inordinate amount of time opening the soda and taking a long sip as she stood near the foot of the bed. "What kind of cards?" she asked warily.

He shuffled the deck. "Choose your game. I'm easy."

"My foot," she said beneath her breath.

"I heard that."

Her impish smile was sudden and brief and utterly bewitching as she scooted around the table to the second chair. "They must've made these chairs in the forties," she said when it wobbled beneath her slender form. "So what *are* we playing?"

"Depends. What's your game? Hearts? Gin?"

"I don't play cards much." She shrugged. "How about five-card draw?"

His hands hesitated, then shuffled again. "What're we playing for? And money," he glanced at her, "or other assets aren't options."

"Why not?" Not that she had a cent she could afford to lose.

"I don't play for money."

That wasn't exactly an explanation. She knew he didn't have any moral objections to poker, because she'd seen Squire, Matthew, Daniel and Jefferson play on a number of occasions. Of course, they always played for chips. And she knew that Matthew almost always won. She shrugged again, absently looking around the spare motel room. "Well, I don't know. Where's the challenge if we aren't playing for *something?*'' Suddenly she jumped up, leaving the chair wobbling. "I know what we'll do."

Matthew watched her rummage through her purse. "What are you looking for?"

She straightened with a triumphant smile and dashed out the door. It closed with a soft *snick* behind her. Shaking his head, he waited. Sure enough, within a minute, she was knocking softly on the door that had locked automatically upon her exit.

He went over and opened it, propping a lazy arm on the jamb. "Need something?"

"Yeah, *in.* It's cold out here."

"Maybe you should have put on your boots," he suggested, glancing down at her vivid socks.

Her toes wiggled, and she folded her arms around her and rolled her eyes. In fact, her entire body wriggled with the cool air in the corridor. Something that his body took extreme notice of, he realized as his amusement faded, only to be replaced by that awareness of her that never really left him. He moved out of the way and headed back to the relative safety of the deck of cards and the wobbly chairs.

She followed and tossed a bag of foil-wrapped chocolate Kisses on the table. "We'll play for those."

Matthew couldn't help it. He looked from the bag to Jaimie's soft, rosy lips. "Kisses?"

Her ivory throat worked as she swallowed, then she sat on her chair, somehow managing to fold her lethally long legs up on the chair along with her sweetly curved rear. She tore open the bag and poured the candy out on the table. "We'll split the bag," she said and her husky tone wrapped itself around Matthew's spine.

He stifled an oath. What was he doing, sitting here in this infernal motel room with a beautiful woman a decade his junior, playing poker for *Kisses,* for God's sake? He should have just bunked down on the floor and gone to sleep, whether he felt bad that she was nervous, or not.

Yet here he sat. Straightening his share of candy into a neat little row of silver-foiled soldiers and absently shuffling the cards while his mind couldn't get past the notion of tasting that chocolate on her lips. He already knew how she tasted flavored with lemon-laced tea. What would it be like if she unwrapped one of those chocolates and placed it in her mouth? The chocolate would soften and melt, sliding down that long, elegant throat. She would taste ever so sweet—

"Matthew?"

He stared at her. "What?"

"You planning to deal there? Or just shuffle all night?"

Her words were sassy enough. But she wouldn't look at him. And riotous color had filled her cheeks. The confounded woman probably knew exactly what he'd been sitting there thinking. What he'd been thinking even before she had drawn off her coffee-stained sweater and introduced him to the visual delights of pink long johns this morning.

He slapped the deck down on the table, waiting for her to cut. "Ante up." He slid a chocolate to the center of the small table before making short work of the deal.

She added her candy to his and picked up her hand. The bracelet circling her delicate wrist caught the light as she arranged the cards.

"What's lucky about it?" he asked abruptly. Surely that was a safe enough topic.

She slowly raised her eyes from her cards. "Excuse me?"

"Your bracelet. Why is it lucky?"

"Oh." She looked at her wrist for a moment, then returned her attention to her cards. "It was my great-grandmother's. On my mom's side." She set two cards facedown on the table. With her head cocked, she looked at the new additions he dealt.

"And it's lucky because…"

"I said so." She slid him an impish look and added another candy to the pot.

He caught himself starting to smile.

"Actually, it was a gift to her from my great-grandfather. She passed it to my mother when she was pregnant with Joe. Now it's mine." Her eyes softened with an expression Matthew couldn't quite read. "It's the only thing I was able to keep of Mom's when she died. Everything else went to auction," she said after a moment. "It's like if I take it off, then she'll be even more gone." She smiled, shrugging self-consciously. "Silly, I know."

"Not so silly," he murmured. Now it was either play the game or continue sitting there watching her. He figured the game was safer and he called her bet. "It's a good thing we're only playing for Kisses," he observed when she displayed her hand.

He laid down his three of a kind and slid the candy to his side of the table.

"Do you cheat?" she asked casually.

"No."

Her lips twitched. "Figures."

He watched her expertly shuffle the deck. "Thought you didn't play cards *much*," he drawled.

Like a waterfall the cards danced from one hand to the other. She shuffled again and presented the deck for his cut, her eyes laughing. "I don't. But I spent a few months in Reno."

He'd played cards nearly his whole life. He couldn't shuffle like that. "What as? A dealer?"

Her laugh was rich. And infectious. "Hardly. A cocktail waitress. But you pick up a few things."

They anted and Matthew picked up the hand she'd dealt. Nothing. He scooted a candy to the pot, anyway. "Sounds like you've had some interesting jobs."

Her smile dimmed. "A few."

Matthew watched her for a moment. "I didn't say there was anything wrong with that."

Her shoulder moved a fraction. "You'd be one of the first who didn't." She looked up and Matthew wondered why it should bother him that the twinkle in her eyes seemed to be a little forced. "Come on," she said. "We playing poker here or having a private therapy session?" She tapped her cards on the table.

Matthew raised the bet. She won back the candies that she'd just lost. Aside from her fancy shuffling, she wasn't a half-bad player, Matthew decided a while later. But she couldn't bluff worth spit. She had only one candy left. He ran his thumb along the edge of his cards. There was no way on earth she had a good enough hand to beat his. If she did, she would be squirming all over in her seat. Still, he felt strangely reluctant to let the game end.

"Losing your nerve?" she asked sweetly when he still hesitated.

"Not likely. Just figuring out a polite way to tell you to kiss the last of your little Kisses goodbye."

"Don't count your chickens before they're hatched," she warned lightly.

He snorted softly. "Red, the Kisses are in my favor, in case you haven't noticed."

Her lashes swept down over her eyes as she pushed her final candy toward the pot. "Would you take an IOU?"

He laughed outright, earning a startled look from her. "What's the matter?"

"You laughed."

He felt the tips of his ears heat. "So?"

She smiled without a hint of her usual sass. "So, nothing. You should do it more often."

"Make me sound like an ogre," he muttered. "Stop distracting me from the game. You can't make the bet."

"You're not an ogre," she protested. "Not all the time,

anyway. And I'll bet you breakfast in bed for a week that I can beat your hand.''

That brought to mind a whole host of unsuitable ideas. ''Sweetheart, you'd have to get your curvy butt out of bed a whole lot earlier in the morning if you want to give *me* breakfast in bed before my day starts.''

She brushed her hair away from her face, her expression confident. ''Name your pleasure, then. Whatever you say. All or nothing. I'll bet my hand beats yours.''

He decided that his brain was suffering from a diminishing blood supply. It was the only explanation. He squared his cards and laid them facedown on the table, then slowly picked up one of the candies from the pot. Eyes narrowed, he methodically unwrapped it, then stretched his arm across the table. ''Here.''

Confusion drew her eyebrows together.

''Eat it,'' he bade her softly.

She lifted her hand to take the candy from his fingers, but he shook his head. ''Open your mouth.''

Her eyes met his. Her lips parted, more in surprise than anything, he figured. He slipped the candy inside, his thumb brushing her soft lips. Then waited. And just as he'd suspected, she didn't do anything. Just let that chocolate soften and melt.

God, he was nuts. A mid-life crisis? No. There wasn't a single part of his randy body that felt remotely close to mid-life. If anything, he felt like a seventeen-year-old kid, with the hormones to match.

After an eternity, she swallowed, and the tip of her pink little tongue sneaked over her full lower lip, leaving a seductive gleam. ''So what's your pleasure?'' she asked again.

''Watching you eat that chocolate,'' he admitted gruffly.

Color flooded her cheekbones. Her eyes seemed to grow even more emerald. ''That's no bet,'' she said after a moment.

The silence of the motel room twined around them. "We're playing for kisses," he finally said.

She moistened her lips again. "What are you saying?"

He shrugged casually, feeling anything but. "You're a bright woman—"

"Never mind. I get it."

"So?"

Now it was her thumb that ran methodically over the edge of her cards. "You're gonna lose."

Whichever way the cards went, he'd win. Because one way or another he would taste those soft lips again. Poker had never seemed such a dangerous game before.

"Kisses are all we're playing for, right?"

He was a fool. Not an idiot. "Right."

She gave a little shake of her head. "Okay. But I'm warning you that there's no way you can beat my hand. So if you want to back out now, I'll—"

He laid out his cards. Four majestic kings marching across the table.

She gave a soft sound of disgust. "I don't believe it!"

"I warned you."

She tossed her cards onto the table. Three queens slithered across the small mound of candies to lie near his kings. Her eyes wouldn't meet his as she squared her shoulders and stood up. "Okay." She marched in front of him and rested her hands on his shoulders. She leaned over him, bringing with her the scent of lemon and chocolate. Then her soft, smooth lips clung to his for an all-too-brief kiss, and she straightened. "There."

He looped his fingers around her wrist. "Not so fast, Red." He tugged and she landed on his lap with a surprised *oof*. The chair creaked ominously beneath their combined weight. He didn't care. "Seems to me you were more than one kiss behind," he muttered, before tilting her chin up to his.

Sweet. Just like he'd known. He nibbled. He tasted. He took.

And she gave and gave.

Kisses, he reminded himself with a tiny portion of dwindling sanity. Only kisses. So why was he slipping his hand beneath her shirt, feeling the satiny warm stretch of her back?

"Matthew," she breathed against his lips. "Oh, *my*—"

With a sudden crack, the chair collapsed and they landed in a heap on the floor, a tangle of legs and arms and cards and Kisses.

Startled, they stared for a long minute at each other. Then Jaimie giggled. Then laughed. "You should see your face," she got out between chuckles.

"You should see yours," he returned. "You hurt?"

Giggles shaking her shoulders, she shook her head. She wriggled around, untangling herself. Matthew dropped his head back on the floor and closed his eyes, thinking about the cooling effects of a six-foot snow drift.

"Matthew, do you hurt somewhere?"

Like you wouldn't believe. He shook his head and finally closed his hands around her arms, setting her safely to the side. He jackknifed to his feet, keeping his back to her. "I'm fine," he said, reaching for another beer. But beer wasn't what he was parched for and he set it back on the table.

"What about the chair?"

He looked back at the destroyed chair, while his common sense came crashing down around his shoulders. "They shouldn't have furniture that is falling apart."

"It didn't collapse until I...well, that is with both of us...mmm." She fell silent, her giggles finally subsiding.

He thrust his fingers through his hair. "Listen, Jaimie—"

"It's all right, Matthew. I—"

"No, it's not all right." He looked at her, then stooped down to collect the pieces of the chair, which he dumped in the round trash container, leaving the intact seat propped against the wall. "I just don't want you to misunderstand what, ah, happened here."

"Matthew, really," she said brightly. Too brightly. "It's just the...situation. I know that." She pushed her hair behind her ears and knelt to scoop up the dozen candies scattered across the floor. "So let's just chalk it up to Valentine's Day, and forget it. It's not as if you...or I...planned to get stuck here, after all."

Jaimie held her breath and reached a trembling hand for the last candy Kiss. She didn't dare look up at Matthew. After what seemed an eternity, Matthew took a step away.

"Right," he said evenly.

Her shoulders nearly sagged with relief. She dropped the candies into the trash, alongside the splintered chair legs and sat back on her heels. Matthew was looking out the window again. Probably praying for morning to come. *Soon.*

She gathered up the cards and set them on the table. "Well—" she pushed to her feet and brushed her palms down her thighs "—think I'll get some sleep," she managed to say cheerfully. "Thanks for the, uh, the game."

He made a low sound that she didn't even try to interpret. Despite the soda she'd drunk, her throat was dry, and she went into the bathroom, drinking down two full glasses of water. Then, calling her procrastination for what it was, she squared her shoulders, tugged off her jeans and went back out into the room. Matthew was still standing in the window, for which she was grateful, and she climbed into bed.

She stared for a long while at the box of Cracker Jacks on the nightstand, not twelve inches from her nose.

She hoped morning came soon, too. Because she would *never* be able to sleep.

Matthew knew the moment she fell asleep. Not that she started snoring, or anything. One moment she was laying there, as stiff as an iron statue. Unyielding…stiff. The next, she sighed deeply and melted against the mattress.

Still dressed, he lowered himself onto the bed, snapping off the light.

Chalk it up to Valentine's Day.

He should be glad that she could so easily shrug off what they'd been doing. He should be glad.

Why on God's green Earth wasn't he glad?

She shifted and he imagined those long legs stretching beneath the covers that he lay atop. Again she sighed deeply and rolled a little more. Her hair drifted across his shoulder. Resigned to a night of torture, he gave up the fight and slid his arm around her waist. In a movement so natural and trusting that his nerves frayed even more, she slipped back against him, bringing the faint scent of lemon. Her delightfully curvy rear snuggled up against him, separated by his sturdy denim jeans and several blankets. He stifled a groan.

It was going to be a long night.

When he awoke, it was to the hiss of running water.

He looked at the wall that separated the bathroom from the main room. She was in the shower. Just the thought of it had his thoroughly unsatisfied body stirring.

He raked his fingers through his hair, realizing that daylight seeped into the room around the edges of the drapes. He leaned over and peered at his watch on the nightstand. Nearly eight. He was usually up by four. He sat up and grimaced, rubbing his face. Then he stood and grimaced some more at the protest his stiff back made.

He hated motels. Hotels. Inns. He hadn't ever spent the night in one with a decent bed. He moved over to the drapes, pulling them aside. Bright light seemed to sear into his brain. He swallowed an oath, then squinting, looked out again. At least it had stopped snowing. Pristine snow blanketed the hoods of the cars and trucks parked in the parking lot. As he watched, someone appeared pushing a snow blower along the sidewalk.

He dropped the fabric. They would get home this morning. He slowly worked his head around, then rotated his shoulders. And tonight he'd sleep in his own comfortable bed.

Alone.

He ignored that stray thought. Just as he ignored the tightness of his jeans. In the cold light of day, he realized that last night *had* been madness. Valentine's Day madness. He was thirty-nine, for God's sake. Not some horny seventeen-year-old kid.

Suddenly, above the steady rush of water, he heard her singing. Enthusiastically. And ever-so-slightly off-key, if he was any judge. His jeans grew even tighter.

He had to get out of there. He shoved his feet into his boots and his arms into his shirt. Leaving it hanging unbuttoned, he rapped his knuckles on the bathroom door. "Hey songbird—"

The singing abruptly ceased. In his mind he pictured her standing beneath the water, her eyes wide and slightly startled at his knock. Her hair streaming in wet tangles down her slender back... "I'm going for coffee," he told her, his voice rough. Without waiting for an answer, he walked to the entryway, yanked open the door and stomped downstairs. He'd noticed the coffee setup in the lobby when he'd found Jaimie playing cutout queen with those kids.

He didn't even much care what the coffee tasted like. As long as it was hot enough to singe his tongue and take his mind off the redhead up in that shower.

He wasn't the only person seeking a morning jolt. Several people stood around the coffee urn, foam cups in hand, as they stood or sat around the small television in the corner of the room. Matt grabbed himself a cup and joined them, his ears perking up as he realized they were watching the local news.

He grimaced when the story turned to a four-car pileup that had occurred the night before on the highway about twenty miles out of town.

Matthew silently sipped his coffee, his eyes turning to the square coffee table where Jaimie had sat the night before. If they hadn't stayed in town, he and Jaimie would've been traveling right through the area where the accident had occurred.

He noticed a bright red scrap of paper sitting among the magazines on the table and picked it up, while his ears listened to the weather report—more snow—from the television. He held the heart between his thumb and forefinger, easily recognizing Jaimie's handiwork. And for reasons unknown to him, he neatly folded it in half and stuck it in his back pocket before finishing his cup of coffee and pouring a refill.

The news had turned to entertainment, and Matt turned to head back up to the room, but stopped long enough to pour hot water into a second cup. He grabbed an individually wrapped tea bag and a packet of sweetener. Surely she would be dressed by now.

She was. In fact, Jaimie met him on the stairs, coming down as he was going up. Her hair hung in a slick, wet rope of fire down her back. Water drops spotted her plain white thermal shirt. Like a lover, the shirt hugged her curves snugly, before disappearing beneath the waist of the black jeans she'd picked out the day before. Two steps above him, she halted, her slender fingers curling over the stair rail.

"Morning," she said breathlessly.

He dragged his eyes up from the twin nubbins taunting him from beneath the white shirt. Didn't the woman know what a bra was? "Morning." He thrust the cup of water into her hand. "Here."

She looked at the water. "Gee, thanks." Green eyes

twinkled down at him from beneath wisps of bangs. "I love hot water in the morning."

Feeling like an idiot with that paper heart burning a hole in his pocket right through to his rear, something which did *not* improve his mood, he handed over the tea bag and sweetener. "The coffee was pretty bad. Are you ready to go yet?" He knew he sounded abrupt. He didn't care.

He saw her cheerful expression tighten. She nodded, taking the packets from him, and flattened herself sideways against the rail as he passed her on his way up. No doubt she was terrified he would throw her over his shoulder and haul her to their room to have his wicked way with her. She caught up to him when he was standing in front of the closed door.

He looked at her. She was definitely ignoring him, taking her time crumpling the tea bag wrapper in her hand and dipping the bag into the hot water. "The key?"

She slowly looked up. "Excuse me?"

"You don't have the key." His fingers curled. "You left the room without the key."

She arched an eyebrow. "So did you, apparently. I assumed you had it." The tea bag took another dunking. "I'll go get another one."

She spun on her heel before he could respond and disappeared, her braid swaying. She returned before five minutes had even passed, a young man hurriedly following her long stride. She stopped beside Matthew and eyed him impassively. The clerk nearly skidded to a halt when he saw Matthew leaning against the wall beside the door.

Not much more than a teenager, Matthew judged, while the kid fumbled with the huge ring of keys he held. Of course, if the kid kept his eyes on the keys and not on Jaimie's chest, perhaps they would be getting somewhere. Matthew straightened from the wall and stepped an inch closer to the clerk. The kid's Adam's apple bobbed, and the keys clattered to the floor.

Jaimie bent and scooped them up, handing them to the boy, an easy smile on her face. The kid practically dropped the keys again, Matthew noted. As soon as Jaimie's eyes turned to Matthew, though, they cooled. She was perhaps an inch or two taller than the clerk, and over the kid's head their eyes clashed.

Finally the door opened and the clerk stepped out of the way, nervously nodding at Matthew before taking off.

Jaimie went inside and started gathering together her things while Matthew stood in the doorway. Aware that he was watching her too closely, he turned his attention to buttoning up his flannel shirt. It took him all of two seconds to gather up his wallet and change. And another couple minutes in the bathroom. When he came out, she was still scurrying around the room.

Hooking his coat over his shoulder, he leaned against the wall and settled his hat into place while she retrieved her socks from beneath the desk. She scooped up the pink thermal shirt she'd worn the day before from the floor where it lay half-buried by the bedspread. Then the T-shirt she'd slept in; the scarf; her gloves; the cards and the beer and soda they hadn't consumed. At last she straightened, her hands clutching the crumpled edges of the shopping bag together. She'd stuffed everything inside. She picked up her coat and purse. "Ready."

Finally. He went out into the hall.

"No, wait," she said just before he shut the door.

"Women," he grumbled as she slipped in and out again. "What'd you forget?"

"*I* didn't forget anything." Smirking, she held up her hand. His watch dangled from her fingers.

Sass. He took the watch from her and slipped it on. By the time they got back to the ranch his morning would be shot. "Hungry?"

Walking away from him, her braid bobbed. "Starved."

He caught up with her at the exit, where they took a

moment to put on their coats. She was humming under her breath. "Are you always so cheerful in the morning?"

Jaimie didn't need to look up at him to know his ice-blue eyes would be filled with irritation. That his lips would be firmly set. "Are you always such a grump in the morning?" She flipped her braid out from her collar. "Never mind," she said as she pushed through the door, gritting her teeth against the cold rush of air that enfolded them. "I already know you're an equal-opportunity grump. All twenty-four hours of the day are good enough for you," she said lightly. Her breath puffed around her head, and her boots crunched in the fresh snow as she crossed the sidewalk toward the parking lot. She would act like last night had been nothing more than circumstances as she'd claimed, if it killed her. "Do you want to eat before we drive back, or are you in a hurry?"

When he didn't answer, she turned around. He was standing at the curb, his expression shadowed by the low hat brim. "Matthew?" He didn't move, and her feet retraced their steps. "Matthew?"

He notched his hat back with his thumb. "Is that really how I am?" His eyes were serious. "A twenty-four-hour grump?"

Her heart squeezed. He hadn't been last night. "Sometimes," she whispered, closing her fingers around the edges of the Cracker Jack box hidden inside the deep side pocket of her coat. "Mostly when I'm around." She'd seen him with his brothers. With Emily. He wasn't a grump with them. He was a decent, hardworking man, full of patience and an easy humor. *She* was the one who seemed to bring out the worst in him.

He seemed to mull over her words. After a moment he jammed his hat down on his head again. "It's cold. Pull up your collar," he ordered, and set off across the parking lot.

For a moment Jaimie hung back, watching him. Dark

brown cowboy hat shading his face. Hands tucked in the pockets of his heavy sheepskin jacket while his long legs ate up the distance toward his truck. Sighing, she followed his footsteps, pulling up her collar as she went.

Chapter Five

Matthew hung up the phone and propped his elbows on his desk, the thumbs of his clasped fists tapping his mouth. He wasn't all that sure he should've made this particular call. Donna Blanchard was a nice woman. She was hanging on to the small piece of land bordering a northeast portion of the Double-C by the skin of her fingernails. Matthew had known her for years.

He'd known her when her father had virtually drunk away his operation. He'd known her when she'd married that good-for-nothing Cliff Blanchard. And he'd known her when old Cliff took off with Suzette Lipton. Suzette had been a waitress, for lack of a more proper term, at Colbys—the bar that comprised half of the dinky town of Weaver, about twenty miles south. If a person wanted booze, poker or pool, Colbys was the place to go. Suzette, however, had been known to provide even more individual pleasures.

No doubt about it, Donna Blanchard had had her share

of troubles. But she'd always been a nice lady. A strong woman. A decent neighbor.

Still, Matthew couldn't shake the vague sense that he should've never made that phone call. If it hadn't been for that annoying *grumpy* thing nagging at him for the past week, he would never even have thought of doing what he'd just done.

There'd been no mistaking the surprise in Donna's voice when he called. Sure, they saw each other now and again, being neighbors and all. They would shoot the breeze over coffee at Ruby's Café in Weaver. Talk about feed, seed, grain and beef. Matthew figured she was pretty well accustomed to a rancher's life. She knew it through and through.

He looked at the tray of coffee that Jaimie had left on the corner of his desk earlier that morning. His empty mug sat in the center of a big white snowflake cutout.

Yes, Donna knew ranch life. And he would bet his first calf of the season that Donna didn't go around cutting holiday shapes out of every piece of colored paper she found, either.

Matthew growled impatiently and leaned back in his chair, glancing out the window. A purple-coated redhead zigzagged across the road, chasing after a streak of gray fur. Sandy bounded behind them both, barking excitedly.

His hands closed over the arms of his chair when he saw her stumble, then fall headfirst into a snowbank. But Jaimie was already flipped over onto her back, the cat in her arms. When D.C. skittered away a few moments later, chased closely by Sandy, Jaimie lifted her head. He was too far to see her exact expression, but he was certain her green eyes would be filled with laughter.

His hands relaxed. He swiveled his chair a little more and watched her head fall back against the snow. Her hair streaked out about her, the white bank making the color appear even darker. Her arms and legs started to move, and a grin tugged at his lips. She was out there making snow angels.

She looked about fifteen.

And he felt like a hundred-year-old lech slobbering over her from his window. Disgusted, he whirled around and faced his desk again. It was a good thing he'd called Donna, he decided. She was his age. They had a lot in common. What harm could a simple dinner do?

Jaimie stared at Matthew, unable to believe her ears. The man had been avoiding her all week, and when he finally did seek her out, it was because of this? Water dripped unheeded from her mop onto her bare feet and the floor. ''You want what?''

''You know how to fix spaghetti, don't you?''

Her grip tightened on the handle of the mop. He was lucky she didn't pitch it at his head. ''Yes.'' She forced the words through her teeth. ''I know how to fix spaghetti.'' And garlic bread and Caesar salad, and she could even toss in a terrific dessert. And hope that they both choked. ''*Who* is Donna?''

''Donna Blanchard,'' he said. ''A neighbor.''

''Ahh.'' That explained it. Matthew had invited his neighbor to dinner. His female neighbor. In all the time she'd been at the Double-C, whether working or visiting, she'd never once seen Matthew invite a woman to the ranch. Neighbor or otherwise.

She shoved the mop into the water, splashing water over the side of the pail. ''Anybody else?''

''Hmm?''

''How many will there be for dinner?'' Jefferson and Emily, hopefully. Maybe Matthew just wanted to have some social interaction. Lord knew that Daniel had been remarkably scarce these days. And Squire had been practically living down in Casper.

''Just the two of us.'' He set down his coffee long

enough to pull on his coat and shove his hat on his head. "Squire's likely to be at Gloria's awhile. Who knows what Dan's doing." Without another glance her way, he took his mug and headed outside.

"Just the two of us." She slopped the mop onto the floor, sending a small tidal wave across the linoleum. "Of all the nerve…asking me to cook for him and his…his… *ooooh*." Jaimie set to mopping the floor so vigorously that she broke out into a sweat and had to peel off her heavy sweater. She tossed it onto the table before plopping down onto a chair.

In all the varied jobs she'd held in her lifetime, a maid had never been one of them. Thank goodness. Oh, it was a perfectly respectable job…just not one of her favorites. She leaned forward in the chair and wrung out the mop.

Of course Matthew expected her to cook his dinner. That's what he paid her to do. She would cook for him and that woman, but that didn't mean she would have to like it. In fact, just the idea of preparing this particular meal pretty well made her want to spit.

She stood up, stretching the kinks out of her muscles. She dumped the mop water and put everything away. Matthew said he wanted to eat about seven, leaving her several hours yet. Matthew and Squire and Dan, if he was around, always ate promptly at five. "He probably wants time to get beautiful," she muttered, her fingernails digging into her palms.

Her stomach twisted. She'd never figured she would be the jealous type. It had never cropped up before. Not even during her doomed engagement. And now it wasn't a pleasant realization. Groaning, she buried her face in her hands. She didn't even have a right to be jealous. Perhaps that's what hurt most of all. To Matthew, that night in Gillette notwithstanding, she was nothing but an employee. An employee he'd been more or less forced to hire.

"Feel a little more sorry for yourself, Jaimie, my girl," she told herself. She would fix his spaghetti dinner. She would even serve it with a smile. And hope that she kept her temper and didn't dump the food right into his lap.

She headed for the dining room. Fifteen minutes later she'd found everything necessary to set the table for a romantic dinner. The only way she'd been able to do it without breaking the china had been to imagine that *she* was the woman with whom he planned to share his table. When she stood back and looked at the gold-rimmed china and gleaming crystal, her chest grew tight.

She wasn't that woman, and it was foolish to even pretend that she could be.

Matthew Clay was out of her league. He could have his pick of women. He certainly wouldn't choose a former city girl who hadn't stuck with one single thing in her life for more than a year.

Clearing her throat, she turned away in search of her socks and boots. Where had she left them? Maybe downstairs when she'd been dusting. Her feet slapped against the cool wood as she went down to the recreation room. Sure enough, her socks were sitting in crumpled balls by the pool table. She shook them out and pulled them on, then stepped into the boots that she still hadn't become accustomed to. It was a shame that her tennis shoes were ruined beyond recognition.

Wiggling her toes in the stiff boots, she leaned back against the pool table. It had been down in this very room only six months ago that Jaimie had shared her one and only dance with Matthew Clay. Her hand absently smoothed the gleaming wood beside her. It had been the night Emily had invited her, Joe and Maggie to dinner. To celebrate Squire's homecoming from the hospital.

They'd all been down in this room. All of Squire's five sons had been home. They were an overwhelming group of men. Each one compelling in his own right. But Jaimie hadn't been able to tear her eyes from Matthew. Music had rocked the room. More than a few beer bottles had been raised. Matthew's youngest brother, Tristan, had been swinging Emily around the room in a wild dance, and suddenly Jaimie had found herself in Matthew's arms.

Her throat tightened. That dance, innocent as it had been, had kept her awake for weeks. Just as the night they'd spent in town had disturbed her sleep every night since. Every time she closed her eyes she remembered the feel of his lips on hers. The broad, strong breadth of his shoulders beneath her hands...

This is ridiculous. She knew that Matthew had felt uncomfortable about the mischief they'd gotten up to. She need only remember the look of masculine relief on his face when she'd told him to dismiss the entire thing.

She stomped her feet inside the stiff boots as if to underline that thought and went upstairs.

Maggie was sitting at the kitchen table in her cozy house when Jaimie headed back over to check on her. Her pen tapped the opened checkbook in front of her, while she peered at the bills scattered across the table.

"Well, you must be feeling better," Jaimie said, surprised. She quickly shut the door behind her and slipped out of her coat.

Maggie shrugged, her attention still on the items on the table.

"Did you eat?"

Maggie shook her head.

Jaimie wandered into the kitchen, passing the round table that filled the small bay. She opened the refrigerator and looked inside. "Do you want something?" She straightened and looked over the open door. "Mag?"

"Hmm?"

"Want anything to eat? Soup?"

"Sure," Maggie said absently. Her pen scratched across the paper next to the checkbook.

Jaimie selected a diet soda for herself and pulled out the

soup that she'd made the day before. Within minutes she set a steaming bowl beside Maggie, along with a tall glass of milk.

Maggie finally looked up when Jaimie sat down at the table. She stared hard at the food. "Is that for me?"

"Mmm-hmm."

"Oh." Maggie rolled her eyes and set down her pen. "Right. I guess I was a little distracted." She scooted the bowl closer and picked up the spoon, gingerly lifting a spoonful of creamy soup to her lips. "This is good."

"Of course. I used your recipe."

"That explains it then," Maggie murmured, smiling slightly. "Did you take any up to the big house? You should," she added when Jaimie shook her head. "Matthew loves broccoli soup." She took another taste. "Any soup, actually."

Jaimie fiddled with the pop top on her can, well aware of Matthew's favorite foods. "He's already asked for spaghetti," she said. "Never mind the fact that I've got a turkey casserole sitting in the fridge over there, just waiting to be baked," she added, disgruntled.

"Matthew's never been fussy. In fact, those men have always seemed grateful just to get something edible and hot. Did you tell him you'd already started supper?"

Jaimie leaned her elbows on the table. "Nope." She sipped at her soda, her eyes narrowed. "He has company coming. Donna Blanchard. Do you know her?"

Maggie set her spoon down and delicately slid the bowl out of her sight. She nodded. "Yes."

"And?"

"She's nice."

"Figures."

"She's lived here for years," Maggie went on. "If Matthew were interested in her, I hardly think he'd have let all this time go by without doing something about it."

"I could not care less if Matthew's interested in Donna

Blanchard.'' Jaimie uttered the lie so blithely, she half expected lightning to strike her down.

''Right.''

''He's a cranky stick-in-the-mud.''

''Right.''

''Well, he is.'' Jaimie raked her hair back from her face.

''You have got it bad, haven't you?'' Maggie leaned forward and patted Jaimie's hand.

There wasn't any point in denying it. Maggie had known her too long. Jaimie looked out the window, thinking how much she'd come to love the ranch. Snowdrifts, incessant wind and all. How much the idea of staying-put somewhere actually appealed. To *her*. She shrugged, not as casually as she would have liked. ''I could tap-dance on his head and he probably wouldn't even notice. He'd just swat me away like some annoying bug.'' She slapped her palms on the table and rose. ''And now I get the pleasure of serving him and his new girlfriend a romantic spaghetti dinner. I'll probably walk in with their dessert only to find them doing that *Lady and the Tramp* thing with the spaghetti noodle.''

Maggie chuckled. ''Somehow I can't see Matthew and Donna doing *that*.''

''I can. I can imagine that. And a lot more,'' she said darkly. After all, what the man could do with a chocolate kiss should be outlawed.

''So do something about it.''

''Like what? Dump the Caesar salad in his lap?'' Jaimie's eyes narrowed. ''Give him an excuse to get out of his pants with Donna Blanchard sitting right beside him? I don't think so.''

''I'm serious.''

''So am I.'' Jaimie's wicked grin died. ''I just need to get over this, that's all.''

''Why? Matthew is a good man. You could do a lot worse.''

Jaimie frowned. ''He's not interested in me that way.

He's made no secret of the fact that I don't belong on his ranch. *Any* ranch. And even if he was interested, well, I'm not cut out for the marriage and kids bit, anyway. I'm not going to apologize for the way I am. Not for him. Not for anyone.'' *Not ever again.* She'd spent enough of her life trying to live it to please other people. It hadn't worked out once.

She went over to the coat rack and retrieved her jacket.

"Jaimie—"

"Mmm?" The zip fastened, she flipped her hair out from beneath the collar.

Maggie tilted her head, her pale, golden hair spilling over her shoulder. "Matthew is not Tony."

Jaimie paused at the mention of her ex-fiancé. Matthew was ten times the man Tony had been. But that didn't change the facts. "I know."

"Matthew's as steady as they come," Maggie was saying. "So are you. He's bound to see that."

"Me steady?" Jaimie managed a light laugh. "You're talking to a woman who's had no less than, hmm… eighteen? Nope. *Nineteen* different jobs." She opened the door and stepped through. "Matthew has his pick of women. Why on earth would he settle for me? I won't even be staying here, once your baby arrives and you're back on your feet." She closed the door before Maggie could respond. Maggie had been the encouraging force in Jaimie's life for a long time now. But not even Maggie could get around that particular fact.

Jaimie had covered the salad with plastic wrap and was sliding it into the refrigerator when the doorbell rang just before seven. She'd never heard it ring in the big house before. Everybody always came around to the back and through the mudroom.

Her lower lip jutted out as she shifted bottles on the shelf to make room for the salad. Was answering the door part of her duties, too? The chimes sounded again, and she huffed. Closing the refrigerator door, she started for the living room, stopping short as she realized Matthew was heading down the stairs to the door. His head was lowered as he buttoned the loose charcoal gray shirt he wore with black jeans.

The smoky silk clung to his broad shoulders, billowing about his hard stomach, yet still managing to emphasize his leanness. The jeans finished the job, hugging his tight rear and muscular thighs.

Jaimie kept herself hidden in the archway of the dining room, slathering over him in his unfamiliar garb. Heaven knew Matthew looked sinful in his usual faded jeans and soft, flannel shirts. But tonight...

Rooted in place, Jaimie watched him swing open the door, his smile easy as he greeted his dinner guest.

Donna Blanchard walked in, and Jaimie bit her lip, her heart sinking. The woman was everything Jaimie was not. Her nut brown hair was sleek, hugging exotic cheekbones and big brown Bambi eyes that Jaimie could see clear across the room. Then Matthew helped the woman off with her hip-length coat to reveal a figure that made Jaimie's eyes nearly pop out. She swallowed, hard, and turned from the sight.

Back in the kitchen she banged a few pots around. Sandy scrambled from her position under the table and trotted out. "They're probably fake," she grumbled to the departing dog. "Real women just aren't built like that."

"Like what?"

She whirled around, knocking the spaghetti pot off the counter. It made an awful racket as it rolled across the floor, stopping at the toe of Matthew's highly polished boot. Her cheeks burned.

He bent and picked up the pot. "Good thing it was empty," he murmured drily, returning it to the counter before opening the refrigerator to pull out two bottles of beer.

Naturally the woman drank beer. Personally, Jaimie hated the stuff. She brushed the bangs from her eyes and turned to fill the pot with water. Resolutely she ignored his freshly showered scent. She'd never before noticed how good a man could smell.

"When do you want to eat?" It was an effort to get out the question.

She could feel his eyes on her back as he twisted open one of the bottles. Unable to stand it, she finally looked over her shoulder at him, seeing him take a long drink. His eyes, always startling in their translucency, steadily watched her. Absurdly she felt her cheeks heat all over again. She swallowed and turned to heft the pot onto the stove. "Well?"

"Whenever it's ready." Suddenly he stepped closer and touched her cheek. She nearly jumped a foot.

Matthew smiled faintly and held up his thumb to show her the smear of chocolate. "Dessert, I presume?"

Jaimie snatched up the dish towel and wiped her face. "Go away. I'm sure you don't want your...date to get lonely."

His smile died, but the watchful look in his eyes didn't. He lifted his hand and tasted the chocolate on his thumb.

Jaimie's heart jerked. For the rest of her life, she knew that she would associate chocolate with Matthew. She turned away, crumpling the towel in her hands.

His voice was quiet. "It's one of my favorites."

Of course it was. That was the reason she'd made it for him. She heard his steps carry him from the room. Back to that woman with the fabulous figure. After adding the pasta to the boiling water, she felt for a chair and sank onto it.

When Daniel came into the kitchen and crouched down beside her chair, she stared at him.

"Hey," he grinned. "Don't look at me like I just sprang from a pod or something."

Jaimie dragged herself together. "Sorry. I did't even hear you come in."

He shrugged and straightened, tossing his hat over to the pegs by the door and landing it perfectly. "Whatcha cooking?"

"Spaghetti and garlic bread." Brushing her hair out of her eyes, Jaimie stood up. Washing her hands gave her something to do. Everything was ready to serve as soon as the pasta was cooked.

Daniel leaned against the counter beside her, crossing his ankles. "Kinda late for supper, isn't it?" He rolled up first one long denim sleeve, then the other.

"Matthew has a, um, a guest."

"No kidding?" He made a surprised grunt. "Who?"

"Donna. Are you hungry?"

"Blanchard?" He rolled his shoulders. "Since when has Matt taken up with the neighbor-lady?"

Jaimie's shoulder lifted. "Who knows. So, are you hungry or not?" She wanted, more than anything, to think that Daniel would be joining the cozy twosome at that elegant dining table. "I can set you a place—"

"Nah. I already ate at Jefferson's."

"Oh."

"I'll have a plate in here, though," he said. "Supper *was* a few hours ago," he added, his lips twitching. "Wouldn't want to interrupt the budding lovebirds."

Jaimie dropped the crystal bowl she'd planned to serve the chocolate mousse in. She cried out when it hit the floor, exploding into a shower of tiny shards.

Daniel scooted back a few inches. "Don't move," he ordered.

How could she? She was surrounded by glass and, as usual, her boots were anywhere but on her feet. Suddenly Daniel reached over and lifted her right off the ground and out of the field of broken glass. Startled, she closed her hands over his shoulders.

"What the hell are you doing?" Matthew paused in the doorway, his fingers curling. Daniel and Jaimie both looked over at him, for all the world looking like they'd just gotten caught with their hands in the cookie jar. His eyes narrowed on his brother's gaze. Daniel's eyes glinted, but he didn't set Jaimie down.

Matthew seriously considered strangling his brother.

"I broke a bowl," Jaimie explained, her color high. Like it had been that night outside the diner. After he'd made an ass of himself kissing her. Before he'd made an even bigger ass of himself in the motel room.

"I heard." Matthew forced his fists to relax. He was vaguely aware of Donna moving up behind his shoulder and then was disgusted with himself that he'd nearly forgotten her, waiting for him in the living room. "Clean it up," he suggested abruptly and turned toward Donna.

"Everything all right?"

He nodded and they returned to the living room. Donna sat on the couch, easily giving him room to sit beside her, if he chose. He stepped around the cherry coffee table and sat in a wing chair. He felt like an idiot. In his own home. And it was all that redhead's fault.

He was aware of Donna asking after Squire. And he was aware of answering. But his thoughts were all on that scene in the kitchen. Of Jaimie.

In his brother's arms.

Eventually he found himself sitting at the table, with Jaimie unobtrusively moving quietly back and forth, serving this, filling that. He wondered if she'd been a regular waitress, in addition to that cocktail stint she'd mentioned. She was good at what she did. If he'd been more interested in his dining companion than his cook, he would have hardly noticed her.

But notice her he did. Even the excellent food failed to distract him.

He shook himself mentally and put more effort into concentrating on Donna. She looked as nice as she ever did. But that spicy perfume she wore was giving him a headache.

It was dark and beginning to snow again when Donna finally announced it was time she went home. In good conscience Matthew couldn't let her go by herself. So he followed her in his truck. He noticed absently as they left that both Joe's and Dan's pickups were gone.

Twenty minutes later he pulled up behind Donna's aging Bronco and walked her to the house. She paused on her porch, her dark eyes looking up at him. With something akin to panic, he wondered if she was waiting for him to kiss her. Good God, what had he gotten himself into? He should've never made that phone call.

Donna smiled slightly. She was old enough to recognize an uneasy male. "It's been an...interesting evening, Matthew."

"Look, Donna...I—"

She smiled again and leaned up to kiss his cheek. "The meal was delicious," she said. "Your Jaimie is a wonderful cook."

"She's not my Jaimie."

Donna merely smiled. She leaned back against the closed door. It would be pointless to ask him in for coffee, and they both knew it. "So, you want to tell me what this was all about?"

He felt like a heel. "Is there a law against asking my neighbor over for supper?"

"No. No law." She shifted, crossing her arms over her chest. "I was a tad surprised though."

He sighed faintly. "I s'pose I should apologize. You know. For being—"

"A bit distracted?" she suggested. Her smile widened. "No sweat, Matthew. I had a great meal. A handsome man to look at across the table." She chuckled when he snorted.

"To tell you the truth, I thought perhaps you were gonna make another offer on this place."

Surprise held him. "Last time I did, you weren't interested."

"Maybe I'm interested now." She shook her head and moved past him to lean against the wooden porch railing that had needed a new coat of paint for about five years now. "I'm getting tired of fighting," she admitted. "The weather. Beef prices." She looked over her shoulder at him. "If you're still interested in buying, I'm interested in selling." Her lips tilted. "At least I can trust you to not run sheep."

At that, his self-disgust over the evening eased. Some. He joined her at the rail. "You're serious about this. What'll you do?"

"Buy a house somewhere. Get a job." She smiled again. "Meet a man."

"Ouch."

A gust of wind blew through the porch, bringing snow with it and rattling the storm door behind them. "So, what do you think? Interested in increasing the Double-C again by a few acres? Good grazing land," she pointed out... needlessly, considering he'd been leasing her land for the past few years.

"Yeah, I'm still interested. I'll get back to you."

"Good enough." She turned and pulled open the door.

"Donna—"

"Yes?"

"Thanks." She smiled again. And if Matthew had a lick of sense in his pea brain, he would be kissing those lips, rather than itching to get his hands on a certain redhead.

"Goodnight, Matthew." She let herself into the house and closed the door.

Matthew watched the snow drift down, big fat flakes that glimmered in the circle of light cast by the bare porch bulb. He sighed, settled his hat and headed for his truck.

Chapter Six

It didn't take long for Matthew to realize that Jaimie had turned the tables on him. *She* was avoiding *him*. For the better part of a week now she'd been anywhere but in Matthew's range. He would walk into the kitchen and she would find some reason to go outside. He would find her in the barn, cooing to the horses and cuddling D.C., and she would disappear into the house. He almost thought he had her when he came upon her cleaning the shower in his bathroom. But the phone rang, and by the time he'd finished the call, Jaimie had gathered her supplies and disappeared again. Even his own dog seemed to have glued herself to Jaimie's side.

It was mighty irritating. A fact that did nothing to improve his mood. For crying out loud, what did it matter to him if she avoided him? He had enough on his plate without messing with that redhead.

Such as working out the details of buying Donna's spread. Such as figuring out why his feed invoices seemed to be skyrocketing for no apparent reason. Such as getting a decent night's sleep, undisturbed by increasingly vivid dreams of a certain sassy female.

Impatiently Matthew shoved the feed records into a folder. He would have to wait for Emily to look them over. She was a CPA. Surely she would be able to spot what he couldn't. If he didn't get himself out into some fresh air, he would start climbing the walls. Never mind the fact that he'd been up, as usual, well before dawn, checking the stock. Tending the new calves that had dropped. Making sure the stock's water hadn't frozen over. Splitting fresh bales of hay.

He left the bulging folder in the center of his desk and headed for the kitchen. It was as clean as a whistle, all signs of breakfast cleared away. He stood in the middle of the empty room, aware that he was listening for some sound. Some indication that Jaimie was in the house. But the only thing he heard was the steady ticking of the clock hanging on the wall.

God, he was losing it.

He grabbed his hat and vest and stomped through the mudroom, the storm door slamming shut behind him. The last few days had been warming, a tempting prelude to spring, and his boots slogged through the slush toward the horse barn. He knew from long experience, though, that even after spring officially began, the snow could still come. Would still come.

He stepped into the barn. The interior was warm, smelling familiarly of horse and hay. His boot heels rang on the concrete aisle between the stalls, and several horses greeted him, their heads bobbing as he stopped to greet each one, slowly working his way to the end stall. When he reached it, Jasper snorted softly and nudged Matthew's palm, looking for his usual bite of carrot.

Matthew obliged, stepping into the stall with his horse. "Hey, Jas," he murmured, running his hand over Jasper's bloodred coat. Jasper shifted, pressing his weight against Matthew's shoulders. "You're sniffing that fresh air out there, aren't you?" Jasper snorted softly. "Me too, bud," Matthew muttered.

He reached around to the halter hanging from a hook and slipped it over Jasper's head, then led the horse out into the aisle before retrieving his tack. Matthew knew Jasper was as anxious to get on the way as he was himself, and in minutes they were heading off across the north pasture.

It wasn't entirely a pleasure ride. Second nature had Matthew's eyes checking fence. Before the snow had gotten heavy, they had moved the cattle to the lower pastures. Now most of the stock congregated near the feed and water, with few venturing out to the farther reaches. Jasper's head bobbed, but Matthew held him to a walk while he worked from one huddle of black-coated Angus to the next. A couple times, he dismounted to more closely check the soon-to-be mamas.

Satisfied at last, Matthew swung back up in the saddle, settled his hat lower, shading his eyes against the sun's glare on the snow, and gave Jasper his head.

Jaimie, arms full with a load of firewood, caught sight of man and horse tearing off toward the trees to the west of the buildings. He was a man entirely in his element. So much so that it made her chest hurt.

What would it be like to belong somewhere the way Matthew belonged to the Double-C? To be part of something so large and beautiful and challenging.

Her arms were straining against the weight of the wood, but she watched Matthew until he was an indistinguishable rider on the horizon. Indistinguishable? Please. She would recognize the way he sat in the saddle, the tilt of his cowboy hat over his brow, even if she was half-blind.

She huffed, impatient with herself, and continued on with her load, shouldering her way through the door of Joe's and

Maggie's house where she stacked the firewood in the wrought-iron box alongside the fireplace.

She straightened her back, kneading her fingertips against the knots there. If Joe had only brought the wood in like he'd promised before he'd gone to town, she wouldn't have just spent the last hour traipsing back and forth to the cord of wood stored on the far side of the big house. He would have been able to carry twice what she could, in half the time.

Oh, well. Dusting her hands against the seat of her jeans, she peeked through the open door to the master bedroom. She was glad to see that Maggie was still sleeping. Jaimie knew for a fact that her sister-in-law had been awake most of the night.

The foreman's house was sturdily built, yet cozy. When one of the occupants was up all night pacing back and forth, it was generally noticeable to the other occupants. Last night Jaimie had finally tossed back her blankets, planning to investigate when she'd heard her brother's voice after he'd come in well after midnight. Only by stuffing a pillow over her head had Jaimie been able to block out the softly hissed argument that had ensued between Joe and his wife.

She'd planned to talk to Joe earlier this morning about it, and to that end she'd pitched in, mucking out stalls. But he'd left her to the chore alone, mumbling something about driving in to Weaver.

She heated herself a mug of cocoa, absently picking a sliver of wood from the sleeve of her dark green sweater. She'd been trying to ignore the tension between Maggie and Joe for weeks now. But it was getting harder and harder to pretend that everything was hunky-dory between the couple. Not while she lived right under their roof.

Too antsy to sit around and be quiet so that Maggie wouldn't be disturbed, Jaimie took her mug and let herself back outside. The air was fresh, touching her cheeks and nose with a brisk bite. Enjoying the freedom of not being bundled inside a heavy coat for the first time in weeks, Jaimie meandered toward the horse barn. Sandy trotted along, her tail going a mile a minute.

She was truly at loose ends. No wash loads awaited her. No dusting or vacuuming or cooking, either. There was an assortment of items packaged in Joe and Maggie's fridge, just waiting for Maggie to be tempted. Squire was still in Casper and Dan was out.

She should have been feeling lonely, Jaimie realized as she drained her cocoa and set the mug on a shelf in the tack room. But she found that she enjoyed the solitude that some of her days brought. She reached for the saddle that Matthew had told her to use months ago.

One thing about Matthew. He wasn't stingy with the horses. Once he'd satisfied himself that Jaimie wouldn't break her neck, he'd given her an open invitation to the horses. Except Jasper, who, beautiful though the horse was, didn't much care for anybody except Matthew...and the mares, of course.

Jaimie left the saddle braced against the wall to retrieve the rest of her tack, her lips twitching. Jasper enjoyed the mares, all right. More than once he'd kicked through a stall or two, anxious to have his way.

She let herself into Daisy's stall, chuckling when the mare butted her shoulder. Sandy waited patiently outside the stall while Jaimie saddled and bridled the spotted gray mare. She led Daisy out into the clear day, smiling when the mare breathed deeply, shaking her head, jangling the bit. Sandy barked and pranced around, anxious to go.

Jaimie laughed at the dog's exuberance. Once she was settled in the saddle, she looked in the direction Matthew had headed earlier.

No. She wasn't going to follow him. She simply wasn't.

Resolute, she headed Daisy in the opposite direction, calling to Sandy who followed along as Daisy leisurely picked her way across the gravel road to the open field.

They wandered contentedly for nearly an hour, staying near the snowplowed road, keeping the outbuildings in sight. Jaimie felt a surge of pride in the well-kept facilities. The strength and basic solidity of the entire ranch. Just as quickly she told herself to get a grip. She had no right to feel so proprietary.

Despite her stern warning, though, she couldn't help enjoying the ride. Couldn't help dreaming, just a little, that the Double-C really was her home. Sandy had stopped following them earlier, and eventually the crisp air started to bite through Jaimie's heavy cable-knit sweater. She clicked to Daisy, who set off in a smooth lope, covering the distance back in a third of the time.

By the time Jaimie dismounted outside the horse barn, her cheeks were cold. She removed the saddle and walked Daisy until the horse had cooled, then led her back into her stall and replaced the tack. Daisy was munching away, seemingly oblivious to the brush Jaimie used to groom her, when Jaimie realized they weren't alone.

She looked over to see Matthew leading Jasper back to that end stall. Daisy lifted her head at the sound. Her tail swished, and she shifted. Jaimie knew how the mare felt. If she had a tail to swish around at the sight of Matthew, she'd be swishing away.

She watched him toss his vest over the top rail, and it occurred to her that he didn't know she was standing on the far side of Daisy four stalls over and across the aisle. Taking shameful advantage, Jaimie looked on silently while Matthew returned a somewhat unwilling Jasper to his stall.

Matthew lifted his hat and drew his arm across his brow, making the fabric of his blue-and-black-plaid flannel shirt tighten across his wide back.

Jaimie swallowed, absently running the brush over Daisy's withers.

Finally Jasper was settled, and Matthew, carrying his saddle as easily as if it were a down pillow, disappeared for a moment in the tack room. She heard him moving around inside for a few minutes. He reappeared within minutes and started toward Jaimie.

She thought he would pass right on by, completely ignorant of her presence. But he slowed, then stopped. He hooked his boot over the lowest slat on the gate and folded his arms across the top. And she knew then that he'd been fully aware of her presence all along.

Jaimie held the brush so tightly, the bristles dug into her palm. She had no escape route here. No chores she could use as an excuse to keep her stupid, foolish heart from tripping all over itself. Maybe if she hadn't gone on that ride just now and let herself daydream about him, she'd have more strength. It seemed all she could do was stare at him.

"You've made a friend."

She nodded, desperately shoring up her resolve. *He wants Donna Blanchard,* she fiercely reminded herself.

He nodded, too, then looked to the side. The toe of his boot tapped against the wooden rail. Her heart pounded, and she was surprised he couldn't hear it in the thick silence. "You've been working hard," he said after a moment.

"So?" Lord, she hadn't expected the word to come out so sharp. So defensive.

Matthew thumbed his hat back an inch. "So…nothing." His shoulders moved, irritated. "Just trying to make conversation. You've been slicker than a greased pig lately."

"Oh, thank you so much." She lifted the brush to Daisy once more. "Women just *love* to be compared to big fat pigs."

"Who said anything about fat pigs?"

"You did."

"I did not."

She shot him a look. "What do you want? Another dinner for you and your new girlfriend?"

His eyes narrowed, icy blue among those curiously dark lashes. "I'm going over to Jefferson's," he said, ignoring her question for one of his own. "Do you want to come or not?"

"Yes."

"Fine."

They glared at each other.

Jaimie was the first to move. She pushed his arms on the gate. "Get out of the way, then."

He didn't budge. "Say 'please.'"

Oh, when did she ever think he was a nice man? "Please." She smiled, saccharine sweet.

He lifted his arms and unlatched the gate, swinging it wide, and she sailed through.

"Sassy brat," he muttered.

She turned, her hand on her hip. "What's that?"

"You heard me, Red. You've been nothing but sass since you put your high-heeled sandals on Double-C soil."

"Well, pardon me," she snapped, stung. "I can't imagine why you'd ask me to go with you if my company is so objectionable."

"The only thing objectionable about you, sweetheart, is your tongue."

One moment she was holding the grooming brush in her hand and the next she'd launched it at his head. Horrified at herself, she could only stare as his hand shot up to catch the missile.

He set the brush on the wide top rail and stepped toward her.

"Matthew—" she lifted her hands. "—I'm sorry. That was in—" she backed up a step "—inexcusable."

"Yup," he drawled.

She licked her lips and backed up another step, bumping her elbow against the row of stalls. "I said I'm sorry. What more do you want?"

His lips quirked, his expression pained. "Sweetheart, you wouldn't believe me if I told you."

"Stop calling me that."

"What?"

"'Sweetheart.'" Her lips firmed. "I'm not your sweetheart," she snapped, wholeheartedly wishing that she didn't want *exactly* that.

He took a step closer, and she nearly jumped out of her skin when he placed his hands on the rail either side of her shoulders. "Okay, *Jaimie.*"

Ohmigod, that was worse. The way his lips closed over her name sent all sorts of yearnings rushing through her. "Look, you just annoyed me, okay?" She hated the way her breath was suddenly rushing unsteadily past her lips. "Calling me a pig and…and all."

"I did *not* call you a pig." He slowly shook his head. "The way your mind works is a complete mystery."

"There you go again!" She pushed at his chest, but he was an immovable object. "Get your hands off me."

"My hands aren't on you," he pointed out reasonably. "But you," he closed his big palm over the fists pushing at his chest, "have yours on me."

She tried to pull her hands away. Futile. He simply wrapped his fingers around both her wrists. Her heart was doing that stupid little jig that happened whenever she stood too close to him. She tossed her head back, her tart response dying unsaid upon her lips.

His eyes. Oh, Lord, those eyes. They seemed to look right down into her very soul. She could no more resist him than she could jump to the moon.

"Ah, Red. What am I going to do with you?" His husky question whispered across her temple.

Her voice was even softer. "What do you want to do?"

Matthew watched the color climb into her cheeks. Self-mockery pulled at the corners of his lips. "Dangerous question." The tiny corner of his brain retaining any measure of common sense told him to stop moving his thumb back and forth across the soft skin of her palm. Her chin lowered and his jaw locked when her lips touched his knuckles. "We're not gonna do this."

Her lashes lifted and she looked up at him. A man could drown in those slumberous green eyes. His thumb touched her lip. Slid to the corner and parted them. "We're not gonna do this," he repeated.

Her tongue flickered across the pad of his thumb, then retreated. She ran her free hand up his arm. Molded his shoulder. Slipped up his neck.

"Jaimie—"

His hat tumbled to the ground. Her fingers slid into his hair. Traced his ear.

He grabbed her exploring hand. Pressed it safely out of the way. "Jaimie—"

"I like the way you say my name," she murmured.

Her head suddenly moved, and he felt her lips touch his throat. He jerked, capturing her second hand safely against the stall, also. She leaned back, her hair tumbling about her shoulders. She looked up at him with such naked longing that it was all he could do not to push her into the empty stall behind her where a fresh bed of straw beckoned. "You started this," she whispered.

Oh, that sassy mouth. "So I did." Though he touched only her wrists, his blood whistled through his veins as if they were plastered together from breast to hip.

"Kiss me, Matthew." Her pupils dilated. "Just a kiss. It's not so bad. You've even done it before."

"Here, Adam, have a taste of this apple."

"Do I tempt you?"

His lips were inches from hers. "Yeah."

"You're not happy about it, though."

He slowly shook his head.

"I won't beg."

"I don't want you to." He closed his mouth over hers.

It was like getting a shot of heaven straight into his veins. He couldn't get enough. A kiss. That was all he would allow. A kiss. That went on and on and on, whittling his control down to a silly, fleeting dream. So much for limits and delusional promises.

Letting her wrists free, his hands slid along her arms, to her waist. She was so slender his hands nearly spanned her waist. All these weeks, months of watching her. Wanting her. It had only gotten worse since the night in the motel.

He wanted to throw her over his shoulder and whisk her to his bed.

He contented himself with cupping her narrow hips in his palms and pulling her tightly to him, acutely, painfully aware of the way her soft curves greeted him.

Jaimie's breath stalled when he pulled her against him. Mindless, she arched against that hard ridge behind his zipper. A moan rose in her when his lips slipped to her throat. His hands, so sure and strong, slid over her bottom, tilting her toward him. Her arms twined around his shoulders, fingers slipping down the back of his shirt, touching his neck, nearly singeing from his searing body heat.

His breath rasped across her ear, and his tongue sent a jolt through her system. His name was a gasp on her lips. He rocked against her, and she could only cling to him. There were too many clothes between them.

As if he'd read her mind, his palm slid beneath her sweater, pulling it up. She leaned back enough for him to pull it from her head.

Time stopped. His eyes clung to her as tightly as the plain white thermal undershirt did. The textured fabric couldn't disguise a single curve. A muscle ticked in his jaw. Just when she thought she couldn't stand still another moment, his hand curled beneath her thigh. Braced between him and the stall gate, she felt him drape her thigh around his hip and press himself against her.

She bit her lip, her breath hard. Her undershirt came free

from her jeans and his palms, calloused and utterly seductive, slid beneath. Her lids were so heavy she could hardly keep them open. But she needed to see his face. Needed to see the heat tightening his features when he closed his fingers over her breast, his thumb rubbing her nipple.

"We've gotta stop," he said roughly. Then pushed her undershirt up enough to reveal her bare flesh. He cradled her bottom against him, and his mouth, warm and wet, closed over first one peak, then the other.

Jaimie arched against him. The seams of their jeans couldn't disguise the warm notch his hips had found. She didn't want to stop. She wanted to get rid of the layers of denim and flannel separating them. She wanted to feel the rough brush of his whiskers over every inch of her skin. Wanted to feel his warm skin against hers. Wanted him to fill the emptiness inside.

An emptiness she hadn't even known existed until she'd met Matthew.

"We've got to—*oh, yes.*" Her fingers convulsed, holding his head to her breast. "We've gotta...stop." Her head knew it. Her heart was slower in following. But already Matthew's head had lifted. He held her against him while their breathing quieted. She unlocked her leg and he set her to the ground, pulling her undershirt into place.

He heaved a rough sigh, his fingers smoothing her hair down her back. "You okay?"

"Yes." *No.* They were both so aroused, the air hummed with it. Beneath her cheek, the flannel shirt was soft. The wide chest beneath that, rock hard. Steady and strong. Her fingers curled into his arms.

"What?"

She shook her head. She would like to burrow right under his shirt and press her cheek against his heart.

"I'm sorry."

The words slapped her like a cold, wet, towel. She opened her eyes wide, unwilling to let the sudden hot tears fall. "I'm not." She lifted her chin. "So if you expect me to apologize, too, you're going to be disappointed."

Matthew studied her from lids at half-mast. "What little wheels are turning in that mind of yours?"

She raked her hair away from her face and sidled past him. By some small blessing, her legs still operated. Embarrassment burned in her, almost—but not quite—replacing the desire still coursing through her. The last time she'd felt even remotely like this, she'd nearly fallen into Tony Dayton's bed. That had been a disaster. But she'd made herself a promise then. Never again would she even contemplate making love with a man unless she knew he loved her in return. If that made her the oldest living virgin on the planet, then so be it. She'd made that promise to herself, and she would be darned if she'd break it.

"Jaimie?"

She closed her hands over the smooth wooden rail, looking at him over her shoulder. Why were some promises so hard to keep?

He seemed to be weighing his words. "You do understand why…we can't—"

She couldn't help it. The man was primed and they both knew it. *"Can't?"*

He propped his fists on his hips, all male. "Won't, then," he obliged. "You're on the Double-C. That makes you my responsibility."

"So?"

"So, I can't very well watch out for you while I'm… taking advantage of you," he said doggedly.

He really believed that. She could see it in his lighter-than-blue eyes. Her heart gave an odd little twist. "I *can* watch out for myself."

"I know that." He raked his fingers through his hair, leaving it standing up in endearing spikes. "But you…well, you're…"

She raised her eyebrows, waiting.

"Jaimie, I'm older than you. A lot older than you. You're—"

"Well over the legal age," she inserted. "For heaven's sake, Matthew. I'm not some teenager that you've hired for the summer. I'm twenty-seven. I do know the facts of life." Maybe not firsthand, she admitted silently. But close enough.

"Don't I know it," he muttered.

"And I can look after myself."

"So you said." He pinched the bridge of his nose, as if he'd developed a sudden headache. "It's stupid pretending there's no…attraction…between us. But that's *all* it is. You deserve more than that."

She knelt and picked up his hat, twirling it in her fingers. Her fingers smoothed over the finely braided hatband. She really loved his hat. It wasn't the hat of a dandy. Sweat had left stains. It was the hat of a hardworking man. The hat reminded her of Matthew, actually. Strong. Protective. And undeniably sexy.

"You know I *am* sorry, after all." She held the hat out for him. "Not sorry for what happened, or for what didn't." She picked her sweater off the rail it had caught on and pulled it over her head.

She tugged her hair out of the collar and shook it free, breathlessly aware of the way his eyes followed her movements. But she took strength in the intensity of his gaze as she stepped close to him, her eyes daring him to back away. Of course he didn't. Matthew had his feet very firmly planted on the ground. Any attraction he felt for her wasn't enough to pull those feet into the clouds. "You want me," she said softly. "We could've made love right here. Right now," she added, wondering vaguely where she'd gotten such courage. It must have come from him. "But we both wanted to stop. We just had different reasons for doing so."

His eyes narrowed as he waited.

"When I make love, it will be with someone who loves

me back,'' she said evenly. ''*That's* what I deserve. And what I am sorry about is that you don't realize that it's also what *you* deserve.''

Matthew watched her wheel around on her heel and walk away. Alone with only his horses to hear him, he swore. The woman was a soft heart just waiting to be smashed. He would be hanged if he would be the one to do it. He plowed his fingers through his hair and slammed his hat back in place. Forgetting all about his plan to visit his brother, he stomped out to the woodpile and, hands on hips, contemplated the already neat stack of firewood.

Calling himself ten kinds of fool, he reached for a log and the ax and started swinging.

Chapter Seven

Matthew counted himself lucky that Squire returned from Casper the next day. Even though his father was in one heck of a temper, stomping around the house grousing about contrary women. Bad temper or not, Squire was an additional presence around the house. A buffer.

He shook his head in disgust and propped his boot on the bottom fence rail he'd just reattached to the post. A grown man, all but hiding behind his daddy.

He straightened abruptly, settled his hat and pushed at the mended post. It didn't budge. Good. He rotated his shoulders, then gathered up his tools and dumped them in the back of the pickup. Sandy scrambled out of the way, whining.

"Sorry girl," he murmured, running his fingers through her silky ruff.

Looking across the truck bed, he contemplated the mile and a half of snow-covered fields separating him from the big house. It was after noon. She would have dinner on the table. Filling, tasty food. She would be pouring Squire's coffee. Her sassy butt swaying around the kitchen, wild hair drifting into her eyes—

No! He had to stop thinking that way. She wasn't a permanent part of the Double-C and she never would be. Maggie would have her baby, and Jaimie would go back to the city. Where she belonged.

And that, as they said, was that.

Jaimie stole another glance at the wall clock. Almost one-thirty. Obviously Matthew wasn't coming in for his lunch. The man's punctual habits about his noon meal were almost legendary. It was bad enough that he'd left the house well before breakfast time. Now he was avoiding another meal.

Swallowing a wad of disappointment, she wrapped what could be saved and tossed out the rest, then fixed herself a thick peanut butter and jelly sandwich and a tall glass of milk.

Comfort food.

She should never have thrown herself at Matthew the way she had in the barn. He was avoiding her. The poor man was probably embarrassed to death.

That hadn't been embarrassment tightening the fit of his jeans when you were plastered against him.

She took a huge bite of sandwich, forcing it down with milk. Well, whatever—she dismissed that contrary voice inside her head.

He could've done whatever in just a few more minutes. You wouldn't have been able to stop no matter what you said...

"Shut up."

"Talking to yourself is the first sign, you know."

She whirled around. Daniel leaned against the doorjamb, the corner of his lip curving.

Jaimie made a face and turned back to her sandwich.

"You've already eaten enough for five men," she pointed out. "Don't tell me you're back for dessert?"

"Not if dessert is—" he cocked his head for a look at her sandwich "—a peanut butter and jelly sandwich."

"Guess you're out of luck then."

"I'm waiting for you to make some more of that chocolate mousse stuff," he said, his voice smooth as butter.

Jaimie cocked an eyebrow. He grinned, unrepentant. "Matt sure did like that chocolate mousse."

"Shut up."

He tsked. "Feeling a little crabby are you?"

Rolling her eyes, she ignored him. But he swung out a chair and plunked right down.

"Old Matt didn't come in for dinner, and you're missing him."

"Hardly."

He laughed, tilting his chair back on two legs. "Sweetie pie, you'd better practice lying through your teeth some more. You don't have it down pat yet."

Jaimie shook her head. "You're rotten."

"To the core." His gray eyes glinted with devilish humor. "You guys oughta just cut to the chase. Get it over with. Then mebbe Matt's mood'll improve, and you'll fix that chocolate mousse for us again."

Jaimie could handle Daniel's teasing. She could handle most men, in fact. Just…not Matthew. "Cut to the chase? Such a way with words you have, Daniel. That type of sweet talk'll get you in trouble if you're not careful."

By his expression, the notion didn't unduly disturb him. She finished off her sandwich and pushed to her feet, casually nudging Daniel's lone boot, planted on the floor to counterbalance his back-tilted chair. He jerked, barely keeping from falling backward.

Jaimie laughed, and quickstepped out of his reach. She opened the refrigerator and pulled out a plastic-wrapped slice of apple pie. A few seconds in the microwave, and she slid it in front of him. ''There you go,'' she soothed sweetly, leaning her elbows on the table.

''Wise woman.'' He reached out and ruffled her hair as if she was Sandy and had performed a particularly smart trick.

Jaimie grinned. The mudroom door squeaked, and she automatically looked over her shoulder.

Matthew towered in the doorway, his dark hat pulled low over his brow.

Her grin died. Great. ''The Look'' was back. She straightened. ''Want your lunch now?'' She couldn't help it that her tone was abrupt. It was all she could do to force two coherent words together.

He planted his hat on the hook by the door and shrugged out of his heavy vest.

''I'll take that as a yes,'' Jaimie said beneath her breath and turned back to the fridge. The oven-fried chicken hadn't yet cooled, and she took out a generous helping. She quickly nuked it, along with the potato she'd baked earlier, and after casually looking back to make sure Matthew wasn't watching, forked fat-free sour cream on top of it. She added some carrot sticks and slid the plate in front of him.

He sort of grunted. *Thank you,* she translated. Of course, it could just have easily been *go away.* He didn't have any problems speaking to his brother, though, Jaimie noticed.

''Where's Squire?'' Matt asked.

''On the phone,'' Daniel said around a mouthful of pie. ''He bought Gloria a new car while he was in Casper, and she went ballistic. Says nothing was wrong with the one she had.''

''It was a rattle trap,'' Matthew snorted.

''That's what Squire told her.''

Matthew grunted.

Women. Jaimie easily read that grunt. She poured him a

glass of milk, set out the last slice of pie for Matthew and a fresh bowl of water for Sandy, then silently escaped.

Matthew jabbed at the baked potato, his eyes on the doorway through which Jaimie had vanished.

"I think it's dead."

"What?"

"You're stabbing that thing like it's the shower scene in *Psycho*."

Matthew looked at his potato. He dropped the fork and leaned back in his chair, rubbing the pain in his forehead. He was beginning to feel pretty psycho himself. If he didn't get a decent night's sleep soon, he was going to start tearing down the walls.

"You eating that pie?"

Matthew dropped his hand. "Have at it." Daniel was pulling off the plastic wrap before Matthew even finished speaking.

"Still haven't bitten the bullet, have you?"

"What are you talking about?"

His brother took a hefty bite of pie. "You haven't taken Jaimie to bed yet."

"It's none of your business."

Daniel shrugged. "Probably not. But we all know you'd be a lot happier if you'd just…take the plunge." He swallowed another bite of pie. "So to speak."

His brother's colorful outlook was nothing new. But Matthew found it irritated him more than usual. "Jaimie's not that kind of woman."

Daniel eyed Matthew for a moment. "Don't get me wrong," Dan finally said before scooping up the last bite. He reached back to set the empty plate and fork near the sink. "I think Jaimie's great."

"Then why don't *you* take the plunge," Matthew gritted, "as you so *poetically* put it. You're the one messing around with her in the kitchen every time I turn around."

"Don't get your shorts in a knot." Dan crossed his arms

and leaned way back in his chair, his eyes alight. "Only guy she's got eyes for is you, brother." He shook his head woefully. "But maybe you're too old and tired to do anything about it."

Matthew's fingers curled. He slowly stood, uncaring that he'd barely touched the food that his stomach had been so all-fired anxious to consume. He glared at his brother. Daniel smiled mockingly.

Matthew drew in a deep breath and let it out slowly, until the desire to pound his brother lessened. As usual Daniel was being...Daniel. Matthew smiled faintly. And with a nudge of his boot, sent his brother's chair toppling over.

Daniel hit the ground with a crash. Sandy barked and ran in circles around the table.

Jaimie came running. She fairly skidded into the room in her hot pink socks. "What on—*Daniel!* Are you hurt?" She caught Sandy's collar, and the dog immediately calmed, leaning against Jaimie's leg, her tongue lolling.

Daniel lifted his head, rubbing it, yet laughing silently. He stood up. "I'm fine."

Hands on her hips, she shook her head. "Keep the chair legs on the floor next time," she suggested tartly.

"Blame Matt," he said, bending over to right the chair. "He did it."

Matthew found himself the focus of those bright green eyes. "Well? What do you have to say for yourself?" she asked him.

She could've been his mother, standing in the doorway demanding to know why he, Sawyer and Jefferson had gotten into some particular piece of mischief. But she was Jaimie. And she was causing him more misery than a man deserved. With a long step, he planted his hands on her arms and hauled her to him. "I may be tired," he growled. Something that was most definitely *her* fault. "But I am not too old."

Jaimie barely squeaked out her surprise when Matthew

closed his lips over hers. It was not the kiss of a boy. It was the kiss of a man in his prime. A kiss that scrambled every sane thought in her soul. As quickly as he'd grabbed her, he let her go, leaving her blinking and fairly swaying on her feet. "Sandy, come," he called sharply.

"Too old for what?" she asked faintly, but he was already gone, the dog at his heels.

Daniel wisely slid a chair beneath her. He patted her shoulder when she sank down. "Hang in there, slugger."

Jaimie stared at the door as he grabbed his coat and followed Matthew's tracks. After an endless minute her heart decided to start beating once again. She took a couple of cleansing breaths, then scooted the chair back to the table. "Well, that was interesting," she said to no one in particular.

She tugged at the suddenly too-warm neck of her sweater and went into the mudroom, grateful for the cooler air as she pushed her feet into her boots. She straightened and pulled open the storm door, standing in the open doorway. A cold breeze washed over her, lifting her hair from her cheeks, and she stood there for a long moment, her eyes closed.

She could still taste him.

"I swear, you don't have the sense God gave a goose. You trying to catch pneumonia?"

Startled, she looked straight into Matthew's translucent eyes, her hand going lax on the door. It slammed shut, knocking Matthew right on the head.

He jerked, one hand shoving the door open and the other going to his forehead. "For cryin' out…are you *trying* to kill me?"

"I'm sorry. You don't have to chew me out! Let me see." She tugged at his hand. "Oh, fudgebuckets. You're bleeding."

"No kidding." He pulled his hand away from hers and brushed past her into the mudroom. He ripped off a paper towel and pressed it to his forehead. It came away bloody. He stifled another curse and blotted. "How deep is it?" He leaned toward her. "Well?"

She swallowed, her green eyes glancing across the cut, then away. "Um, maybe you, uh…you…ought to sit down."

Throbbing from the outside now as well as the inside, Matthew's head felt about ready to explode. He yanked off another paper towel and went into the kitchen, heading for the bathroom near the stairs. "How deep? Stitches deep?"

Jaimie hovered behind him. "I don't know. Maybe."

With his luck? Probably. He snapped on the light and looked into the mirror. It was more of a split than a cut. Directly over his right eyebrow. He dropped the paper towels into the trash can. "Get the first aid kit from my office." She didn't move. "Jaimie?"

He turned just in time to catch her as her eyes rolled and she pitched forward.

His heart jumped into his throat and he cursed. He squinted down at her, closing his eye against the drop of blood creeping past his eyebrow. She was out cold. Keeping her weight propped against him, he impatiently swiped his forehead, then lifted her into his arms and carried her around the corner to his office.

He bent over, depositing her on the scuffed leather couch. A drop of blood fell from his forehead to her sweater. He reached for the first aid kit.

"Come on, Red," he murmured as he ripped open a gauze pad and slapped it over his cut, followed hastily by a strip of adhesive. "Where's that famous sass of yours?" He yanked off his coat and tossed it onto the desk, crouching down beside the couch. Her cheeks were pale and cold.

"Come on, sweetheart." He picked up her limp hands, chafing them in his. "Don't do this to me."

Cursing under his breath, he dragged the first aid kit down beside him and pawed through the contents. "Smelling salts. Smelling salts. Where the h—there.'' He broke the little tube and waved it beneath her nose. "Okay, sweetheart, wake up now."

She made a face, turning away.

"That's it, sweetheart. Come on now."

She grimaced again, a protesting sound on her lips. She pushed away his hand, and a glimmer of green appeared between her lush lashes.

Matthew nearly collapsed with relief. And he hated that weakness. "Are you crazy?" he demanded.

She stared blankly.

"You nearly gave me a heart attack."

She blinked and glanced around. Her legs swung and she sat up like a bullet. And cracked her head soundly into his jaw.

"Oh, shioot." Pain exploded in his brain and he sat back down. Hard.

"Matthew. Oh, Lord, Matthew—'' Jaimie scrambled toward him and he held up his palm.

"Don't move," he ordered grimly. "Just don't move."

"I'm so sorry."

He gritted his teeth. "Are you doing this on purpose," he asked wryly, "or do you just have a knack for it?" His head was pounding so viciously he wasn't sure the little food he'd managed to consume was even going to stay put. "Don't move," he ordered, seeing her start for him again. "Get your bearings first."

She pressed a hand to her head, clearly still off balance. "You're bleeding," she said faintly.

"You...don't—'' he pushed himself to his knees and reached across for the scattered first aid supplies "—say." He snagged a couple more paper-wrapped gauze pads and tore them open. Then wearily leaned his head back against the side of his desk. He replaced the bloody gauze and tape with fresh ones. "I guess you're not up to putting a few stitches in my hard head," he murmured, deliberately light.

Dan was more than capable of doing whatever first aid might or might not be necessary.

He heard her sniffle and looked over only to swallow a heartfelt groan. Huge glistening tears had turned her eyes to glittering emerald. She blinked and a diamond-bright tear slid down her cheek. "Oh, come on, sweetheart. I was kidding. Don't do that." *Please.*

She sucked in a shuddering breath. And another tear slipped free of her spiky lashes. "I'm…sorry," she whispered.

A twenty-person drum line was rehearsing inside his brain. But he absolutely couldn't stand to see Jaimie's saucy eyes filled with tears. Somehow he ended up kneeling in front of her, holding her chin still while he kissed away the tears.

His name was a whisper on her lips when he finally lifted his head. He looked long and hard at those soft lips. It didn't matter, just then, why he needed to stay away from her. He wanted those lips on him.

All over him.

"Matthew," she whispered again.

"Hmm?"

"Matthew…"

His thumb traced the full curve of her lower lip.

"Matthew," she tried again. "You're bleeding. You need—"

He'd like to blame his weakness for her lips on his loss of blood, but knew he hadn't lost that much. He leaned forward and tasted her kiss, anyway.

"A doctor." Her lips moved against his.

"No." He slipped his hand along her jaw and arrowed through the silky waves to cup the nape of her neck. Like modeling clay, she tilted her head in accordance with the slightest movement of his fingers. "Open your mouth," he murmured against her lips. "Let me in."

"Matthew—"

It was all the opening he needed. Her fingers crept up his shoulders. Slid behind his neck. Before he knew it, he was pressing her back against the couch, his cut, his chin and her fainting all forgotten in the drugging pleasure of the thrust of her breasts against his chest. Of her fingers slipping past his shirt collar. The soft sounds coming from her slender throat.

She shifted, and he moved reflexively. Her leg—her long, long leg—bent at the knee and pressed against his hip. Just then it didn't matter what they'd said in the barn.

"Jaimie—" That distracting leg had slipped over him. "Wait." Clothes. They had way too many clothes on for the things he wanted to share with her. He groaned and lifted himself up on his elbows. Her eyes were slumberous. A blush of color rode her high cheekbones.

And a dark smear of blood marred her smooth forehead.

He sprang off her, sucking in a gulping breath of air. All he could taste...could smell...could breathe...was flavored with her scent. What was he doing? Had his brain gone south for the winter? The phone rang once. Sharp and loud. Then it was silent.

She made a strangled sound and sat up, too. Somehow or other her sweater had become twisted high around her abdomen, and she yanked it back into place. She pushed her heavy hair away from her face.

He saw her looking down at her hand. A smear of his blood was on her fingertip. Her teeth worried her lower lip.

Matthew found another sealed packet and ripped it open. She started when he knelt in front of her and daubed the smudge from her forehead. Then he picked up her hand to wipe away the smear with the moist paper. "Don't worry, sweetheart," he told her.

Jaimie couldn't tear her eyes from the vivid stains he'd wiped from her fingers. The sight of blood had never bothered her before. But seeing *Matthew's* blood oozing from his forehead... Maybe he was right about her. That she really was out of her element on the ranch. "What about your forehead?" she asked.

Matthew moved behind his desk and sat down. He leaned his head back against the chair. "What about it?"

Jaimie's hands twisted. This was all her fault. "I'll see if Dan's still around. He's had lots of first aid training, hasn't he? I, uh, think…yes, he told me that once." Aware that she was babbling, she swallowed. "Want me to get you some aspirin or something?"

Matthew grunted. "There are packets of aspirin scattered all over the floor in here."

Another mess she was responsible for. Jaimie hastily knelt and scrambled everything she could reach back into the first aid container. She found two packets and set them on the desk near his propped boot. "I, uh—" she cleared her throat "—I'll get Daniel."

"Fine."

She hung in the doorway for a moment, looking back at him. A long strip of adhesive stretched haphazardly across his forehead, holding the blood-spotted gauze in place.

Her stomach lurched warningly, and she silently escaped. She stuck her head in the barns and nearly cried with relief when she eventually found Daniel in the machine shed. His head was buried in the depths of a tractor. She quickly explained, and he headed back to the house, wiping the grease from his hands with a rag, while she tagged after him.

They found Matthew once more in the bathroom. He'd pulled off the lopsided adhesive and was wiping the cut clean. The bleeding had finally stopped. "I think I can get by with just a butterfly strip or two," he said, turning to toss the used gauze into the trash.

Daniel tilted his head in agreement. "I'll adjust the tension on the storm door," he said, turning to go. "Oh, yeah. Donna called a little while ago. I picked it up in the barn. Said she needed to talk to you pronto."

Matthew nodded, eyeing his reflection in the mirror as he placed a butterfly strip to hold the edges of the cut together. He followed it with a square bandage and turned to find Jaimie hovering in the hall, her arms curled over her chest. He expected the aspirin to kick in soon, and he had to curtail the instinct to tug her back against him. Up the stairs and a few steps down the hall, and they would be in his bedroom. "Don't you have something to do?"

Jaimie reacted to his curt demand just as he'd known she would. The worry in her eyes slid behind a tart glint. "See if I try to apologize to you anymore."

"Accidents happen all the time on a ranch." He stepped past her toward the kitchen.

"What's that supposed to mean?"

"It means what I said." He reached for the phone. No doubt Donna had some detail to discuss about the sale.

"You mean, since *I* came."

His fingers hovered over the dial. "Did I say that?"

"It's what you meant." Eyes defensive, she waved at the phone. "I suppose *Donna* never put a scratch on your precious truck."

"True." Donna had never even driven one of the Double-C vehicles. He punched out the number.

"And she could probably stitch up a bloody gash ten inches long without turning a hair."

At his ear the phone began ringing. A curl of basic, male satisfaction wended its way through his gut. "Jealous?"

"Not in this lifetime," she sniffed haughtily. And huffed her bangs out of her eyes. She bowed mockingly. "Since you're not likely to bleed to death, I'll leave you to your girlfriend."

"She's not—oh, hi, Donna. It's Matt. What's up?"

The mudroom door slammed shut when Jaimie stomped out.

He didn't see her stride across the road and angle toward

the fence post—the first one—that she'd knocked down that unforgettable day. He didn't see her stare at it for a long moment, only to swing her foot back and deliver a solid, bone-jarring kick.

Chapter Eight

Jefferson and Emily dropped by the Double-C right after dinner that evening, Emily bearing a plastic-wrapped plate, mounded with still-warm brownies. Jaimie had just finished giving the kitchen counters one final swipe when the mudroom door creaked open.

Squire and Daniel were still seated at the table. Both men had been noticeably silent through the meal. But no more so than Matthew had been. After Squire had irritably told her to sit down and eat with them, Matthew had barely looked her way during the whole dinner. Then as soon as he'd finished nudging his food around his plate, he'd disappeared.

Emily and Jefferson settled themselves at the table. Jaimie automatically poured coffee for Jefferson and milk for Emily, then excused herself.

"Oh, Jaimie, don't go," Emily invited. "Join us. I wanted to talk to you about my plans for òur nursery. You have such a wonderful eye for color."

"Better submit now, Jaimie," Jefferson murmured, reaching for his second brownie. "Otherwise she'll just keep hounding you until you give in."

Emily shot Jefferson an affectionate glare. "You."

"It's true, isn't it?"

Emily pointedly ignored her husband, looking at Jaimie. "Please?"

She smoothed her palms down the sides of her jeans. "I really should check on Maggie."

Squire snorted. "Checked on her fifteen minutes ago, and she was sleeping like a baby. Lord, girl, you're as jumpy as a prize-winning frog. Have been all through dinner."

Emily caught her gaze, her eyes rueful. "I thought we'd stake out the comfy couches in the basement. And leave the guys here—" she tilted her head toward the three men "—to fend for themselves for an evening." She touched the zippered binder she'd set on the table. "I've brought a bunch of samples that I ordered from a shop in Cheyenne."

Jaimie's fingers pressed into the counter behind her. She managed a smile. "Sure."

Emily hopped up, bumping her growing tummy against Jefferson's arm. "Oops. Sorry, darlin'."

Jefferson looped his arm around her waist and pulled her close. "You can apologize to me. Later."

"Gawdalmighty, Jefferson. You've already gotten the girl pregnant," Squire complained, testy as he'd been all day.

"Shut up, old man," Jefferson said mildly. "Get your own love life and stay outta mine."

Squire harrumphed. He snatched up another brownie and devoured it in two bites. He wiped his mouth and tossed his napkin into the trash, then bent and kissed the top of Emily's dark head. "Thought you'd taught that long-haired son of mine some manners." He harrumped again, more for effect than anything, and stomped toward the door. "Poker," he announced. "Ten minutes."

Jefferson and Daniel both groaned softly.

Emily chuckled, her eyes on the doorway that Squire had disappeared through. "He having a disagreement with Gloria again?"

"Yeah. And I wish he'd just get it over with and marry the lady," Daniel said feelingly as he followed his father. "I'd better find a new deck of cards. You know Squire's tendency to cheat. See if you can roust Matt from his office, why don't you," he said to Jefferson. "He'll keep everyone honest."

Jaimie watched, fascinated, as Jefferson caught Emily's slender hand and kissed her knuckles. She felt sure the man wasn't even aware of the tenderness he displayed. Would Matthew be the same with the woman he loved? With... Donna?

Jefferson brushed a kiss over his wife's lips, then gently set her aside to rise. Though Jaimie had begun to wonder if they even remembered her presence, she realized at once that Jefferson hadn't forgotten. He smiled faintly at her. "Bet you think the Clay men are a strange lot."

Jaimie shook her head, feeling her cheeks fire all over again. Darn her fair skin, anyway. Personally, she'd adored each and every one of the Clay men. It was just one particular Clay who was wreaking havoc with her mind. *And heart,* a tiny voice whispered.

"Jefferson, get your carcass in here!" Squire's bellow could've been heard all the way to Colorado.

Jefferson made a face. "Nice to know some things don't change. Think I can keep the old man honest?"

"Probably not." Emily picked up her binder and milk glass before heading toward the back staircase. "Just don't bet anything more valuable than our firstborn here."

"If Matthew's playing, it'll be for matches or chips," he predicted as he slowly headed out of the kitchen.

"Grab yourself something to drink," Emily suggested as she flipped on the light and slowly descended the stairs.

Jaimie dragged her mind from the poker game she and Matt had played. She heard the men laugh and the scrape of chairs as they settled around the dining room table. She closed the refrigerator and slowly opened the pop top on her soda. The low tones of the men's voices were audible, the words indistinct.

Until Matthew joined them. She easily picked his voice out from the others.

She closed her eyes and held the can to her forehead. Emily called up to her, and swallowing the knot in her throat, Jaimie headed downstairs.

Emily had spread her samples out across one of the low coffee tables situated in front of a deeply cushioned couch. She was perched on the edge, her hands folded over her tummy. "I feel like Buddha," she grinned.

Jaimie couldn't help smiling. "You look like Buddha," she agreed, joining Emily on the couch. "You and Maggie could almost be twins."

"How is she doing?"

"Still getting sick a lot. She's not supposed to do anything much, other than get up to use the bathroom. I think it's getting on her nerves."

"I'll bet. I'd be nuts. I learned the other day that if I lean back into these couches that are built for people the size of my darling husband, it takes me a week to get back to my feet." She smoothed her palm over the swell of her child. "Pretty soon Jefferson's going to need to hook me up to a crane just to get in and out of bed."

Jaimie swallowed a mouthful of soda. "I'm pretty sure Jefferson's more than capable of getting you into…and out of bed all on his own."

"True." Emily grinned delightedly. "Very true. Now." She pressed her hands to her knees and scooted forward an inch toward the coffee table. "Tell me what you think of this fabric. So far it's my favorite."

* * *

Upstairs in the dining room, Matthew sat back, absently studying his cards. The double dose of aspirin had finally begun working its magic, and his headache had lessened.

He glanced up, waiting for Daniel to decide what to do. But his mind wasn't on the game. Proof of that was in the diminishing pile of plastic poker chips near his elbow. Daniel raised the bet. Matthew folded.

"That's three hands straight that you've folded on," Squire remarked as play continued. "That conk on your noggin musta scrambled your brains, boy."

Matthew tilted his bottle and let the cold beer slide down his throat. "Can't fight the deal." He looked at his father pointedly. "I don't have any aces up my sleeve."

Squire raised innocent brows. "Neither do I."

Matthew shook his head, catching Jefferson's expression. Everyone and their mother's brother knew that Squire was an inveterate poker hustler. He crossed his arms and slouched in the straight-backed dining room chair. It was too hard to concentrate on the cards when his mind kept straying to the last poker game he'd played. Within minutes Daniel had scooped up the pot, adding the chips to his not inconsiderable pile.

Matthew knew the moment Jaimie appeared in the doorway behind him. Not that she made a single sound. But the hairs on his neck tingled, and he caught the lemony scent of her hair. He tossed down two cards, scarcely noticing their value.

Emily glided past him to take up her post behind Jefferson. She folded her arms over the back of his chair and watched over his shoulder, making a soft sound now and then until Jefferson turned around. "Go away, would you? I can't concentrate, and you're giving away my hand."

"I am not."

He eyed her. Grimacing with good nature, Emily straightened.

"Don't stand by me," Daniel warned.

"Or me," Squire added. "I love ya, girl. But you couldn't play poker to save your soul. We can read every card right in your eyes."

"Well, fine then," Emily retorted. "See if I bring you a batch of fresh brownies again, if you're going to insult me."

Jefferson laid his cards facedown on the table and caught his wife's wrist to pull her down onto his lap. "Your talents lie in other areas," he assured her, his tone dry. "And you hate playing poker. We all know it."

Emily grinned. "So, Matt, how come you're not cleaning up the house tonight? Looks to me like Daniel's whipping everybody."

Jaimie watched Matthew's wide shoulders lift in a lazy shrug. The golden light of the chandelier centered over the big dining room table tossed glints over his gold hair. She tucked her fingers into her back pockets, hovering at the edge of the room.

Yearning, hard and tight, knotted in her stomach, but she didn't belong here any more than she'd ever belonged anywhere. No amount of dreaming would change that inescapable fact.

She moistened her lips and silently left the family gathering. In the chilly mudroom, she slipped on her coat and picked up D.C., who'd followed her out from the kitchen. She would've put her back into the other room, but the bundle of fur curled into Jaimie's arms, purring contentedly.

Stroking the cat's dainty head, Jaimie let herself out into the night. Her nose wrinkled at the cold air, and her steps quickened as she headed home.

"Where are you going?"

She whirled on her heel. "Matthew."

He continued walking toward her, shrugging into his heavy vest. "Why'd you leave?"

She hugged D.C. a little closer. "I...you...well—"

"Cat got your tongue?"

"Ha-ha."

His teeth flashed for a moment, and he tilted his head back, looking up into the wintry night sky. "We're in for more snow," he commented after a moment.

"That's not what the weatherman said on the news this morning."

He peered at her from beneath that ever-present cowboy hat. "Sniff," he said.

"Excuse me?"

"Sniff the air," he said patiently. "You can smell it coming. I don't care what the weatherman predicted. Try it. Tell me what you smell."

Not sure if he was pulling her leg or not, she gave a quick sniff.

"Well?"

"I smell the cattle," she told him truthfully.

His eyes crinkled. "It's hard to miss," he agreed. "Beyond that. Try again."

She did, closing her eyes this time as she concentrated. Her nose wrinkled at the brisk cold. She could smell the smoke from the fireplaces burning in the big house, and from Joe and Maggie's place. She tilted her head slightly. She could smell something pure and cold. But mostly, she could smell the intensely seductive scent of him. Of denim and leather and soap. Her eyes flew open.

"Smell it?"

Grateful for the cover of darkness that hid the heat in her cheeks, she nodded. "Yes."

"So you going to tell me why you left?"

She let D.C. jump to the ground when the cat pushed at her. Without the protection of that warm, furry body, Jaimie pulled her coat closer about her. "I just thought I should get back. You know. See to Maggie and all."

"Joe's with her, isn't he? His truck is there."

Jaimie looked over her shoulder. Sure enough, her brother's truck *was* parked outside the foreman's cottage.

He'd been gone so much lately, she was actually surprised to see it there. So much for that excuse.

"You were welcome to stay. You could have joined the game."

She shook her head. "I don't think so."

"Why not?"

"How's Donna?" She cursed the waspish question that escaped without thought.

He nudged his hat back. "Fine, far as I know. Tell me why you left."

She yanked up the zipper on her coat. "Just because. All right?"

"No, it's not all right."

"Why do you care?"

He shook his head. "Don't know. But I do."

"Sure, because I'm your employee."

Beneath the cold white moonlight, she saw his jaw cock to one side. "That'll do for a start," he finally said.

"Okay, then how about *because* I'm your employee."

He studied her. "What are you trying to say? That you're not welcome among my family because you're the house-keeper? Where the heck did you get a crazy idea like that?"

"Come on, Matthew. I'm good enough to…to pass a few hours with…but I'm still the housekeeper." And you're dating the neighbor-lady.

"That's what you think? That I was just *passing* a few hours with you?" He settled his hat firmly. "Well, hell, darlin'. Why didn't you just say so. We could've skipped all this foreplay and gotten right to it. Saved ourselves a lot of grief."

She sucked in her breath, feeling the cold air freeze its way down into her lungs. She'd offended him. Even in the darkness she could see it. "Matthew—"

He waved his arm toward the cottage. "Mebbe you'd better just go home," he said.

"That's where I was *trying* to go when you stopped me."

"You'd try the patience of a saint, do you know that?"

"Then just think how nice it'll be when Maggie has her baby and you can get me out of your hair." She whirled on her heel and stomped across the slushy gravel. The door to the foreman's cottage slammed shut behind her.

Matthew stared at the small house for a long time, his jaw tight. If all went well, Maggie was due to have her baby in April. Soon after she would probably be able to return to her duties. But the idea that Jaimie would be leaving then was losing its appeal.

And that was the most dangerous realization of all.

Not ready to return to the house and the curious eyes of his family, he headed toward Joe's office, partitioned out of a corner of the barn, stopping short when he found his foreman there.

Joe's head lifted, his tanned hand tightening around the telephone receiver held to his ear. "I'll get back to you," he said into the receiver and hung up.

Matthew had no desire to interrupt Joe's conversation. "I need the file for Wayland's."

Joe slowly reached for the file drawer. "Problem?"

Matthew shrugged. "Em's looking into something for me."

Joe eyed him strangely, then turned to paw through the file folders. Eventually he drew out one and extended it.

Matthew tucked it under his arm, wondering why Joe was still in his office at this time of the evening. "Maggie is hanging in there pretty well, isn't she?"

Joe nodded, silent.

"We'll all be happy when she can get up and about again."

Joe eyed the stapler he was aligning with the edge of the desk. "If Jaimie's not working out—"

"I didn't say that."

"You don't have to keep her on," he continued, as if Matthew hadn't spoken. "I heard in Weaver that a new couple has moved to town. The wife is looking for work. She might be interested.''

''Why wouldn't I keep Jaimie?'' The words rang in his ears. He hadn't meant that *quite* the way it sounded, he assured himself silently.

The chair squeaked when Joe leaned back. ''Well, you know. She never sticks to anything for long. Never has. I think the only time she's ever quit before getting fired was when she worked for Bennett Ludlow before coming here to take over for Mag.''

Bennett Ludlow, Matt knew, was a skirt-chasing fool. Naturally he wouldn't have fired Jaimie. Personally he was glad Jaimie had been able to quit. She was a heck of a lot safer working on the ranch.

He went still for a moment. Jaimie was a city girl, he reminded himself grimly. And a ranch was not a safe place for city girls.

''Crazy kid,'' Joe continued with a heavy dose of brotherly disgust. ''Don't know why she doesn't just find a job and stick to it. Preferably something that pays better 'n baby-sitting a buncha rug rats. Kid never did finish anything.''

Matthew swallowed the words that sprang to his lips. He didn't need to defend Jaimie to her own brother. Nor did he want to stand here and listen to more of Joe's disdain, either. ''Thanks for the file.'' He settled his hat and turned for the door, then abruptly turned back. ''And just so it's clear, Jaimie's doing a fine job.'' Matthew left his foreman sitting in his desk chair, speculation growing in the man's eyes.

He returned to the big house in time to hand over the file to Emily as she and Jefferson were leaving. Too keyed up for bed, he poured himself the last measure of coffee still in the pot and headed out to check on the new calves he'd brought in that morning.

In the barn he studied the newest additions to the herd.

Despite their early birth in the middle of a snow-covered field, one of the calves was doing just fine. The little guy's Mama leisurely looked Matt's way, her big brown eyes velvety soft, undisturbed that he was messing with her baby. Satisfied, he turned to the other. If the cow didn't accept the little orphan soon, the second calf wasn't going to make it. He pushed the cow's hind quarters with the flat of his hand to move her out of the way. She flicked her tail once, then shifted, turning her attention to the grain in the bin attached to the solid rear wall.

He filled a clean pail with warm milk from the cow and hunkered down in the stall, patiently coaxing the small calf to drink by dipping his fingers into the milk and drawing the calf to the pail.

He'd been annoyed with Joe's attitude. Oh, sure, Jaimie drove him nuts. Okay, maybe not *all* the time. As for all those jobs he'd been hearing about…well, she obviously hadn't found her niche with them.

It seemed to Matt that, despite Jaimie's…exuberance… once she set her mind to learning how to do something, she worked at it until she had it mastered. She might be a city girl, but hadn't she more than pulled her weight baling hay at the end of last summer when she'd been visiting Joe and Maggie? Even Emily, who'd pretty much grown up on the Double-C, was a menace when it came to haying. But Jaimie—

Well, Jaimie sure as shootin' hadn't managed yet to drive one of his trucks without bringing it back sporting a dent or a new scratch.

But she cooks hash browns just the way you like 'em, and the big house hasn't looked so cared for since… since…

All right, so he couldn't remember a time. Maybe before his mother had died. Emily was a terrific housekeeper— homemaker, he amended—but Squire had shuffled her off to boarding school when she'd been a teenager, and she'd never really had the opportunity to take charge of the Double-C's household. And Maggie did a great job. But…

He swore inwardly.

There had never been many woman around the Double-C. And Jaimie, with her wildly waving hair and impractical diamond bracelet, her green Christmas tree cutouts and red hearts everywhere, was like a breath of fresh air.

Matthew pinched the bridge of his nose, his headache's foothold gaining ground. He was crazy, he decided abruptly. His brains were scrambled, just like Squire had accused earlier. He wanted her. That was all. He certainly wasn't going to entertain the absurd notion of her becoming a permanent part of the Double-C.

The last time he'd considered such foolishness, he'd been in college and idealistic as a new pup. What had happened? He'd gotten his guts stomped on by a pair of Italian high-heeled size sevens, that's what had happened. Because the girl, BethAnn Watson, the first female Matthew had ever loved, had made it plain that she had no intention of languishing away on a remote Wyoming ranch.

He'd been good enough to sleep with, but not good enough to marry. She'd sure proved that, when she'd ended up marrying his good buddy Bill Pickett.

Matthew shook his head. BethAnn should have stuck to the excuses she'd used with Matthew. Because she'd only made it through two harsh winters before she'd driven her truck into a tree. It might have taken Matthew a while to realize it, but he did believe that she really had fallen for Bill. Nothing less would have ever budged her on her opinion of ranch life. But even then she'd been unable to stand the loneliness. Being away from her friends. From malls and movie theaters. She'd ended up using liquor to ease the loneliness.

In the end it had killed her.

Since his experience with BethAnn, Matthew had been excruciatingly careful to keep his heart uninvolved. There'd been women here and there. Women he shared common interests with. Women who knew that a pleasurable night or two didn't mean breakfast together in the morning. Much less orange blossoms and babies.

But Jaimie was different from those women. What he felt for Jaimie…well, he'd admit to a certain affection if pressed, but it was pure want. Impure want, if a person wanted to get technical. And as soon as Jaimie went on her way, things would get back to normal.

Barely a fourth of the milk was gone when the calf refused any more. Sighing, Matthew ran his palm over the little body, then pushed himself to his feet, cleaned up and retrieved his now-cold coffee from where he'd set it on a corner post.

He hated losing a new calf.

Blaming his unsettled feelings on that, he sucked down the dregs of coffee and headed back to the big house. The clear night sky stretched out forever. Golden light gleamed from several windows of the big house, and he stopped cold as he saw a familiar figure pass by the large window over the kitchen sink. She reappeared in the mudroom, her head bent as she concentrated on something out of his vision.

His fingers curled around the empty mug. Who was he kidding? He wasn't sure he even knew what normal was anymore.

A half dozen long strides carried him to the house and through the newly adjusted storm door. Jaimie looked over her shoulder when he entered. She flushed to the roots of her auburn hair and looked at the bundle of blue jeans in her hands. Water rushed through the pipes, filling the machine.

"It's a little late for laundry, isn't it?"

Avoiding his eyes, she busied herself pulling scraps out of the pockets before adding each pair to the wash. "It's ours," she said. "I, uh, hope you don't mind. Maggie's machine stopped working the other day. Doesn't agitate. Joe was gonna fix it, but—''

"Jaimie." Her eyes glanced his way then bounced back to the laundry. He wiped his boots on the little rug, leaving a streak of mud behind, and moved over to stand by the dryer. "Use whatever you need. I'll get someone to take care of Maggie's machine this week."

"I'm sure Joe will get to it."

Matthew shrugged. Maybe Joe would, maybe he wouldn't. In the meantime, Matthew would make sure that the machine got fixed. By someone. Daniel was a whiz with all sorts of machines. He caught a pair of jeans before it hit the floor, and handed them to her.

"Thanks," she murmured, her fingers searching. She pulled out several small packages, glancing at the items before she set them on the shelf above the machines. Matthew watched the hectic color leave her cheeks just as quickly as it had arrived. He looked at the contents in her palm.

"Yours?" he drawled.

Jaimie closed her fingers over the packets, feeling the foil crinkle. "That's none of your business." Matthew's pale eyes were expressionless. She hated it when he did that. Not that she was very good at reading what he was thinking, anyway.

She pushed the packets into her front pocket and shoved the jeans into the washing machine just as it began agitating. She hastily shut the lid, stifling a wince at the noisy slam.

He rubbed his forefinger across the edge of adhesive tape on his forehead. "They're not yours."

She moistened her lips, prepared to argue. But she couldn't. She'd never been good at lying. Knew it never served a good purpose. "No," she admitted. Her stomach clenched as she waited for some comment.

But Matthew simply looked at her. "Well," he said after a long moment. "Good night." He turned on his heel and left her standing in the cool mudroom.

With her brother's condoms burning a hole in her pocket.

Chapter Nine

When her alarm chirped a few minutes past five the next morning, Jaimie was sure she'd never felt more tired in her life. Still, she dragged herself out of bed and into the shower. Ten minutes later, conscious if not quite coherent, she emerged, clean and dressed. Joe sprawled across the couch, a lit cigarette propped between his fingers.

She halted in front of him. Disgust mingled with love. "Trying to burn down the place?"

He blinked, then jackknifed forward to dump the long ash into the beer can sitting on the coffee table. "Hey, sis."

She added dismay to the emotions tangling through her. "You're drunk."

He shook his head, focusing carefully on her. He lifted the cigarette and took a long, deep pull. "Nope."

Jaimie glanced at the door to Maggie and Joe's bedroom. At least it was closed. She nudged aside several empty beer cans and sat on the coffee table. The memory of what she'd found in his jeans burned fresh in her mind. "Joe, what's wrong? This isn't like you."

"Nothing's wrong."

She wished that she weren't so familiar with the actions of a man bent on being unfaithful to his wife. Unfortunately she'd had years of experience as a teenager, watching her parents. "I washed your jeans last night," she said.

"Gee. Thanks. Am I supposed to give you a gold star for the day?"

"No." She stifled the anger rising in her. "Why don't I give you these, instead?" She pulled the small packets from her pocket and held them out to him.

Seemingly unconcerned, he took another drag, then pushed the butt into an empty can.

"Don't insult me by saying they're not yours," she warned softly.

He snatched the packets from her. "It ain't your concern." He stood and walked out, pulling on his coat as the door slammed shut behind him, leaving her no opportunity to respond.

Jaimie wrapped herself in her own coat and scarf and quietly cleaned up the mess he'd left on the coffee table before following him out into the dark morning. The sight of the lights in the rear windows of the big house didn't soothe her this morning.

Squire would already be in the kitchen, drinking his coffee from that crazy saucer, while Sandy slept under the table. Matthew and Daniel would probably be out checking the stock. It might be Saturday, but that didn't mean diddly to a cow bringing a new calf into the world.

She should be grateful that Matthew would be busy. That he wouldn't be sitting at the table, watching her cook his breakfast as he'd done so many mornings in the past. Moving carefully, she headed toward the house. The snow Matthew spoke of hadn't come in the night, but the ground was covered with slick patches of ice. A soft meow distracted her, and she stopped, peering into the darkness. "D.C.?"

The cat sprang across the build-up of crusty snow at the edge of the gravel road. Jaimie bent down and picked her up, carrying her toward the house. "What did you do? Ditch Sandy for a while? I'll bet you're hungry." She rubbed the cat's head. "Want me to find you some tuna?"

"You're spoiling that animal."

Jaimie startled, her foot sliding on the step, and Matthew steadied her with a quick arm. She jerked her elbow out of his hand. How could such a large man move so quietly? "She's pregnant. She deserves some spoiling."

Matthew narrowly missed the storm door as it slammed shut behind Jaimie. He sure didn't need another close encounter with that bloody door. He let himself into the mudroom, watching her croon to the cat as she passed through to the kitchen, leaving her coat and scarf piled on the washing machine. "What's eating you?"

Jaimie slammed the tuna can onto the counter and attacked it with the can opener. "Nothing."

"Right."

She sliced him an irritated look before scooping the tuna onto a plate, which she set on the floor. D.C. practically climbed onto the plate in her haste to eat. Jaimie's hair, unruly and damp at the ends, swayed about her back as she filled Sandy's bowl with dry food, then yanked the waffle iron from the cupboard and plugged it into the outlet above the stove. She jerked open the refrigerator with enough force to rattle every bottle stored in the door shelves. Eggs, milk and margarine found their way to the counter. "Where's Squire?"

"He decided to drive down to Casper. Left late last night."

Her shoulders sagged. Then she shoved back the long sleeves of her plain gray sweatshirt and pointed to the growing pile on the counter. "Squire always wants waffles on Saturday morning."

"I imagine he can persuade Gloria to meet his needs," he assured her drily.

Rolling her eyes, she sniffed. "Well, do you want any? Waffles that is?" Pink climbed into her cheeks.

He was hungry. He could've easily fixed himself something to eat and saved himself this grief. But this was his house. His kitchen. And he *paid* her to cook. "Sure." He pulled out a chair and sat. "Dan is out, though. He's heading over to Jefferson's with a load of hay." It didn't take a rocket scientist to recognize the dismay in her expression.

Sipping his coffee, he reached for the file folder he'd laid on the table earlier. Receipts and invoices practically sprang from the confines when he opened it. "How's Maggie?"

"Still pregnant. So you're still stuck with me for a few more weeks." She punctuated her words by cracking an egg. Which promptly dripped down the side of the bowl onto the counter, since she'd split it clean in two.

Matthew clamped down on his ire. "Maybe you'd better go back to bed and climb out of the other side. The right side this time."

"Maybe I don't need your advice." She reached for another egg. At least this one ended up inside the bowl. Though he saw her carefully pick out a piece of shell and flick it into the sink. Then she added flour.

"Maybe you don't need this job." He regretted the words as soon as he said them.

Her shoulders stiffened. "Go ahead. Fire me. It certainly won't be the first time I've been canned." She turned to face him, bits of egg and flour clinging to her fingertips. Defiance colored her features, but it was the expression in her eyes that made him hold his tongue.

Fear.

In fact, her green eyes, usually vivid and full of sass,

looked whipped. She fully expected him to tell her to start packing her gear.

"Sit down."

"I prefer to stand when being fired."

"I'm not gonna fire you," he said, irritated. "Sit down." He closed the file abruptly. "Please," he tacked on after a long moment.

She picked at the sticky flour. Worrying the inner corner of her lip, she rinsed her hands, then sat.

"What's bothering you?"

"Nothing."

"You're as antsy as a cat in a roomful of rocking chairs. Is it cabin fever? It probably gets pretty boring for you here in the dead of winter."

Her lashes dipped. That cloud of pink bloomed on her cheeks again.

"You haven't had a day off in weeks, have you? Not since we—" He broke off. He didn't want to bring up that night in Gillette. He didn't want to bring up a whole passel of things. "That's my fault," he continued, determined. "I should've told you that you weren't expected to stay on the ranch seven days of the week. Even Joe takes off on Friday nights."

Her expression tightened, and he wondered what on earth he'd gone and said this time. Lord, the woman was prickly. "You, uh, could use one of the trucks, if you needed." *What* was he saying? She'd used one of the trucks to drive Maggie to that one doctor's appointment. He hadn't been able to miss the fresh scratch stretching down one side of the vehicle when they'd returned.

Her lashes lifted, and he nearly groaned. Tears swam in her eyes, turning the dark green to shimmering emerald.

"Don't," she warned, her voice husky. "Don't start being nice."

He didn't want her to cry. Oh, man, he did *not* want her to cry. "Yeah, well, I don't want it to get out, either." Her tongue sneaked out, leaving a glistening lower lip when it retreated. He shifted in his seat. "Might ruin my image."

It was such a ridiculous statement that Jaimie couldn't help feeling her heart lighten. It wasn't his fault that she couldn't be around him without wanting to throw herself in his arms. It wasn't his fault that her brother was acting like an idiot. Or that, once Maggie's baby came, she would no longer have a reason to stay at the Double-C.

She swallowed that worrisome detail and concentrated, instead, on the here and now. "You are a nice man." Before she could help herself, she leaned across the table, touching his jaw. Golden stubble prickled against her palm. "The nicest man I know."

"Don't fool yourself."

Jaimie's breath caught. Then he glanced away and she decided she'd imagined that sharp, hot look in his light eyes. She brushed her tingling palm against her jeans and rose. "Look, I know I'm not much use to you around here." Working at the counter, she measured and poured. "But you've let me stay for Maggie's sake." She blindly reached for a wooden spoon and started stirring the waffle batter.

"You're even paying me." She watched the batter drip from the spoon when she stopped stirring. "I just…well, I should've said thank you a long time ago." She heard his chair scrape and looked over her shoulder.

"I don't want your thanks." He gathered up the folder. "And you're earning your keep," he said gruffly. Then, without looking at her, he strode out of the room. A moment later she heard the distinctive, woefully familiar, sound of his office door slamming shut.

Jaimie's shoulders sagged. Silently she turned to the waffle iron and poured the smooth batter into the center. Fifteen minutes later she checked the table over once more. Hot, crispy waffles. Two eggs, sunny side up. Maple syrup, still warm from the microwave. Orange juice. Counters clean. Dishwasher unloaded.

She went through the dining room and back behind the wide staircase to Matthew's office door. She nibbled the corner of her lip, then quickly rapped her knuckles on the door. ''Breakfast is on the table,'' she called.

Feeling like a ninny, she hightailed it up the stairs before he even answered. She stopped at the linen closet at the top of the stairs and pulled out a stack of fresh sheets. She heard Matthew come out of his office just as she went into Daniel's room.

Matthew stopped short at the sight of the laden table. Hunger curled through his stomach and he sat down at the lone place setting, forking a waffle onto his plate. ''Nice,'' he muttered, sliding an egg onto the waffle before dumping syrup over the whole thing. If he was nice, he would go upstairs and tell her to come down and eat, too. He could hear her moving around above his head. How easy it would be to go up there…behind a closed door…

He slammed an iron door over that notion. He sliced into the waffle and shoved a huge bite in his mouth. *Nice.*

The storm door squeaked and he looked up when Daniel entered. ''Figured you'd be gone all day,'' he commented when his brother pulled out a chair and reached for a waffle. ''You get that load over to Jefferson's?''

Daniel nodded. ''Ran into Joe on my way back. He was heading out to check the south section for calves. Said the one you brought in yesterday is still holding on.''

''Fed him about two hours ago. He took a little more this time.''

Dan nodded as he folded the waffle in half, then wolfed it down, plain, in three bites. ''Good,'' he commented and reached for another. ''You know, Matt, you oughta marry the girl. We could eat like this every morning.''

Matthew glared at Dan. He slid the second egg onto his

plate before his brother could reach for it. Daniel pointed at the last waffle. "You eating that, too?" He reached for it when Matthew shook his head. "Saw Bill Pickett the other night at Colbys."

Matthew knew Daniel was waiting for a reaction at the mention of BethAnn's widowed husband. "So?"

"Had a hot game going. Old Bill was winning, too. Bragging about how he won that car off you."

"Pretty pitiful if Bill has to brag about a poker game that happened more 'n fifteen years ago."

"Joe was there, too."

Matthew eyed his younger brother. Daniel's grin was gone. He knew his brother didn't much care for Joe, though Matthew had yet to figure out why, and Daniel had yet to say. The two men usually steered pretty clear of each other. It didn't matter much to Matthew how they acted, as long as the work got done. "Were you playing?"

His brother nodded.

"Thought pool was your game."

Dan held up his hand and reached into his pocket before Matthew could vent his opinion. He took out a wad of bills and tossed it on the table.

"Guess you won." Matthew studied the money spilling across the empty waffle plate.

"Bill didn't go home empty-handed either," Dan said. He jerked his chin toward the money. "But that there is most of what Joe lost."

Matthew flicked the bills. "Must be close to his entire paycheck there."

"Yup." Dan pushed back his chair and stood. He headed for the door. "Make sure Maggie gets the money back," he said quietly. He jammed his hat on his head and pushed his arms into his battered coat. "Might be best if she... keeps it to herself." Daniel's eyes skipped past Matthew. "Morning, Jaimie," he greeted, his usual, devilish grin back in place. "Mighty fine waffles."

Her eyes were glued to the pile of money sitting in the middle of the table. "Glad you liked them," she said faintly, unaware that Daniel had already gone outside.

Matthew scooted back his own chair. He scooped up the bills, folded them and shoved them in his front pocket. He wondered if Jaimie knew her brother had a penchant for card games. He wondered what he was going to say to Maggie when he gave her back the money.

He realized that Jaimie's eyes were on the pocket where he'd pushed the money. And he wondered what Jaimie would do if he yanked those bunched up sheets out of her hands and carried her back up to his bed. "Jaimie."

"Hmm?" Her eyes jerked upward. "What?"

"Do you...would you—" He broke off when the phone rang. Had he really been going to ask her out? Out where? Colbys? The place was a dive. Ruby's Café closed in the afternoon. Swallowing an oath, he yanked the receiver off the hook. "Double-C," he barked. "Oh, hi, Donna."

Jaimie passed him with a rustle of sheets, and the door to the mudroom closed behind her resoundingly. He heard the washing machine start and forced himself to pay attention to what Donna was saying. He quickly provided the information she'd called for, then yanked open the door to the mudroom. The room was empty.

He raked his fingers through his hair. It was just as well. He was supposed to stay *away* from her. Not encourage this madness between them. He returned to his office in time to see Jaimie through the windows as she trudged across the road. Her chin was tucked into the upturned collar of her coat, and her long hair streamed behind her on the breeze.

The never-ending paperwork spread across his desk held even less appeal than usual. Maybe he should go ahead and see if Emily really was interested in taking over the Double-C's books. At least a portion, he modified. It wasn't his nature to give up complete control, but spring was getting closer by the day and he would soon be hiring on more men. It would be nice not to have to divide his time so much between the pain-in-the-butt bookwork and the real work.

He found himself at the window again. Jaimie was leaning over the top rung of the fence. The trio of horses inside the corral trotted toward her, jockeying for first crack at whatever treat she was offering them on her outstretched palm. He glanced at the computer sitting on the corner of the desk. The cursor blinked steadily, waiting for him to start punching keys.

Ah, the heck with this.

Without further thought, he reached over and shut off the computer and that annoying cursor.

His bootsteps seemed to echo throughout the quiet house as he walked back toward the kitchen. He paused by the foot of the staircase. The wood banister gleamed. The living room off to his left was as neat as a pin. When he passed through the kitchen, he wasn't surprised that Jaimie had already restored it to order.

She didn't even give him a fleeting reason anymore to complain about her housekeeping. In fact, these days she didn't give him a reason to complain about anything.

Except her sass, which had been noticeably absent this morning.

Obviously he was suffering from cabin fever himself. Why *else* would he find himself missing it?

Must be those infernal dreams he kept having about her.

His shoulders moved restlessly. What he needed was some fresh air. That was all. Some fresh air, and he'd be able to rid himself of this impossible…attraction.

He checked the new calves again, giving another round of feeding his best efforts, before heading over to the horse barn and saddling up. He could've driven a snowmobile out to check on the small cluster of stock that habitually found themselves stuck in Dawson's bend, but he would rather ride.

During the winter, the acreage near the border of the Double-C and Jefferson's spread was a headache. The terrain was rougher than usual. Cattle effectively got snowed in. They were forever trying to knock through the fence rather than figure their way through the snowdrifts blocking their way to lower ground, unfrozen water and ready feed. He spent an hour rounding them up, forcing them through the narrow, rocky passage, toward the lower pastures.

Stupid cows.

Not as stupid as sheep, of course.

Not as stupid as he was. The snowmobile would've been faster.

Maybe he oughta just transfer that land over to Jefferson and Emily. Originally it had been owned by George Dawson, the man Jefferson and Emily had bought out, but the land had been transferred to the Double-C years ago.

He ducked his head beneath a bare, gray-tinged tree limb. Squire had never admitted it, but Matthew was pretty certain the transaction had had a lot to do with a certain poker game.

Jasper's hooves clopped and scrabbled across a patch of rock, but Matthew barely noticed. His pocket, and mind, were still heavy with the money Daniel had given him.

Poker.

One of the most insane things Matthew had ever gotten himself involved in had been poker. He'd been far too good with the cards. He'd been young and cocky, and thought he would never lose. He had. But not until he'd watched Bill Pickett haul in the pot that Matthew had confidently tossed his precious car keys into, had he realized that sooner or later the odds caught up. His pride had taken quite a beating. It hadn't helped that BethAnn, who'd run off and married Bill only a month before, had been sitting in that room, watching. He remembered thinking...wondering...whether BethAnn felt strange after that, riding next to her brand-new husband in that car that she and Matthew had made love in more times than he could count.

As for poker, Matt had dragged his obsession with it under control. For a long time, he hadn't even allowed himself to touch a deck of cards. As time went on, though, he'd learned that he could still enjoy the game without the added edge of gambling.

Too bad he was plagued now by dreams of the poker game he and Jaimie had played.

He felt Jasper gather beneath him and launch himself over a fence. Then he was racing along the snow-plowed road leading to the stable. Matthew settled his hat, and slowed the wild ride. Jasper snorted impatiently, but he complied, eventually settling into a walk. By the time Matthew returned Jasper to the stable, he was cooled and settled, contemptuously ignoring Matthew's grooming for the feed which he dove into with gusto.

Finally Matthew couldn't put it off any longer. He shoved his heavy gloves into the pockets of his coat and headed on foot toward Joe and Maggie's house.

Jaimie, sitting on the kitchen counter in the big house, saw Matthew pass by the window. She leaned across the sink, almost pressing her nose against the glass. His coat hung loose around his narrow hips, and she sighed faintly when he was no longer in sight. She looked down at the grocery list she'd been making.

She wondered what it would be like to be writing such a list for her very own family.

Then she snorted. She was an employee. A temporary one, at that. She would do well not to imagine anything else. Matthew and she might click on a physical level, but that's *all* they did. If she needed proof of that, all she had to do was remember that Matthew was still seeing Donna Blanchard.

She renewed her efforts and scratched down a few more

items. It wasn't as if they needed any staples. But if she didn't get some fresh vegetables soon, she would go crazy. A person couldn't very well freeze salad greens.

Maybe she could borrow Joe's truck and drive into Weaver. No way was she going to ask Matthew. Not for the first time she wished she still had the little compact car she'd owned in Phoenix. It had been a clunker, true, but it had made her mobile. Then she'd found herself out of a job. Again. And Maggie had coaxed her to move to Wyoming, reasoning that Jaimie would surely be able to find work.

And there had really been nothing keeping her in Phoenix any longer. Her engagement had been off for more than three years. The circle of friends she'd thought she shared with Tony had drifted away after the breakup.

They probably would never understand why Jaimie had called off the engagement. And, once the initial shock of it all had worn off, Jaimie found she didn't care. She wasn't the prim and proper wife-to-be that Tony had tried to mold her into. She wasn't cut out for tennis lessons at ten and doing lunch at noon. She hadn't wanted to quit her job at the children's center because he told her it wasn't in a decent area of the city. She hadn't wanted to cut her hair into a smooth, controlled bob, and she had refused to sell her lucky bracelet just because Tony told her it would be more financially responsible to take the funds and invest it in blue-chip stocks.

So Jaimie had sold the little car that Tony had never liked, paid off the rent she still owed and bought a one-way ticket to Wyoming. And she still didn't have a car; the salary she'd earned from Bennett Ludlow had barely covered the essentials, much less a car and auto insurance.

She didn't have many expenses now, working for Matthew. But this job was only temporary. Once Maggie was back on her feet, she would have to hit the pavement again, looking for more steady work. Perhaps she would try Gillette. She wouldn't be too far from the ranch then. Not so far that she couldn't visit Maggie and Joe and the baby on weekends or something.

Or catch a peek at Matthew, either.

She hopped down from the counter and tucked the pen above the message pad by the telephone. Pulling on her coat, she headed back to the foreman's cottage. Her nose was frozen and showing a distinct tendency toward running when she scurried into the snug warmth of Joe's house. She pulled a tissue out of her pocket and tossed her coat onto the couch.

Just when she'd blown her nose, she realized that Matthew and Maggie were sitting at the table, watching. She barely contained a groan, feeling her cheeks fire. She mumbled a greeting, spun and headed for her bedroom. Why did it seem as if she couldn't go anywhere these days without tripping over that man?

Because he runs the place, idiot.

Because you can't last two hours without needing to see him. Even if only from a distance, watching from the house or the gravel road, while he headed out into the range, disappearing into the gray dawn.

She'd never once stood rooted in place watching Tony drive away, nor had Tony ever suggested that Jaimie ''sniff the air'' to catch a whiff of the coming weather! And if he had done so, she would have wondered what on earth it was that *he'd* been ''sniffing.''

Shaking her head impatiently, she threw away the used tissue and looked at herself in the small mirror over the dresser. Her hair looked like a band of gypsies had been dancing in it. She didn't have on a speck of makeup. Her nose, as expected, was still rosy from the cold, and her lips were red and chapped.

It was enough to scare Frankenstein's monster. She tamed her hair back into a neat French braid, then quickly smoothed on lotion. A touch of mascara, blush and lip gloss and she looked more like the self she was used to.

She flattened her palms on the dresser and stared for a moment at the box of unopened Cracker Jacks that sat in a position of honor in the center of the small bureau. Stifling a sigh, she carefully tucked the box into her lingerie drawer.

Then she noticed her fingernails. She had healthy, strong nails. But her work on the Double-C was definitely taking its toll. She contented herself with smoothing the jagged edges with an emery board. One of these days she would give herself a proper manicure. Then she replaced her shapeless sweatshirt for a bright blue turtleneck that hugged her figure.

Definitely better.

Nothing like a touch of makeup and colorful clothes to brighten a person's outlook on life.

Yeah right. That's why she was pressing her ear to the bedroom door, trying to decide whether she'd killed enough time for Matthew to leave. As far as she could tell, not even a mouse was stirring out there.

She opened the door and peeked out. "All clear?"

Maggie's head jerked up. "What?"

There was no sign of Matthew. Her sigh was one of relief, she told herself. She walked into the living room. "Matthew left."

"Mmm-hmm." Maggie leaned against the counter, rubbing her palm over her swollen abdomen.

"Are you all right?"

"Just a few false labor pains."

"How can you be sure they're false?" Jaimie asked. "With the problems you've already had…maybe I should find Joe?"

Maggie shook her head. "My OB warned me about them. They'll go away in a few minutes. And Joe's in Weaver, anyway."

"You should be lying down."

With a grimace, Maggie nodded and slowly returned to her bedroom. Jaimie watched, still concerned.

"I'm fine," Maggie called through the open door.

In other words, stop hovering. She could take a hint. She quietly let herself out of the cottage. At loose ends, she wandered into the barn, thinking that she would look at the calf she knew Matthew had brought in. Then she would go back and check on Maggie, no matter what her sister-in-law said.

Inside the barn she stopped in surprise at the sight of Matthew sitting on the hard-packed ground. A small calf sprawled across his lap, all gangly legs and mouth. Captivated by the sight, Jaimie walked over to the stall and folded her arms across the top rail. "How is she doing?"

The brim of his hat tilted up, and his eyes skipped over her face. "He."

"How is *he* doing, then?"

The calf lowered his head to Matthew's knee. Milk dribbled from his fuzzy mouth. Matthew tried unsuccessfully to get the calf to drink more. "Not great," Matthew finally said. "He should be drinking all of that." He jerked his chest toward the small pail of milk.

Jaimie slipped into the stall. "Can I try?"

He eyed her, then shrugged. "Can't hurt."

"Such faith," Jaimie murmured, lowering herself to the ground several feet away from where Matthew sat. "What do I do?"

"See if you can get him to drink." He smiled faintly at the look she gave him and moved closer to her, bringing the calf with him. "Go ahead and touch him," he encouraged softly. "He won't hurt you."

Jaimie touched tentative fingers to the calf's head. He looked at her, his eyes soft and brown, and Jaimie's heart melted. "Oh, Matthew, he's so sweet." She scooted around until she lay on her side with the calf cuddled next to her.

His little body sighed, and more like a puppy than a calf,
he nudged his head against her stomach.

Matthew propped his wrist on his bent knee and shook
his head. "I should've known," he muttered. Naturally she
would react like the calf was a beloved pet. "He's probably
not gonna survive." She gave him a look of such horror
that he felt like a heel. But facts were facts. "Sweetheart—"

"He *is* going to make it," Jaimie stated firmly. She lay
right down with the calf, presenting Matthew with a close-
up view of her denim-covered derriere. Dipping her fingers
into the milk, she touched the calf's mouth.

And darned if that little beggar didn't follow her fingers
right back to the pail of milk like he'd never eaten before.
Like Matthew hadn't been trying that very same thing.

A short while later, she set the empty pail aside and sat
up, her eyes sparkling. "Sometimes it takes a woman's
touch."

Loose bits of straw clung to her bright blue shirt, and
strands of her vibrant hair had worked loose from her thick
braid, curling along her throat and temple. "Sometimes,"
he agreed, feeling something old and tight start working
loose in his chest. He reached over and brushed away the
smudge of dirt on her cheek. She went still, her eyes dark-
ening.

"Matthew, I—"

"Shh."

"But—"

"Just…shh." He curled his hand behind her neck, and
she rocked toward him, bracing her hands on the ground
between them. The calf grunted and scooted away. Jaimie's
head tilted and he covered her inviting lips with his own.

Then, before he really succumbed to the madness careening through his blood, he set her from him, settled his
hat and stood. "He needs to be fed every few hours," he

said gruffly. "If you want the job during the daytime, it's yours."

Her eyes shimmered. She nodded and rose, too.

"Jaim—"

"Matt—"

They both stopped. Matthew's lips twisted. "Ladies first."

She blinked. Despite the yawning barn around them, the walls of the stall seemed far too close. "I, um, just wanted to say…you know…thanks. Again."

He shook his head. "And I told you that you were earning your keep."

She nodded and swallowed. He was too nice for his own good. Jaimie knew that she could never hope to fill Maggie's shoes around this place. The silence lengthened. Thickened. She looked down at the calf. "Well, I should, you know. Get going."

"Right."

But he didn't move out of her way. Just stood there until she felt the need to wipe her cheeks of the dirt that surely must be there for him to watch her that way.

"What are you doing this evening?"

She barely kept from jumping out of her skin when he spoke. "I…what?"

"Tonight? Do you have plans?"

She braced herself. No doubt he wanted her to prepare another dinner for him and that woman. "No," she said, wishing she could say otherwise.

"Then we can ride over to the cabin," he said. "You haven't been there yet and the view is terrific."

She blinked. "Cabin?"

"Yeah." He waited a beat. "Unless you're not interested."

"*No*. No. Sounds, uh, great."

His jaw cocked. "Good. Good. So, let me know as soon as you're ready. We'll take one of the snowmobiles." He shoved his hands in the pockets of his down vest and stepped out of the stall. "And get a coat on, before you catch pneumonia."

Alone with the calf, Jaimie leaned her forehead on the rail. Had she just dreamed that conversation with Matthew? Or had he really asked her out? To the cabin, no less. Squire had told her about the cabin, located several miles from the big house. She'd gathered it was a retreat for the Clay men. It was where Squire went when he was particularly grouchy after a tiff with Gloria. She wondered if it was a haven for Matthew as it apparently was for his father.

Then she willed her silly heart to just calm down. He was just being nice again, she told herself firmly. It wasn't as if he would take her out there to...to...try to seduce her or anything like that.

Unfortunately, her stern talking to herself didn't keep her stomach from tightening with anticipation as she raced through the rest of her few chores and prepared a cold supper for Maggie and Joe.

She didn't dare take time to change her clothes again. There was certainly nothing wrong with her bright turtleneck and jeans. And she didn't want Matthew thinking that she was, well, primping or anything. For all she knew, he would change his mind about the entire thing.

It was not quite evening when Jaimie came across Matthew, sitting at the table in the kitchen, drinking a hot mug of coffee. She braced herself, nearly convinced that he *would* call off the outing. But he didn't. He just asked if she was ready, and before she knew what had happened, she was sitting behind him on a big, hulking snowmobile, flying across the snow-covered fields.

It took longer to reach the cabin than she'd expected, and if it weren't for the searing warmth of Matthew as she huddled close to him on the ride, she would have been frozen to the bone.

He, on the other hand, didn't seem fazed by the cold at all as he ushered her inside the rough-hewn cabin. He lit two gas lanterns and laid a match to the firewood stacked in the cabin's stone fireplace.

Shivering inside her coat, Jaimie stood near the fire, anxious to feel its heat.

The flames started licking at the kindling and soon the warmth of the fire battled the cold interior of the cabin and he rose and turned to her.

"Your nose is red."

She managed a smile, even though her cheeks would surely crack. "The rest of me is probably red, too." She scooted closer to the fire, holding out her mittened hands. "Maybe this wasn't such a good idea," she said around her teeth which were chattering annoyingly. "We still have to drive *back* again."

"You should have worn your gloves we bought," he said as he tugged off her mittens and folded her cold hands in his.

She sighed at the welcoming heat on her hands. "Hey, come on. You don't like my purple mittens?"

He tucked her palms against his thick, knit sweater. "They do seem to suit you," he admitted. "Your Arizona blood just hasn't acclimated itself yet to Wyoming winters."

"You're telling me." She looked around the cabin with forced interest. Truthfully, she was far too interested in the broad chest where her hands lay sandwiched between wheat-colored knit wool and his callused, warm palms. Finally she couldn't take it a second longer and slipped her hands free with a murmured thanks. "The ride was fun, even if it was cold," she admitted. "Have you always had snowmobiles?"

"For the past ten, fifteen years or so."

She nodded. "Do you always use them for work?"

"Tonight's not work," he pointed out after a moment.

She smiled faintly. She was still chilled, but she walked around the cabin, anyway. Considering the Clay wealth, she was rather surprised at the sparseness of it. A single bed was situated against one wall. Near the fireplace, a battered sofa and two chairs faced each other, separated by a rough wood chest that bore the obvious marks of boot heels. The only item seemingly out of place was the telephone that sat on a three-legged stool next to the bed.

"So this is where Squire comes to go fishing, then."

Matthew nodded and moved his coat and gloves from the couch to hang them from the empty hooks on the wall by the door. "The creek comes up pretty near here. When the moon comes out more, you'll be able to see it better."

Jaimie knew with certainty that looking at the creek by moonlight with Matthew Clay would be a dangerous pastime. But then, coming here to this quiet, out-of-the-way cabin wasn't exactly one of the most sensible things she'd ever done, either.

Suddenly feeling much warmer, she pulled off her coat and scarf and hung them beside his.

The fire snapped and crackled cheerily, and she turned to see Matthew sitting on the couch. With *lots* of empty space beside him.

Reminding herself that Matthew had made his preference for Donna quite plain, she walked over to one of the chairs and sat there. Matthew's eyes seemed even more translucent in the golden light from the fire and the lanterns. She folded her hands in her lap. Crossed her legs. Looked into the fire.

"Well."

"Well."

They smiled faintly, though Jaimie felt little amusement. She felt...antsy. Embarrassingly tongue-tied. An ongoing amazement to her, considering the fact that she'd verbally gone toe-to-toe with this man more than once. Not to mention tongue to—

No. She really couldn't start thinking that way. *Start*

thinking? What a laugh. She brushed her palms down her thighs and drew in a breath. "Do you fish a lot, too?"

"Now and then."

She pressed her lips together, nodding. "Um...what kind of fish?"

"Is that what we came up here to talk about?"

Her mouth ran dry. "Well, I don't know," she answered slowly. "You invited me. Remember?"

His lips twisted. "That I did."

"And now you wish you'd kept your mouth shut," she concluded. "Why did you, anyway? Was Donna busy?"

His eyes narrowed. "You do have a mouth on you."

Her cheeks flamed. She curtailed the impulse to get up and walk out. She would be lost in the dark within two minutes.

"You ever notice how we usually end up arguing?" he asked after a long silence.

Pretending an avid interest in the fraying weave on the arm of her chair, she lifted a shoulder. What she noticed was that he hadn't denied her crack about Donna.

"Ever wonder why that is?"

She moistened her lips. "No."

Matthew watched her face and knew she was lying. Her eyes were far too expressive. She knew the answer as well as he did. They either argued, or they kissed.

And kissing was definitely on the list of things they shouldn't do here in the cabin where no one could possibly interrupt them.

Perhaps he should start an argument.

"So what *do* you do when you come to the cabin," she asked. "If you're not fishing, I mean."

He shrugged. "Play cards. Read. Vegetate."

"Somehow I can't see you vegetating," she said drily.

He'd spent hours here doing just that after BethAnn dumped him. And two days straight when she'd married Bill. When she'd died, he'd closed himself up here for a week, with only a few bottles of whiskey to keep him company. "You'd be surprised," he murmured.

"So what do you read?" Jaimie looked around. "I don't see any books."

"There's a whole stack in that closet over there. Books. Magazines. Stuff that has collected over the years."

"Or cards. Solitaire?"

"No one around to play poker with." *Well, that was brilliant, Matt, old man. Bring up poker, why don't you?* He shot to his feet. "Hungry?" He didn't wait for her answer, but went to the closet he'd just mentioned and pulled it open. "I'm starved."

Naturally the woman was curious. Of course she had to follow him and stand right behind him, the lemon scent of her hair filling the room along with the smell of wood smoke.

"What do you have in there?" She peered around his shoulder. "Good grief! It's a whole pantry."

"Squire spends a lot of time here. Remember?"

Jaimie reached past him to run her fingertips along the neat stack of bottles and cans. "A person could live out here."

"Yeah." All of his brothers and he had more or less done that at one time or another. Sometimes together. Sometimes not. "See anything that takes your fancy?"

She looked up at him, and something shifted in her eyes. They went from bright and inquisitive to slumberous and enticing in less than a blink. Thankfully, she moved away with a shrug. "Anything. I'm not fussy."

Matthew stared at the cans, then blindly reached for a few. He had them opened and in pots, which he heated over the fire before he realized he'd at least had the sense to choose soup and pork and beans. The way his mind shut off, he'd fully expected to be heating up a can of fruit cocktail.

As if by silent agreement, they ate their meal and cleaned

up the few things that needed cleaning, without conversation.

He knew it was getting late and that they should be getting back. He'd already let the fire die way down. Yet the fact remained that he was reluctant to leave.

Jaimie stood at the one window the cabin contained. The one that overlooked the creek. "You're really blessed," she murmured.

"You don't think it's too...isolated?"

She looked at him in surprise. "Well, we are pretty far from civilization. But sometimes civilization is overrated. Don't you think?"

"I barely tolerated college," he admitted.

"It's hard to picture you sitting at a school desk." She grinned crookedly. "I think you're more the outdoors type."

BethAnn had cried and whined and complained when Matthew told her he was not going to stay in town and planned to return to the ranch after finishing his education.

Jaimie had turned around again, holding her hands around her eyes so she could see out the window that her nose pressed against with innocent delight. "It's so beautiful out there. Like a postcard."

The firelight flickered over her luxurious, wavy hair, and Matthew figured it was pretty darn beautiful in here. He banked the fire building in his gut as thoroughly as he banked the one in the fireplace. Though it took quite a lot more effort. Then he handed her coat and scarf to her. "Wear this one, also," he said, holding up a second, larger coat. "You won't get cold with both coats on. It'll reach your knees, and the sleeves will cover your hands."

She pulled her own coat on and wrapped her black scarf around her head and neck. He helped her on with the additional parka. "Whose is it?"

He left her to fasten it and pulled on his own coat and gloves. "Mine."

Her fingers paused for a moment, then continued fastening. ''Thanks.''

''For the coat?''

She pulled her knit cap over her ears. All he could see of her were her deep green eyes and her inviting lips. ''For sharing this place with me.''

As simply as that she'd put her finger on the lingering question in his mind of why he'd brought her here. To share it with her.

Except for his brothers and his father, he'd never once brought a female to the cabin. Not even BethAnn. She would have turned up her nose at the rough simplicity of the place.

Not Jaimie, though. She considered it a blessing.

He tugged her scarf up over her chin, covering those soft pink lips before he succumbed to their temptation. ''You're welcome.''

Chapter Ten

Late Sunday afternoon arrived, and so did Squire. Jaimie came upon him sitting at the kitchen table in the big house working a crossword puzzle, cursing beneath his breath. She sat down beside him, looking past his arm to the puzzle. *"Hover,"* she said, pointing.

"I know, I know. Dang it all, girl, would ya let me do this?" But his eyes twinkled, and Jaimie knew he wasn't really annoyed. He wrote in another word.

Jaimie held her tongue. For all of ten seconds. "I think nineteen down is supposed to be *erstwhile.*"

He clicked his pen a few times. "Hmm." He scratched the correct word over his previous answer. "Can't read this at all."

"That's what you get for doing a crossword in pen."

He grunted. "Pencils are for pansies."

It was such nonsense, she thought with a grin.

Tossing his pen onto the paper, Squire leaned back in his chair. "So what all's been going on here while I've been down courtin' the most prickly woman on the face of the earth.''

''Gloria's not prickly.''

''She's as prickly as a porcupine.''

''Didn't fix you waffles, huh?''

He shook his head. ''Tried to pawn off that putrid decaffeinated coffee on me, too.''

Jaimie pressed her lips together, trying vainly not to chuckle.

''Don't you laugh at me, missy. Someday a man's going to lead you a merry chase, and I'm gonna sit back and laugh like a hyena. Hey, don't look like that. I'm just teasin' you, child.''

She brushed her hair behind one ear. ''I know.''

''So what's stuck in your craw?''

''Nothing.'' She rose and refilled his coffee cup.

''My foot. My boy Matt still giving you a hard time?''

She felt her cheeks heat, thinking about Matthew taking her to the cabin. ''No. Of course not,'' she managed. ''But I think he'll be happy when Maggie's back on her feet and things get back to normal.''

''Normal is often overrated,'' Squire murmured. He frowned, wrote, then scratched it out two seconds later.

The mudroom door slammed open, startling them both. Matthew stomped inside. His jeans were soaking wet, as was the lower edge of his parka.

''What on earth?'' Jaimie jumped up, grabbing a handful of dishcloths from the drawer.

''Hell's bells, boy. It's a tad cold for swimming ain't it? What happened?''

Matthew clenched his teeth together to keep them from chattering. ''Don't ask.'' He turned, stiff with cold, and tossed his hat onto a peg. Jaimie was mopping at his legs with her little dishcloths. She was at his knees now. God help him if her fluttering hands went any higher. ''That's not helping,'' he gritted.

She snatched her hands away, bright color flooding her cheeks. "Ex...*cuse* me."

He stifled a curse. A man just didn't swear around women. Yet Jaimie goaded him to all sorts of behavior he wasn't accustomed to. Like taking her out to the cabin last night.

Squire thumped his chair down on all four legs. "Jaimie, go up and start a bath for Matt. Not too hot, he's probably close to frostbit."

Avoiding his eyes, she left the towels on the table and hustled out of the room. Matthew shivered. His fingers were numb, but he managed to undo his coat and he let it drop to the floor.

"What happened?"

Matthew grimaced. "I got wet."

Squire grunted. "Did something stupid, didn't you."

Matthew didn't have any intention of answering. No one ever had to know that his mind had been so completely filled with Jaimie that he'd fallen in the water trough through his own clumsiness. At least he'd been spared the indignity of any witnesses other than Sandy. And she'd figured he'd invented some new game.

He sat down and worked off his wet boots and sopping socks. Overhead he heard the sound of water rushing through the pipes.

"Well, don't just sit down here," his father finally said. "Git yourself warmed up. And be nice to that girl," he ordered, when Matthew headed for the stairs.

He stopped and looked back at Squire. "What?"

"I said, be nice to Jaimie."

Matthew closed his eyes, calling on reserves of patience he wasn't sure he had anymore. "You know, Squire, sometimes you're a real pain in the neck," he finally said. Slowly and clearly, so there was no misunderstanding.

The sound of Squire's laughter followed him up the stairs and down the hall to his bedroom.

Jaimie was leaning across the oversize claw-footed tub, her hand stuck in the gushing stream of water. Matthew's fists tightened and he closed his eyes, reminding himself that he was *freezing*. He opened them to see Jaimie looking up at him, her green eyes wary. And no wonder, considering the way he'd barked at her.

"Thanks," he muttered, hoping she would take the hint and leave. Soon. This little scene here was way too similar to the dream he'd had last night. A dream that had left him hard and aching and alone with only a cold shower for comfort.

She nodded, bracing herself against the tub as she straightened. "I, uh, hope it's not too hot."

His lips twisted. "I'm sure it's fine," he managed to say. A portion of his brain wondered when his bathroom had gotten so small. He tried unbuttoning his flannel shirt, but his numb fingers couldn't manage the simple task.

She glanced back at the filling tub. "Here." She brushed his hands away and began undoing the buttons herself. Her pearly teeth sank into the soft flesh of her lower lip.

He dragged his attention upward. "I can manage."

"Mmm-hmm." She pushed the flannel from his shoulders and started tugging at his thermal undershirt.

He had to get her hands off him before he did something even more stupid than falling in that trough. He yanked the shirt over his head, and her eyes went wide. When he deliberately reached for his belt, she made an interestingly strangled sound deep in her throat. The belt jangled as he slipped it out of his jeans and it, too, joined the pile on the floor. Suddenly she was taking a keen interest in twisting her bracelet round and round her wrist.

"You joining me?"

Her eyes flew up. "What?"

"In the tub."

Her mouth opened, yet no sound came out. He leaned over her, deliberately torturing himself with the fresh scent of her wildly waving hair as he turned off the rushing water. Then he reached for the first button of his fly.

She flushed and fled, slamming the door shut behind her.

He sank down on the edge of the tub, his head lowered between his hunched shoulders. He didn't know whether to be relieved or disappointed.

An hour later his fingers and toes were still cold. He added an extra pair of socks and shoved his fingers in his work gloves, then headed back out. He stopped to check on the calf.

His dark mood took a nosedive when he found Jaimie sitting in the stall, her head bent over the calf she cuddled like a newborn babe. "You're just s'posed to feed it," he said. "Not make a pet out of it."

She looked up at him, tears in her eyes. He stifled an oath and joined her, crouching down. He pushed her hands out of the way and felt the still calf.

"Ahh…hell." He pulled the calf off her lap and carried him into the tack room, swiping his arm across the wooden bench to clear it of the clutter. He heard Jaimie crying quietly behind him, but couldn't take the time to see to her. Not while there was still a chance to save the calf. He yanked off his gloves, searching again for the faint pulse. "Go bring me a blanket," he told her. "There's a stack in the closet beneath the stairs."

"But he's already—"

Matthew looked over his shoulder. "Not quite. Now *go.*"

She went. And Matthew turned his attention to the dying calf. A year didn't go by when calves didn't succumb to the harsher elements of nature. He hated it as much now as he always had. But it was a fact of life. Animals died.

Good grief, he raised beef cattle. Sooner or later they were all going.

The truth didn't slow his steady, fervent efforts to save the calf. By the time Jaimie reappeared, holding two checkered blankets in her hands, the calf was kicking his spindly legs. Weakly kicking, true. But kicking.

He picked up the calf with half-frozen hands. "Wrap the blanket around him," he told her. She did so, snuffling all the while. He headed back to the big house. It wouldn't be the first time they'd cared for an ailing calf inside. It wouldn't be the last.

Jaimie scurried ahead of him, opening the doors for him. He deposited the calf on the floor in the kitchen near the hot air vents, then straightened, arching his tired back. He shrugged out of his coat, and Jaimie hung it in the mudroom, along with his hat. She came back, then crouched down by the calf, crooning under her breath to it.

D.C. padded into the kitchen, took one look at the interloper and turned on her heel, slinking right back out again.

Jaimie's eyes met his. She swallowed visibly and turned back to the calf. "Now what do we do?"

"Keep him warm and fed."

"I thought that's what we were doing in the barn," she whispered. Her hand smoothed over the calf's head. Then she looked up at him. "You saved him."

The wonder in her eyes made him feel about ten feet tall. And lower than a snake, when what he wanted most was to carry her up to his bed. He wanted to sleep with the woman, but he had nothing more than that to offer her.

She wouldn't last on the ranch any better than his mother had. Any better than BethAnn had. So he'd bloody well better learn to keep his hands to himself.

Turning away from those eyes, he yanked open the refrigerator and despite the fact that he still felt cold to his bones, pulled out an ice-cold beer. He viciously twisted off the cap and tossed it on the counter. "What's for supper?"

She blinked. With a last pat for the calf, she stood up and moved around to the sink, washing her hands. In minutes she'd set a place at the table. "Squire ate while you were in the bath,'' she murmured. ''Said he wanted to go to the cabin. Do some ice fishing.''

Matthew remembered Squire mentioning it earlier. ''Where's Dan?''

''He went into Weaver.''

She pulled out a pan from the oven and served up a generous serving of some turkey-and-rice concoction she'd prepared a few times before. A salad joined the meal, as well as several fragrant rolls. She started to pour him a glass of milk, then with a look at the beer bottle, put the carton back in the fridge.

Matthew's jaw cocked. So. They were alone in the house. Except for D.C., Sandy and the calf, and they sure as shootin' weren't great chaperones.

He pulled out the chair and sat down. The food smelled terrific. But then everything that Jaimie cooked smelled terrific. She had been fussing around the calf, arranging the blankets around his skinny body. Now she stood up and pulled her bright coat off the peg.

''Where're you going?''

Her hand closed over the doorknob. ''To the cottage.''

He noticed she didn't refer to it as ''home.'' ''What for?''

Her chin came up. ''Did you need something else?''

Only your warm body next to mine for the night. He shook his head and picked up the fork.

''Then there is no reason for me to stay, is there?'' Still, she didn't open the door.

He stabbed a tender chunk of turkey. ''If you want to stay, then stay.''

''What do *you* want me to do, Matthew?'' she finally asked irritably. ''What? Do you want me to stay and watch out for the calf? To clean up the dishes when you're finished eating?'' She pushed at her hair, and it rippled over the shoulders of her pale yellow thermal shirt. She clutched the coat to her, and the nylon crinkled under her grip. ''Or do you just want a warm body next to you for a while? Because if that's all you want, call Donna Blanchard. I'm sure she'd be happy to oblige.''

His fingers tightened on the fork. When he remained silent, she just shook her head and turned the knob.

"I don't want Donna," he said abruptly.

She stopped, but didn't look at him.

"I want you," he gritted. "And you want someone to sweep you off your feet, like in some fairy tale." He tossed down the fork and shoved away the plate. "There's no happily ever after for you here, Jaimie. You wouldn't last past the first hard winter before you'd hightail it back to the comfort of the city." She would go and find someone else and take his fool heart with her, just like BethAnn had done.

Color rose in her cheeks. "Trust me, Matthew Clay. You're not my idea of Prince Charming."

"Then why do you look at me the way you do?" He rounded the table, his boots scraping against the floor. "Sweetheart, you've been sending vibes my way since the very first day you stepped foot on my property."

"Like you haven't, too? I didn't invite *you* to the cabin." Humiliation burned inside her. "Oh, you're insufferable." She yanked open the mudroom door.

He stopped its progress with the flat of his hand. "Yeah, but I'm right." He lowered his head toward hers. "So unless you're set to share my bed for a while, I suggest you keep your soft looks and sweet touches to yourself. Or I'm gonna take you up on your invitation."

"Go soak your head," she hissed. Then arrowed her elbow into his hard midsection. He barely *oofed*. But she managed to squeeze into the mudroom and out into the evening. Her chest hurt from the tears she refused to cry.

It seemed as if the temperature had dropped twenty degrees since the day before, and her boots slipped and slid on the icy gravel as she hurried down the road to the cottage.

As she half ran, half stumbled, the snow that Matthew had predicted started to fall. If she had a home in the "comfort of the city" as he'd so derisively put it, she would have run all the way there.

Jaimie hardly spoke to Matthew the next morning at breakfast. It was fine with him. As long as she did her job, he didn't care if she ever uttered a word. He'd been harsh the night before. But it had done the trick. She hadn't even met his eyes once since she'd come in at five to feed the calf. But he'd already fed it. As he'd done several times throughout his sleepless night.

Over the rim of his coffee mug, he watched her back as she stood at the sink, washing the skillet she'd used for hash browns. It was still early: that time of morning when dawn has arrived, but the sun had yet to break over the horizon. The ceiling light was on, and it washed over her head, highlighting the sheen of her hair.

His eyes narrowed and he realized, not for the first time, that her hair was almost the same color as Jasper, his bay.

He rocked his chair back on two legs, absently rubbing his finger over the bandage on his forehead. Jaimie's attention was still on the dishes in the sink, and he looked his fill. Well, hell, he was a man, wasn't he? Hadn't he told her that in no uncertain terms, not even twenty-four hours ago?

His eyes ran from the waving locks clinging to the shoulders of her thermal shirt—a white one this time, one he could see the outline of a tiny bra beneath—to the slender waist accented by the unbelted jeans. She moved to a cupboard and knelt down to put away the heavy skillet, and the jeans gapped at her waist in the back as they tightened over her rear.

The front legs of his chair hit the floor with a thud. Despite everything, he was getting turned on watching that infernal woman do dishes in his kitchen. Stifling a curse, he shoved to his feet. By the time she left the ranch, he would be a madman.

Jaimie whirled around at the sound of chair legs squeaking on the floor. She'd had a terrible night's sleep. And now, Matthew's expression was tight, but he couldn't mask the naked desire burning in his eyes. Her fingers clenched the wet dishcloth she held, and her breath stuck in her throat. She couldn't tear her gaze from his. Her feet had even taken a step toward him when the mudroom door suddenly bounced open and Daniel stomped into the kitchen.

She swallowed, watching Matthew's head slowly turn to his brother.

The hat Daniel tossed at the pegs missed, and he stood staring at it for a moment, his attention very focused. Then he grabbed it and shoved it onto a peg so hard Jaimie wondered why the wood didn't poke through the hat. He glanced at Matthew, then moved past Jaimie to reach for the coffeepot. His movements were slow and concentrated, and as soon as he came within a foot of Jaimie she realized why.

He'd been drinking.

She bit her lip. Daniel's face was pale, his eyes bloodshot. Matthew watched his brother's careful motions, thunderclouds gathering in his expression. She handed Daniel a mug after he fumbled the first one, and it rolled into the sink with a splash of water and suds.

The corners of his lips lifted as he took the mug from her, then he poured his coffee and sank down at the table. He slouched back in the chair, his eyes at half-mast. He lifted his mug. "Cheers."

"For God's sake, Dan, it's not even seven in the morning. What's gotten into you?"

"Not enough," Daniel closed his eyes.

"Where were you? Colbys?" Matt got no answer. "I told you I wanted your help moving that old tractor to Jefferson's this morning."

Daniel's mug hit the table, and coffee sloshed over the side. "I said I'd help."

"In the shape you're in?"

"I *said* I'll do it." He shoved back from the table.

Jaimie caught the back of his chair before it could slam into the refrigerator.

"You're not fit to stand up straight, much less drive."

"Get off my back," Daniel growled.

Matthew's jaw cocked. "You are not getting behind the wheel of any vehicle on this property."

"Trucks your personal property now?" Daniel crossed his arms, leaning against the refrigerator. "You own it all, do you?"

The two brothers were suddenly nose to nose, both big, determined and angry. For heaven's sake, Jaimie thought, Matthew and Daniel always got along. Without thinking, she slipped between them, afraid that their clenched fists would start flying. She braced a palm on each chest, wedging herself between them. "What do you think you're doing?"

Matthew set her aside as if she were an annoying fly.

"Stop it!" She pushed between them again. "Now you just cool off."

"This doesn't concern you," Matthew gritted.

She hadn't expected the pain that came with his words. It yanked and twisted her insides into a knot.

Matthew saw her features blanch. Her eyes stood out vividly, bruised emeralds.

Lashes suddenly shielded her expression and she scooted away, grabbing her coat. "Beat each other to a pulp then." The mudroom door slammed behind her.

"Nice touch, Matt."

"Shut up." Matthew glared at his brother. Despite the years between them, he and Daniel had always been in tune with each other. But lately...

"You oughta go after her. Kiss and make up."

"You're the one who carries her around in the kitchen."

"Jealous?"

"Not bloody likely," he snapped.

"Right. I almost believe you." Daniel's bloodshot eyes narrowed, mocking. "Except for that vein about ready to pop outta your forehead there."

"Do you *want* me to hit you?"

"Maybe," Daniel growled. Then he cursed long and low and turned away, slamming his fist into the wall. The skin over his knuckles split and blood coursed down his hand.

Matthew pulled a clean dishcloth out of a drawer. He tossed it on the table. Something had been nagging at Daniel for a long time now. Matthew wasn't particularly surprised that it was finally boiling over. "Feel better now?"

Daniel snorted derisively. He picked up the cloth and wrapped it around his fist. "No."

"You want to talk about it?"

"No." He hooked the chair with his boot and swung it back to the table to sit down.

Matthew sighed. Talking had never much been Daniel's way. Truth be told, it wasn't the way of any of the Clays. He stuck his finger into the hole Daniel's fist had left in the wall. He'd have to get some chicken wire and patch it. "You break anything?"

"Probably. Won't be the first time."

"Nope."

"You oughta go after Jaimie, Matt." Daniel's voice was quiet. "She looked like she's the one who got punched."

"I know."

"What's stopping you?"

Matthew turned to see Daniel adjusting the towel. Blood seeped through the white cloth. "I'm not starting anything with her I don't intend to finish."

"At least she's free," Daniel murmured under his breath.

"What?"

The mudroom door flew open, and they both looked up.

Jaimie stood in the doorway. "Maggie's bleeding," she said baldly. "Her OB said she had to get to the hospital." She looked everywhere but at Matthew. "I don't know where Joe is. His truck is gone." Daniel was out the door before Jaimie had even finished speaking. "I called the emergency helicopter, but it's up in the mountains looking for some idiot camper. Who camps in the snow? I need to use—" Her voice broke.

Matthew pulled her against him, and her shoulders trembled. She didn't even have on her coat, the little fool. "I'll drive," he said gruffly. He reached around her and pulled down a set of keys. "Come on."

She stiffened, pulling away from his hand on her shoulder, and hurried outside. He swiped several coats from the hooks in the mudroom and followed.

The snow had stopped falling during the night, leaving a pristine white blanket behind, marred only by their footprints from that morning. They climbed into his Blazer and Matt tossed the coats onto her lap. "Take one." He started the engine.

Jaimie separated a battered wool coat and pulled it on, shivering all the while. She waited impatiently for the engine to warm up. Daniel strode into view, carrying a blanket-bundled Maggie.

Matthew drove forward and met them halfway. Jaimie hopped out, pushing the seat forward so that Maggie could lie on the back seat. Her sister-in-law was pale, her expression stoic. Jaimie swallowed the lump lodged in her throat and moved aside as Daniel gently maneuvered Maggie into the Blazer.

"She's supposed to keep her legs elevated," Jaimie told him. Daniel bundled up the blanket that Matthew always kept in the vehicle and placed it, along with the extra coats, under Maggie's knees. Maggie's eyes were closed, but Jaimie saw a tear slowly trickle down her pale cheek. She swallowed, fighting tears herself.

Daniel finished tucking blankets around Maggie's feet and straightened. He moved out of the way, catching the blood-stained towel as it started to slip off his hand. Jaimie sucked in her breath, seeing the split knuckles. Her gaze flew to Matthew. Had they really been fighting?

"Get going," Daniel said abruptly, deadly sober now.

Maggie's eyes opened. "Your hand—"

"It's nothing."

Jaimie snorted. This macho stuff was for the birds. She climbed in the front seat, scooting to the center. "Get in."

Maggie's voice was soft. "Please, Daniel."

A muscle ticked in Daniel's jaw. But he got in. Matthew turned the vehicle around and headed out to the highway.

Everyone was silent as Matthew broke more than a few speed postings as they headed for Gillette. Tension was so thick that by the time Matthew pulled up outside the emergency room entrance, Jaimie wondered why the truck hadn't simply exploded.

"I'll get a wheelchair," Jaimie said when they climbed out. Daniel just shook his head and, despite the pain his hand must be in, he lifted Maggie out and carried her inside. Jaimie hurried after them, leaving Matthew to park the truck.

When he joined them, Daniel was standing at the chest-high counter, drumming his good fingers on the surface. "They've already taken Maggie back," Jaimie told Matthew. "But they need her insurance information."

Matthew pinched the bridge of his nose. This, at least, he could help with, since he was the one who paid for the policies. He took the form from Jaimie and started filling it out. "Get your hand taken care of," he told his brother.

Daniel nodded, his attention on the double doors separating the waiting area from the exam rooms. Jaimie touched his elbow, distracting him.

"So, what'd you do?" she asked, striving for a touch of levity. "Punch a wall?"

"Yeah." Daniel slouched into one of the hard plastic seats.

"Excuse me?" She'd been joking, for heaven's sake.

"Guess you didn't notice the hole he left in the kitchen wall," Matthew said, joining them. He sat down next to his brother.

"I hate hospitals," Daniel muttered eventually.

Silently Matthew agreed. He glanced at the big clock high on the wall for about the fiftieth time. His first introduction to hospitals had been when his mother died. Then, too, was the all-too-fresh memory of the day last year when Squire had his heart attack. He'd sat for hours in this very waiting room, waiting for word on whether his father was going to live or die. Two days later, stabilized but still unconscious, Squire had been transferred to a hospital in Casper.

"So what happened?" Daniel finally asked. "Did she fall or something?"

Jaimie shook her head. "It just…happened." She stood up, restless.

A nurse approached. "Are you Jaimie? Your sister-in-law is asking for you."

Jaimie couldn't help glancing at Matthew. His eyes were focused on the toes of his boots. She wiped her palms down the sides of her jeans and followed the nurse.

The double doors swung closed behind them. Matthew sighed. He stood up and fished some change out of his pocket. Going to the machine in the corner, he inserted the coins. Carrying the sodas with him, he opened one and handed it to his brother. Then he pressed the other to his throbbing forehead right on top of the bandage.

They sat in silence for a long while. Daniel had taken to pacing the waiting room, and Matthew's head was propped in his hands as he tried to press his headache out with his fingertips when the same nurse that had taken Jaimie back poked her head out, calling Daniel's name.

He followed her through the double doors. An hour later he returned, sporting a brand-new cast.

"Guess you did it up good," Matthew greeted him. "How many casts does that make now?"

"Who can remember?" Daniel rubbed his eyebrow. "I saw Maggie back there."

"And?"

His brother was silent for a long moment. "They're admitting her," he finally said, his voice gruff. "Jaimie'll be out soon."

"The baby?"

"There's still a chance. Her obstetrician is here. If the baby comes now, the chances—" He shook his head and scrubbed his good hand across his face. "Maggie's asking for Joe."

"I'll take care of it. Look, you're beat. Take the truck and go on home. Or call Jeff. I'm sure he'd drive up and take you back."

"I'll wait."

"Dan—"

"I'm not leaving. Not yet."

Matthew knew that look of Dan's. There wasn't any point in arguing.

A movement by the double doors attracted their attention. Jaimie came through and walked toward them. "I'm gonna see if I can find some place to get cleaned up," Daniel said. He passed Jaimie and went back to the examining area.

"How's she doing?"

Jaimie hugged her arms close, rubbing her hands over her elbows. "I don't know. I mean, obviously, they're doing what they can." She shook her head. "She's not saying much at all, really." She drew in a shuddering breath. "This baby means everything to her. She's waited so long."

Matthew ached at the misery in Jaimie's eyes.

Jaimie sniffed, dashing her fingers beneath her eyes. "I

don't know why I'm the one crying so much. Maggie's the one in there. I wish— Oh, God it's too early." Her voice broke.

Matthew pulled her against him. She was so desperate for his comfort that she let him. Her forehead pressed against his chest, her fingers curling into his shirt. His hands smoothed up and down her back. The wad of tears threatening to choke her slowly abated. She still didn't want to leave his arms. It was that very reason that had her stepping away from him.

She cleared her throat, feeling awkward. "I have to find my brother. Maybe he's back at the Double-C by now."

"Maybe," he agreed. "I'll see if I can round him up."

"You don't need to. I can manage," she said.

His eyes glided over her face. He gently lifted a strand of hair away from her cheek. "I know."

Speechless, she stared at him. Watched his head lower and felt the gentle kiss he brushed across her lips. The caress was so sweet and pure it stole her breath and made tears threaten all over again.

"Why don't you go back in with Maggie," he suggested.

"I, uh, can't." She realized she'd lifted her fingertips to touch her lips, and shoved her wayward hand into her pocket. "Not yet, I mean. They're moving her to a regular room."

He gave a nod, obviously in thought.

"I'm sure you want to get back."

His eyes focused on her face. "You're sure, are you?"

"Well—" She gestured toward the door. "I mean you're probably wanting to get that tractor to Jefferson's. And… and…I have no idea how long Maggie'll be here before…well before. I know you've got things you want to get back to. Once Joe gets here—" she swallowed "—it's not really your concern."

Matthew's jaw tightened. "Touché."

She huffed. "That's not what I meant."

"It's exactly what you meant."

"Excuse me." They both turned to see a young candy striper standing nearby. "Your friend is in her room now," the girl said, her wide eyes staring at Matthew. As if he were some movie star or something. "It's on the next floor—212. Turn right off the elevators. I'd be happy to show you the way," she added breathlessly.

Jaimie shook her head. "That's not necessary." Of course the teenager was slathering over Matthew. The man could turn a solid block of ice to mush. "Thanks, though." She moistened her lips, sliding a glance Matthew's way when the candy striper trailed away, casting a lingering gaze over her shoulder. "I'll go up now," Jaimie told him. "Thank you for bringing us."

"Such politeness. Are you in shock or something?"

"Fine. Forget I said anything. You can go now."

A muscle ticked in his jaw. He tucked his hand around her upper arm and bent his head close to her ear. "Let's get a few things straight, shall we? I'm not leaving until I'm good and ready." His hold wasn't painful, nor did he let her scoot away when she tried. "I'm sorry for what I said this morning in the kitchen. Accept it or not. I drove Maggie here because I'm concerned, too. She's as much a part of the Double-C as Dan or I."

"Let me go," she hissed, painfully aware that he didn't consider *her* a part of the Double-C, too.

He abruptly did so. "Go on up to Maggie's room. I'll let you know when I've gotten hold of Joe."

His implacable suggestion stirred her vocal cords. "But—"

"Go!" Her eyes shot daggers at him as she turned and went. He figured it was better than tears.

Now it was up to him to find his foreman. He sighed and went in search of a phone.

Chapter Eleven

Matthew hung up the pay phone with a final click. He rolled his head side to side, loosening his tight neck as he walked back toward the row of seats against the wall of the small waiting room located down the hall from Maggie's private room.

He and Jaimie were alone now in the room. Had been for an hour or so. But before that, he'd watched Jaimie curtail her own worry as she charmed and soothed two children who had been waiting with their stoic grandmother for news on their parents, who'd been involved in an accident. Those kids, a boy and a girl, couldn't have been more than seven, and they'd been scared out of their minds. The grandmother hadn't been any help. Jaimie had sat right down on the floor in the corner over there by the stack of books and assorted toys, and within ten minutes the kids had been singing soft songs with her and shy smiles had replaced their tears.

Finally the parents had been deemed stable, and the

grandmother had carted off the children, but not before they'd given Jaimie a hug so heartfelt that even Matthew had felt it.

He stopped several feet away from the chairs, his eyes on Jaimie's slender form stretched across several seats. She was exhausted. He'd tried to get her to eat something around lunchtime, and then again at suppertime, but she'd merely picked and poked at the food. Her worry over Maggie was palpable. Within two hours of being admitted, Maggie had developed a fever. The doctor hadn't yet been able to determine why.

He sat down in the chair perpendicular to Jaimie's head and curtailed the urge to smooth the long tangle of hair from her sleeve. He stretched out his legs and leaned his head back against the wall, watching Jaimie through his lashes.

Her arm was draped across her eyes and her knees bent toward the seat backs. Even uncomfortable as he knew the seats to be, she was graceful in her fitful sleep. Her arm moved and she murmured.

Matthew's hearing had always been acute. His jaw tightened when he realized the name on her lips was his. Silently he rose to his feet and moved across the room to the windows. It wasn't quite dark yet, and he wasn't the least bit surprised to see a few snowflakes drifting to the ground from the gray sky.

He'd talked to Jefferson earlier that afternoon. Between his brother and Squire, who'd returned from the cabin, the Double-C would be taken care of until he, Dan and Joe returned.

He hadn't been able to turn off one disturbing realization since Maggie had been admitted: the fact that he'd have been tearing down walls if it had been Jaimie lying in that hospital bed.

Within minutes she was shifting, drawing his thoughts away from that dangerous turn. She lowered her arm and looked around, her eyes becoming shadowed when they rested on him.

With some difficulty he focused his thoughts. "I found Joe."

She blinked groggy eyes, then swung her legs to the ground. Her long fingers raked back her hair. "Where was he?"

Matthew tugged at his lower lip. She'd had to ask. Joe's activities had been varied that day—starting at the only motel Weaver possessed and ending hours later in Casper. He settled for the easiest answer. "In Casper."

Her eyebrows shot up. "Casper? Whatever for?"

Matthew made himself shrug. "Supplies."

Her eyes lost the haze of sleep clinging to them. "Supplies." She sniffed and stood up, smoothing her palms down her jeans. "Is he coming here?"

"I arranged a charter. He'll be here anytime now." It had taken him hours to track down his foreman. He'd found himself wishing he had the bloodhound instincts of Jefferson or Tristan. But his persistence had eventually paid off.

"A charter. Oh. How nice of you." She swiped at her hair again. "What time is it?"

"Dinnertime."

Jaimie didn't seem to hear him. "I wonder if that guard-dog nurse of Maggie's will let me in there yet."

"She was pretty adamant about observing visiting hours."

"Adamant? The woman was positively rabid. I still can't believe she wouldn't let those little kids see their parents. It would've been better for them to see the casts on their legs and arms, than sit in here wondering…well, you know." Jaimie paced to the doorway and looked out. "Where is Daniel, anyway?" Her restless pacing brought her back in front of the chairs. "Did he go back to the Double-C?"

"He took a couple rooms at the hotel across the street."

She stared at him. "For who?"

"Us."

Heat swept into her cheeks. "Oh." Jaimie suddenly wished there was somebody else in the waiting room with them. Anyone else. Just so she didn't go making a fool of herself again. The idea of hotel rooms had her at a complete loss. Her brain simply shut down. That's all. Just…shut…down.

"Jaimie."

Lord, the way he said her name. As if to back away from the thought of Matthew and hotel rooms, she physically backed away from him even though there was no room in which to back. "Yes?"

"What's the matter?"

"Nothing. Look, I'm just, just worried about Maggie."

"I know. We all are. Why are you trembling?"

"I'm not," she lied. "Look, if you must know, I'm worried about Joe, too. Does that satisfy you?" She *was* worried about her brother. But she couldn't stop her hands from shaking, because she simply couldn't get past that hotel room thing.

He brushed his thumb down her cheek. "I haven't been satisfied since the day we met," he mused. "And no matter how hard or which way I try to twist it, it always comes back to that."

Her mouth ran dry. She could only stare at him. At his sharply angled jaw, liberally dusted with golden stubble. At the surprisingly lush lashes surrounding his white-blue eyes. Eyes that studied her beneath heavy lids. "What are you saying?"

Matthew closed his hands over her shoulders, molding the delicate curve of muscle and bone. He swallowed, feeling more awkward than he could ever remember feeling. "I, uh, I care about you, is all."

Her eyes closed for a moment. When she opened them

again, her attention was turned toward the floor. "Is it so hard to say?"

He cleared his throat and slid his hands down her arms to catch her hands. "Yeah."

She moistened her lips, seeming to study their linked fingers. "Are you involved with Donna Blanchard?"

Now where was that mind of hers going? "Well, yeah, you could say that. I thought you knew."

She jerked her hands from his and tucked them in her stiffly crossed arms.

"What? What did I say?"

Her eyes glittered. "Leave me alone, Matthew."

He raked his fingers through his hair. "Why are you upset now?"

She gave him a look that should've scorched him to his heels. It merely made him want to toss her over his shoulder and haul her off somewhere more private than this bloody hospital waiting room. Thankfully, his common sense overrode the caveman instinct. He drew in a slow, deep breath and looked at this woman who'd turned his entire world inside out. "My involvement with Donna is only—"

"I don't want to hear about it."

"Too bad."

She sniffed imperiously and stepped to the side. He followed. She glared at him.

"I'm buying Donna's spread from her."

"So? She wouldn't sell it to you until you slept with her?"

"I'm not sleeping with Donna Blanchard! Gawdalmighty, woman, where do you come up with this stuff?"

"You just told me you were involved with her!"

"SSHHH!"

They both whirled to see the nurse standing in the doorway, giving them a disapproving look. "This is a hospital," she said crisply. "We can hear you all the way down the hall.'' She wheeled around on her crepe-soled shoes and squeaked along the tiled floor as she left.

Jaimie crossed her arms. ''Move out of my way, please.''

He didn't budge. ''I'm involved with Donna only because I'm buying her property. I'm not sleeping with her now. I have never slept with her. I don't *want* her. I want you,'' he growled. ''I can't think straight for wanting you. I close my eyes and see you etched on my brain. I wake up looking forward to seeing your little face across the breakfast table. I go into my office, and there's one of those crazy hearts or shamrocks you've cut out lying around.''

He nudged her chin up with his thumb when she moved restlessly. ''I'll be out on Jasper, and his coat is the same color as your hair. I go to bed and my sheets smell like you. Even my own dog follows you around like a shadow. I haven't had a decent night's sleep since we met, and until I get you in my bed for the night, I'm not likely to.'' He made an impatient sound and turned away, thrusting his fingers in his pockets.

Stunned, the only word she could summon was his name.

He whirled on his heel, his eyes intent, his beautifully molded lips drawn tight. ''Is that clear enough for you now?'' He hauled her close and kissed her as if he'd never kissed her before.

''Well, now. Ain't this sweet.''

Slowly Matthew lowered Jaimie until her feet hit the floor. His hands at her waist kept her against him, and he looked over his shoulder at Daniel. ''Go away.''

Daniel's grin didn't fade as he shook his head and straightened from the doorway. ''Can't do that,'' he said regretfully as he walked toward them. ''The way you two're going at it, somebody might walk in when things are *really* interesting.'' His smile widened at the heat that climbed into Jaimie's cheeks.

''Jaimie, there you are.'' Joe appeared in the doorway

behind Daniel, his dark hair rumpled, his cheeks unshaven. "Where's Mags?"

Matthew's arms dropped from her, and Jaimie felt suddenly cold. She moved over to Joe and hugged him. No matter how he behaved, he was still her brother. And no matter how much she wanted to pretend that she and Matthew were the only people in the world, how much she wanted to explore what he'd begun, there were other things that needing tending. "She's in her room," she said huskily. "Come on, I'll show you where." She could feel the heat of Matthew's eyes on them. Flushing, she pulled Joe down the hall but spotted Maggie's doctor first.

She hurried after him, nearly skipping in her haste to catch the doctor before he reached the elevator. "Doctor Foster," she said, skidding around beside him. "How is Maggie?"

He looked at Joe, clearly not recognizing him, then at Jaimie. "You're the sister-in-law," he remembered aloud. "We've managed to stop the contractions. But her fever is still rising. We're running an IV and have started a course of antibiotics," he told them, glancing at the gold watch circling his wrist.

"Wait—" She grabbed his coat sleeve when he punched the elevator call button. "What about the baby?"

He paused, his glance over the top of gold-rimmed glasses not unkind. "We want to put off delivery for as long as possible. Every day at this point increases the baby's chances. I'll want to keep her in the hospital until she delivers."

Beside her, Joe swore beneath his breath. Jaimie tightened her hand on his.

The elevator doors slid open. "I'm due in delivery," the doctor said as he stepped inside. "Right now I'm concerned about clearing up the infection causing her fever." He nodded toward them as the doors slid shut.

Jaimie turned to find Daniel standing a few feet behind

them. He looked at Joe, and his gray eyes turned to cold chips of slate. "Maggie's asking for you," he told him.

Jaimie pointed toward the room, and her brother went inside. When she looked back for Daniel, though, he was gone. Matthew walked toward her. "You okay?" he asked.

She nodded. "Her doctor wants to keep her here until the baby comes."

"Then she'll be here for whatever care she needs."

His voice sounded oddly hollow, and she looked up at him, for the first time noticing how pale he was. "Are you all right?"

"Fine." He planted his hat on his head. "Just need some fresh air. You want to come with me or wait to see Maggie?"

"Now that Joe's here," she said, "Maggie will be fine. I'll check on her later."

His expression was tight, but he nodded and handed her coat to her. "Let's get some supper, then. You didn't eat enough food earlier to fill a thimble."

They stopped at the nurses' station and Jaimie told the nurse assigned to Maggie where they'd be. They rode the elevator down, and Matthew hustled her to the café located on the main floor of the hotel across the street. *Keep it simple,* she told herself. Simple, so that perhaps she could maintain some semblance of dignity. "Did Jefferson check on the calf?"

"Emily did. He was fine. Took him back out to the barn. He's drinking on his own."

Jaimie nodded, relieved.

"Daniel took the truck back to the ranch."

She toyed with her napkin. "Why didn't you go with him?" His eyes met hers and her mouth went dry. She reached for her water glass and sucked down half of it. So much for dignity.

She looked scared out of her mind, but her determined expression told Matthew she was battling it down. His lips twisted. "Relax. I've got some business to take care of. Since I'm already here, might as well tend to it now." It wasn't a complete lie.

She moistened her lips, thrusting her slender fingers through her hair. It tumbled down her back, glowing deeply beneath the lamp hanging over their table. He stifled the want that chugged hot and slow through his veins and turned his attention to the menu in his hands.

They had just ordered when Jaimie realized they were being stared at. She looked at the man who was eyeing them from the entrance and knew she'd never seen him before. "Matthew, there's a man…oh, he's coming this way."

Matthew looked up and his eyes, which had been filled with heat a moment before, cooled. A large man to begin with, his mile-wide shoulders seemed suddenly even more imposing against the back of the booth.

The stranger who'd been staring stopped at the table. "Matt."

"Haskell."

Jaimie wanted to shrink back in her seat at the tangible dislike between the two. It rolled off Matthew's shoulders in waves.

The man, Haskell, turned his pale brown eyes toward Jaimie. "Howdy, ma'am."

For no reason that she could fathom, Jaimie didn't like him. His greeting had been friendly enough. She made herself nod. "Good evening." Then the man turned his attention back to Matthew and she was relieved.

"Hear you're sniffing around the Blanchard place," the man murmured crudely. "You Clays not satisfied owning nearly every piece of land in these parts? You gotta cheat some poor woman outta her place?"

Jaimie swallowed a gasp and watched Matthew's fist slowly curl. She held her breath.

"Hear you had to go all the way to Arkansas to find a job," Matthew returned. Calm. Cold.

"Thanks to you."

"You should have stayed there."

"I don't gotta do nothing," Haskell retorted.

Matthew didn't respond and Haskell smiled nastily. He looked back at Jaimie. "You ought to find yourself a better date," he suggested. "One that's not ice all the way to his bones."

"Haskell."

The man went still as Matthew said his name. He suddenly turned on his heel and stalked out of the restaurant.

Jaimie blinked. She looked at Matthew. She'd never heard him sound so menacing. And all he'd said was the man's name. She moistened her lips. "*What* was that?"

His fist uncurled and he picked up his water, drinking. "A snake," he finally said. "Don't let him ruin your appetite."

"But—"

"He worked for us once," Matthew provided shortly.

"Once? Good grief, Matthew. You looked like you wanted to squash him under your boot."

"An appropriate action," he said. He set down his water and shifted his shoulders. "He tried to rustle Double-C cattle," he said after a moment.

"Tried?"

"I stopped him."

Jaimie decided she really didn't want to know *how*. "I thought rustling was a criminal act," she said instead. "Was he convicted?"

"Haskell and I went to school together. We used to be friends. He thought that would make a difference." His lips twisted. "We handled it ourselves."

"Oh," she said faintly. "How long ago did this happen?"

"A long time ago. Haskell and the likes of him know better than to mess with the Double-C," he said softly. "Now, can we talk about something more pleasant?"

Jaimie toyed with her water glass. She nodded. "Please." She didn't want to think too hard about what she'd just witnessed. She didn't *need* to think hard on it. Just as Matthew would never leave the Double-C, he would never stand for anyone harming it, either. Not an old schoolmate. Not anyone.

Thankfully, the waitress arrived with their meal, and Matthew seemed to set himself the task of erasing the brief, unpleasant episode from existence with his casual banter. He did such a good job of it that Jaimie actually managed to eat her entire meal and the dessert that he ordered for her.

When they returned to the hospital, they learned that Maggie's temperature had risen even higher. Jaimie wouldn't be allowed in to visit her that night. Through the small window in the door, they looked in. Joe sat beside his wife's bed, an unopened magazine on his lap.

Jaimie turned to Matthew. Everything he'd said in the waiting room was suddenly fresh in her mind. "It's getting late," she said. "There's no reason for you to stay. Go on over to the hotel. You'll be a lot more comfortable there than in the waiting room here."

"So would you." He tipped her chin up and studied her face. "You haven't been sleeping much lately. You've got circles under your eyes."

Because every time she drifted into sleep it was to dream about him. About his body lying next to hers. She turned her head, and his hand fell away. "I should wait for Joe."

Matthew's expression seemed to tighten. He pulled a key from his pocket and closed her palm around it. "The room number is on the key," he said. "Get some sleep sometime."

His glacial eyes were anything but, when they ran over her face once more before he headed for the elevators. Jaimie watched him go, her finger running along the jagged edge of the key. Then she tucked it in her pocket and slowly walked back to the waiting room.

Matthew knew he was dreaming. It was all very logical. He *knew* it was a dream, no doubt spurred on by the afternoon spent in the hospital, but he couldn't get it to stop. So he braced himself for the visions that engulfed him. Memories that were so vivid he could still smell the piney scent of the Christmas tree in the big house, feel the way the cold snow stung his cheeks. So vivid that he could taste the coppery tang of fear when he stood at the top of the back steps, looking toward the old barn.

His heart thudded painfully in his chest as he took those steps down, fear growing with every step he took. He'd had the dream so many times in the past that he knew what he'd see when he got to the barn, and that knowledge just made his guts twist even tighter.

He broke out into a sweat when he saw himself fall to his knees. Blood soaked through the new Levi's he'd just opened a few hours ago.

He tried so hard not to cry, but failed miserably. Clutching her hand in his as he tried to wake her. Then her eyes opened and she softly whispered his name.

Matthew bolted out of bed, nearly stumbling over his boots that he'd left lying on the floor. Sweat cooled rapidly on his bare chest and he raked his fingers through his hair, pressing the heels of his palms into his eyes.

Tension twisted and twined inside him and he stepped across the hotel room, yanking back the drapes to look out. His room faced away from the hospital across the street, looking over a parking lot instead.

Heart thundering, he pressed his forehead against the cold window-pane.

God. He hadn't had that dream in years.

He'd spent thirty years of his life without a mother. And now, to have that dream again. After all this time...

Making an impatient sound, he dropped the drapes back into place and headed for the bathroom. It was nearly 2:00 a.m. And he sure as shootin' didn't want to go back to sleep just now.

He flipped on the shower and stepped in. A solid twenty minutes later, he mentally blessed hot water heaters and wrapped a towel around his waist. He was heading back to bed when he heard a soft tapping on the door. He yanked it open.

Jaimie gaped.

It was a wonder he didn't have a heart attack, considering the way his heart was getting a workout tonight. "What's wrong?"

She dragged her eyes up to his and visibly swallowed. "Nothing. I, um, was going to my room." She looked over her shoulder at the room directly across the hall from his. "I thought I heard you."

"You've been at the hospital all this time?"

She nodded. "Maggie's temperature is almost back to normal. And she hasn't had any more contractions."

"That's good."

"They, um, let Joe sleep in her room."

Matthew wasn't ready to think too kindly on Joe yet. Not after what he'd learned had gone on in Casper. He nodded, absently wiping at the water dripping down his chest. "You look exhausted."

She crushed the wool coat to her chest. Her eyes skittered over him. "Yeah. Well, I don't think I can sleep. I'm too keyed up. Why are you still awake?"

He had never told anyone about the nightmares. He didn't intend to start now. "Couldn't sleep, either."

"Oh." She moistened her lips and rocked on her heels. "Well, I guess I'd—"

Before he knew what he was doing, he'd captured her arm and pulled her into his room. The only light came from the one he'd forgotten in the bathroom. But he could see her startled expression. The color that rose in her creamy cheeks.

He dropped the Do Not Disturb tag on the outside of the door and closed it, soundlessly sliding the security lock in place.

"What...what are you doing?"

He pulled the coat from her hands and tossed it over a chair. "We're both gonna get some sleep tonight," he murmured.

Her hands warded him off. Or reached for him. He wasn't sure which. Either way, he didn't think he could handle her touch just then. Not when he was standing there with only his towel protecting her modesty.

He bent down and tapped her boot. "Lift." She did so, wobbled and grabbed his shoulder. He pulled off one, then the other. They hit the floor with a thud and he stood up, molding the smooth angle of her shoulders through her thermal shirt with his palms. "You've got a choice here, Jaimie," he said gruffly. "One night. We're either gonna sleep in that bed together and just sleep. Or we're not."

Her mouth parted soundlessly.

"It's up to you." His jaw cocked.

Jaimie trembled. No false promises would fall from Matthew's lips. Everything that was sensible and sane inside her told her that she shouldn't do what her heart was yearning for her to do. He would hold her through the night, make love to her if she wished...*oh how she wished*...and in the morning they would go about their business.

Could she do that? Could she go back on her promise to herself?

In the dim light, she looked at him. He was good and honest. Honorable and kind. He was everything that her father had not been. That Tony had not been. And even, painful as it was to suspect, what Joe was not.

I care about you, is all.

No, there would be no fairy-tale promises of love from

Matthew. But, for this night…this one night…he would be hers.

And she would be his.

Wasn't that really the only thing she wanted?

She lifted her hand toward him.

His eyes closed briefly, then he folded her hand in his. Her head tilted back of its own accord when he covered her lips with his. Sweetly and gently he kissed her, as if he sensed she was ready to bolt. A curious ease spread through her even as her blood warmed to his touch.

Kissing Matthew was like coming home, she realized hazily.

His big hands slid around her back, cradling her against him, and she wrapped her arms around his neck, her thoughts short-circuiting. His skin dampened her through her shirt, and her fingers slipped through the strands of his silky wet hair. She pressed her mouth to the pulse that throbbed beneath his hard jaw, breathing in deeply that wonderful scent that was Matthew.

He made a rough sound and tipped her head back. His lips burned over her temple. Her jaw. The edge of her collarbone bared by the scooped neckline of her shirt. Her fingers grasped his waist, encountering the damp terry cloth tied there.

She went still and his head lifted.

"I'll take care of you," he murmured.

She wanted to return the words, but found herself incapable of speech. When he tugged the hem of her shirt from her jeans, she mindlessly lifted her arms. His hands traced the strap of her lacy bra. She could feel the heat of his intent gaze and her breathing quickened.

Matthew actually trembled at the vision before him. Thirty-nine and comfortable in his life, he was trembling before the sight of a beautiful woman.

There she stood. A warm living statue as his eyes roved over the lacy bra covering her deceptively full curves. As he watched, her nipples pebbled and peeked through the ivory lace. He traced one narrow strap, watching her lips part soundlessly.

He flicked open the tiny clasp in the valley of her breasts. The two cups separated an inch, cradling her peach-tinted skin like two loving hands. His body tightened and he slid his fingers into the waist of her jeans.

Her breath hissed as he popped open her button fly to display the edge of panties the same color as the bra that cupped her breasts. Capturing her palms against his, he sat on the edge of the bed, drawing her between his thighs. She slipped her fingers through his hair and smoothed it back, then leaned forward and pressed her lips to the vein throbbing in his temple.

His eyes narrowed as he absorbed the scent of her. He touched the long strands of hair swirling down her back. It was like running his fingers through liquid silk. She made a soft sound deep in her throat as he smoothed her hair behind her shoulders and ran a fingertip along the upper edge of that tantalizing bit of lace barely cradling her breasts.

Her breath came a fraction faster, harder, her eyes wide on his when he slipped his finger beneath the lace and traced the satiny smooth skin. Her fingers flexed into his bare shoulders. She breathed his name.

"Shh," he soothed, gliding his hands down her narrow rib cage and slipping beneath her jeans. With just a nudge, they slipped over her hips, and he pushed them down past her knees. She stepped out of them and Matthew sucked in his breath. Her panties were cut with a flirty edge of ruffle high on her illegally long legs. The ivory lace was sheer, and his attention whisked over the shadowy down at the juncture of her thighs.

Her fingers curled around his biceps and tugged. He stood up and sucked in his breath when her knuckles grazed his abdomen as they slipped the knot of his towel free. The terry tumbled to the floor and he sprang free, his hard length grazing that sassy ruffle over her thigh.

Her soft lips parted. Her green eyes snared his as her fingers intimately traced over him. He closed his eyes and started counting backward. It was entirely possible that he would disgrace himself at any moment. He stilled her hand, linking her fingers with his.

"Please," she breathed. "Let me."

He groaned faintly, and she traced his length, his hand resting atop hers. "You're killing me here," he muttered.

She lifted his free hand and placed it over her thundering heart. His little finger teased the turgid peak still protected by that sheer lace. He scraped his finger over and around that tight little point, and she moaned, her fingers clutching him spasmodically. "Matthew."

He tugged the two halves of lace apart, exposing the high swells to his eyes. The lacy confection drifted down her elbows. She let go of him and the bra whispered to the floor. He sat back down on the edge of the bed, his knees feeling like rubber. Curving his palms around her thighs, he pulled her closer until her knees met the bed. "I've dreamed about these legs of yours," he admitted gruffly. "Wrapped around me. I've dreamed of touching you like this." His fingers slipped up beneath the taunting little ruffle. "Tasting you."

Her breath whistled past her teeth. "I've had dreams, too." Her hands smoothed along the heated golden skin stretching across his massive shoulders. "I've never… felt…like this." His tantalizing touch swirled and she thought she might go up in flames. She'd never dreamed…never expected the drugging madness sweeping through her. Had she even lived before this moment? "Oh…*Matthew*."

He pulled her head down to his. Their tongues tangled. She wrapped her arms around him, marveling that she had the power to make this man, so strong and proud, tremble in her arms. His open mouth burned along her jaw, closed over her earlobe. His breath was harsh in her ear, and delight danced along her limbs. His palms slipped over her bottom. "Part your legs for me, Jaimie."

She shivered like a leaf borne on the wind. She inched her feet apart. His fingers urged more. She could do nothing but follow his lead.

Matthew kissed her again and slipped his palm over her. Her fingers clutched his shoulders. He groaned softly, nudging aside the moist lace. A soft keening cry escaped her lips. His eyes snared hers. Her eyes were deeply green, the pupils dilated. He murmured her name, letting his fingers delve into her slick heat.

She whimpered, her head falling forward. Her hair tumbled over him as she arched against his hand. His breath hissed between his teeth when her searching hand closed over him, matching the slow, drugging rhythm he'd set. He caught a tight nipple between his lips and tugged gently. She cried out, moving urgently.

"Enough," he growled, tugging off the sexy panties and tossing them aside. He reversed their positions and she sank onto the bed, holding her arms up to him. The diamonds circling her wrist caught the subdued light and glistened.

"Please," she breathed.

Sheathing himself, he came down to her, holding his weight on his arms. He groaned, bowing his head when he nudged against her swollen flesh.

She moaned.

"Look at me."

Her heavy eyelids lifted and she stared into his eyes as he slowly filled her. A tear slid from her dark eyes and disappeared in the fire-tipped hair spread around her.

Tight. Wet. Oh, she was so tight. He flexed and her lips parted on a soundless cry. "Am I hurting you?" *Please no. Stopping now just might kill him.*

Her legs hugged his hips. "Don't stop," she gasped.

He took her hands in his, linking his fingers with hers. He pressed them gently to the mattress beside her head and slid fully home.

His mouth swallowed her harsh gasp. Then she was straining closer and closer, driving him to the edge of sanity. He loved the incoherent sounds welling in her throat. Would remember to his dying day the way she absorbed him, savored him. Moved with him.

His jaw locked as her muscles suddenly clenched. She cried his name and he looked into her beautiful, glowing eyes. His feeble control had no defense against the sight of her exquisite pleasure, and he felt everything within him, everything he *was,* straining for her.

Boneless, Jaimie pressed her lips to his chest as Matthew went rigid, his back bowing. Tears leaked from her eyes, but she didn't care. He collapsed with a heavy groan, and her arms cradled him to her. Then he shifted from her, pulling her tightly against him.

Long minutes passed. He left the bed for a few moments then returned, sliding her boneless figure against him. When their breathing had slowed, and their bodies had cooled enough for him to drag a blanket over them, he thumbed the tear tracks drying on her face. "You should have told me," he murmured, his voice low and husky.

There was no point in pretending she didn't know what he meant. "Would it have made a difference?"

He breathed deeply, his broad chest moving beneath her palm. "I don't know," he said quietly.

Jaimie closed her eyes and pressed her cheek against the steady beat of his heart. "That's what I thought," she whispered.

He brushed her hair away from her cheek and finally, exhausted, satisfied and warmly twined together, they slept.

Chapter Twelve

Once again Matthew found himself oversleeping. It must have something to do with the person who'd shared his bed, he acknowledged wryly, as he read the note Jaimie had left him. She'd already gone over to the hospital.

He sprawled back on the rumpled, tangled sheets, covering his eyes with a bent arm. So much for good intentions. He knew what it was like to be obsessed. He'd conquered his penchant for poker, though. Hadn't he? Which meant that he could conquer this…need…for Jaimie, too. And he would. Soon.

Right now, though, it just wasn't in him to be sorry for what they'd done. The regret could come later.

Right now, he felt like he'd tasted heaven.

He dropped his arm with an oath. He wasn't going poetic, was he?

He got out of bed and took a quick shower, trying not to acknowledge the wish that Jaimie was still here in the room. In the shower with him. He'd been stupid enough to think that one night would satisfy him.

A week of nights wouldn't satisfy him, now that he knew. Knew how the earth rocked when she opened herself to him. Generously, seductively. Giving everything she was to him.

He stared at himself in the foggy mirror over the sink. He needed a shave. And though he'd had his first decent stretch of sleep in weeks, he still looked haggard.

What could she see in him?

He peeled off the wet bandage over his healing cut and dropped it in the trash. She was young and vibrant. Beautiful and sassy. She belonged in the city. Not on the ranch. Where life wasn't easy or soft and gentle. Where calves died in the ice and snow. Where even his mother hadn't been able to survive.

He raked his fingers through his short hair, leaving it standing in spikes, and turned to find his clothes.

One night, he reminded himself as he yanked on his jeans. One. Night.

The door opened and Jaimie slipped inside. Her cheeks were rosy. From the cold or from last night, he didn't know.

"I thought you might still be sleeping," she said, setting the room key on the dresser. She held up a small white paper bag. "I brought coffee."

He slowly finished buttoning his jeans, then took the foam cup she held out. "Thanks."

She blushed and busied herself with removing her coat and hanging it over the back of a chair.

Matthew's eyes caught and held on the sway and gleam of her hair. He jerked his attention to his coffee. "How's Maggie?"

"Better. Her OB was already there this morning. Maggie knows she'll have to stay here until the baby comes. She's not exactly thrilled, but it's necessary." Jaimie sat in one of the upholstered chairs near the window and lifted the plastic lid off her coffee. She cautiously sipped, then smiled slightly. "This place is a tad nicer than—"

"Yeah." Matthew didn't need any reminders of the other time they'd shared a room.

Her gaze grew thoughtful. Then she turned her attention back to her coffee. "Will you be able to take care of your business without your truck?"

He stared at her. "Oh. Yeah." He set aside his cup and snatched up his shirt, shoving his arms into it. "I'll get Dan or Jefferson to drive up and get me later," he said.

She set her own coffee down and pulled her hair away from her face, letting it cascade down the back of her shirt. The movement drew Matthew's attention to the thrust of her breasts beneath that textured weave. Her lacy bra peeked out from beneath a pillow that had fallen to the floor.

He stifled an oath. One night did not include the morning after. No matter how soft and sexy she looked. "What about you?" he asked abruptly. "Do you want to stay here or go back?"

"Joe plans to stay," she said after a moment. "Unless you need him at the ranch."

"No. We'll manage." Matthew didn't know what he'd say to his foreman when the time came. He'd always made a point of staying out of Joe's personal business. But after what he'd learned, he figured sooner or later he'd have to. And wasn't that ironic when he himself had taken the virginity of the man's little sister last night, with nothing more than the promise of a good night's sleep in return?

"Matthew, are you all right?"

"Why wouldn't I be?"

Her shoulder lifted. She reached out and touched the brim of his hat that sat on the table beside her. Beneath the snug shirt, her breasts moved enticingly. Pink rose in her cheeks. "You seem…I don't know. Tense, I guess."

He watched her slender finger smooth over his cowboy

hat and knew he surely was tense. In fact, he felt like a rubber band stretched five times too tight. And the only relief in sight was her. He picked up the coffee. Maybe if he concentrated on the tongue singeing he'd get from drinking it, he'd get his mind above his belt.

Jaimie stood up suddenly and yawned. "I guess I'll come. With you back to the ranch," she added when he shot her a startled look. She squelched the nervousness bubbling inside her. Matthew was tense enough for the two of them without her adding to the mixture. She couldn't contain another yawn, and slid a look toward the bed. She could use another hour or two of sleep. Perhaps if she used the room across the hall that Matthew had originally intended for her...

Oh, who was she kidding? She didn't want to climb into bed for sleep or anything else. Not unless Matthew was there with her.

What a foolish thing she'd done. Foolish and wonderful and perfect. If only she had some experience with "morning afters," she'd know better how to behave. When she'd awakened beside him, she'd been so close to waking him...begging for his love...that she'd had to leave the warmth of his arms, if only to retain some small portion of her dignity.

Even now, all it would take would be one crook of his finger, and she'd willingly go to him.

Instead, she would go back to the ranch for as long as they needed her. She'd take care of his house. Prepare his meals and wash his clothes. And she'd save their one night together to keep her warm in the lonely nights ahead.

She capped her coffee, leaving it on the table, and picked up her coat. "Well..."

The corner of his lips lifted, but Jaimie couldn't see any humor in his clear eyes. In fact, the only thing in those barely blue eyes was the same heat that had been there in the wee hours of the night.

Her fingers curled.

"What are you going to do when you leave the Double-C?"

She felt the blood drain from her head. "What?"

"After Maggie's back up to snuff," he said. "What do you plan to do?"

Her breathing started up again. For a moment she'd thought— She moistened her lips. "I'll play it by ear," she managed truthfully. "I thought I'd try to find something here in Gillette. I think Weaver is pretty well tapped out. Colbys doesn't need waitresses and the general store and the café aren't even open full-time."

"You don't want to go back to work for Bennett?"

"No, thanks. I'd go back to Phoenix before I'd work for that octopus-armed man. I guess even attorneys aren't above the desire to play chase-around-the-desk."

"What kind of work would you want?"

Jaimie shrugged, feeling suddenly restless. She didn't want to think too closely about when she left the Double-C. "I don't know," she said. "Why?"

He frowned into his coffee. "No reason. I've just seen the way you gravitate toward kids. You know. That night when we got snowed in at the motel. And then those kids in the waiting room."

"Well, yes. I like kids. But…"

"But what?"

"Oh, nothing. Just something my dad used to tell me."

"What's that?"

She was ready to shrug it off. But he watched her steadily, and she realized that Matthew really wanted to know. He was truly interested in what motivated her. She rubbed her forehead. "I loved to baby-sit when I was a teenager," she finally said. "And I thought about going into teaching or something. But Dad, well he discouraged it." Talk about an understatement. "He insisted that I needed a business degree if I was going to get anywhere in life." Of course, she hadn't ever earned that degree, either. And even if her dad had lived, Jaimie knew that she *still* wouldn't have gotten a business degree. She'd hated every minute of her classes.

"The schoolteachers in this world would probably disagree with that," Matthew pointed out reasonably.

"I know. He just kept telling me to…get a *real* job." She folded her arms across her chest. "I guess if you hear something often enough, you start to believe it."

"Maybe if you found a job that you really enjoyed, you'd be able to stop searching. There's plenty of things you could be doing that involves kids. I know a lot of people in Gillette."

And a good word from Matthew Clay could probably about guarantee her a job somewhere. "I'll find something," she assured him. She always did.

"I never said you couldn't. I just—" He sighed. "If you needed something, once you…go. All you'd have to do is ask."

Of course he would want her to have some means of supporting herself. Matthew wouldn't turn a dog out into the cold, much less his…what? What term did she use to identify herself now? Soon-to-be-former temporary housekeeper? One-night stand?

She surreptitiously wiped her palms down her jeans. "I'd better get back to the hospital."

"I suppose so."

She had to walk by him to get to the door. She paused. "Matthew, I…I wanted to say that I…" She closed her eyes, and her ears started to burn. "Thank you for last night," she finally whispered. "For being there." She swallowed. "No one has ever—"

"Don't," he growled. "Don't thank me, like I did you some favor. We both know I didn't. And we both know that I'm standing here wanting you just as bad as ever. Worse, because now I know how it is between us."

Her legs went weak.

"You'd better go to the hospital right now, sweetheart."

She stood there, unable to take a step to save her soul.

He cursed softly, his knuckles white around the foam cup. "Jaimie."

She set aside her coat.

"You don't want to do this."

"And you don't know as much as you think you do," she returned.

He shook his head. "This is madness," he muttered. "Unadulterated madness."

Jaimie shored up every bit of courage she possessed and reached out. She took his coffee from him and set it aside. Then, painfully aware of his absolute stillness, she slowly pushed his shirt back off his shoulders. "Can't we have this one day, Matthew? One day without should-haves and shouldn't-haves?"

His head tilted back and he heaved a sigh. Then he looked down at her. "What am I going to do with you?"

She smiled faintly, gliding her palm over his forearm. "I'm sure you'll think of something."

His half chuckle was wry. "No doubt." He ran a possessive hand over her shoulders, then cupped his palms over her breasts. "You wear these thermal shirts to torture me."

She struggled for breath. "No. They're warm."

"They're tight. Like you are." His breath warmed her neck and his teeth captured her earlobe, nibbling gently. "Are you sure you want to do this?"

Her fingers slid through his hair. "The only thing I'm sure of right now is that if you stop, I'll have to kill you."

"Well, now I'm shaking in my boots."

"You're not wearing any." Her fingers were busy fumbling with his fly, and Matthew wondered if it was some new kind of torture specifically designed to make him crazy. He swallowed a groan and captured her hands.

"Lift." She raised her arms, allowing him to remove the body-hugging shirt.

He'd thought he could take his time. Leisurely explore her body. But as her hair tumbled down around her shoulders, settling like silk over her breasts, all visions of long, slow, languid loving flew out of his mind.

Jaimie gasped when he swept her off her feet and tumbled her onto the bed. Their clothing disappeared in a flurry. His urgency set off an answering chord within her, and she clung to him, crying out when he took them on a head-long race to heaven.

When they finally fell back on the mattress, dazed and exhausted, Matthew scooped her close to him. "You should be illegal," he murmured against her temple.

Jaimie tightened her arms around his slick shoulders. Pressing her head to the uneven beat of his heart, she closed her eyes. "You, too," she whispered.

Just before supper time, Jefferson arrived to drive Matthew and Jaimie back down to the Double-C. Jaimie left Maggie in the hospital with her assurances of returning within a few days with Maggie's own nightgowns and toiletries.

The tension in Maggie's face hadn't eased, even though the baby seemed to be out of danger for the time being. Jaimie knew how Maggie dreaded staying in the hospital. But for the safety of the baby, her sister-in-law would endure anything. Heaven knew that these last seven months hadn't been a walk in the park.

The drive back to the Double-C was an exercise in torture. Every time the truck hit a bump, Jaimie swayed against Matthew's rock-hard shoulder. Every time the truck slowed or turned, his strong thighs pressed against her.

By the time Jefferson dropped them off in front of the big house and drove home to his own place, Jaimie was a bundle of frayed nerves. More so, even, than when they'd driven Maggie to the hospital in the first place.

With hardly a glance in her direction, Matthew wasted no time in closeting himself in his office. Jaimie could tell that Daniel and Squire had made some attempt at feeding themselves dinner. Matthew would certainly be hungry, since they hadn't taken the time to stop for a bite, so she fixed him a tray and carried it to his office.

He thanked her brusquely and she returned to the kitchen to clean up the mess, wondering edgily if she'd dreamed the last twenty-four hours with him.

Then she reminded herself that he had given them one night. *And the morning after.* No promises, she reminded herself firmly. So she'd better learn to pretend nothing had transpired between them, and quick, or she would be ready for a rubber room by the time Maggie came home with the baby.

When she finally turned in for the night, the little brick cottage seemed large and empty. Lonely.

Jaimie had never denied the fact that she was a social creature. She enjoyed the company of others. But in the past several years, since the fiasco with Tony, she'd learned also that her own company wasn't too awful. She seldom felt lonely. Separate or apart from others...the rest of the world.

Tonight, however, as she crawled in her narrow bed in the second bedroom of her brother's house, she was more aware than ever before just how alone a person could feel.

Turning on her side, she tucked her arm under her head. She had pulled back the curtains at the window before climbing into bed, and now the moonlight bathed the shadows with cool white light. Half a mile away, Matthew would probably be turning in himself. She couldn't help the futile wish that he would be thinking of her when his head hit the pillow.

She made an impatient noise and turned on her other

side, punching the pillow into place. Nothing in her life had turned out the way she'd expected. There was no point in indulging in wishful dreams.

No matter what had happened between Matthew and Jaimie, no matter how wondrous and fulfilling, the fact remained that Jaimie wasn't cut out for ranch life. And in her wildest dreams, Jaimie couldn't imagine Matthew ever leaving the Double-C, so she'd better get her wayward emotions under control, and quick. He'd even warned her. No fairy-tale endings.

Matthew stood at the window in his bedroom and looked out over the moonlit fields of white, reaching desperately for the calm it usually provided. He had tried to sleep, but couldn't. He'd had the dream again. Two nights in a row now. But something had changed. And it was *that* which had him even now sweating like it was the middle of August and not the dead of winter.

For when, in his dream, he'd fallen to his knees in the snow beside the still, bleeding woman, and she'd opened her eyes to look at him, they hadn't been the gentle blue eyes of his mother.

They'd been green. As green as the moss that grew on the rocks down by the swimming hole in the springtime.

He braced his clammy hands on the sides of the windowsill and bowed his head. His mother had gone away. BethAnn had died, too.

God help him. He couldn't bear to see the same fate befall Jaimie. She *had* to go before something tragic happened. It was that simple.

Shoving away from the window, he yanked on his jeans. As he did so, a few papers fluttered from his nightstand to the floor, and he bent and picked them up. One of them was the little red heart he'd found that one morning in the motel lobby. His fingers tightened around the heart, crumpling it into a ball.

She *had* to go.

* * *

A few days later Jaimie went back to the hospital with Emily and Jefferson. Emily had her own doctor's appointment to attend, and it was logical for Jaimie to ride along with them. Matthew was particularly busy, with Joe still in town, and Jaimie knew he couldn't really spare the time to drive her himself.

The sensible logic did little to quell her disappointment.

Maggie was with her doctor when Jaimie arrived, so she left the bag of clothing and toiletries she'd packed for Maggie at the nurses' station, then wandered around the hospital, killing time. When she found herself standing outside the windows of the nursery, Matthew's suggestions about finding a suitable job lingered in her mind.

She didn't want to leave the Double-C. But Maggie *would* have her baby. And soon. She had to be realistic about that.

Knowing that, however, didn't keep her feet from dragging when she went in search of the human resources department to check out the job postings, before going back up to visit with Maggie.

It was time to start supper when Jefferson and Emily finally dropped Jaimie off at the Double-C. They'd made only one stop after leaving the hospital and that was to pick up groceries and supplies.

After taking her own load over to the cottage, she carried the bags of produce she'd bought in town for the big house into the kitchen. Already her mind was busy planning the meal. Liver and onions, of all things.

She stopped short at the sight of Matthew and Donna Blanchard sitting cozily at the big table. Then she quelled her knee-jerk reaction with the reminder that Matthew had business dealings with Donna. So she greeted the two and went about her own business, putting away the fruit and vegetables she'd purchased. The two at the table continued their discussion and Jaimie couldn't understand a word of their technical talk. But she kept the phrases in her mind so she could ask Squire later.

She was folding the reusable canvas bags she'd used when Donna scooted back her chair. Matthew helped her on with her heavy coat and then the other woman was gone. Leaving Jaimie alone with Matthew.

Thank goodness she had supper preparations to keep her hands busy. Otherwise they'd be doing something embarrassing. Like reaching out and smoothing back the heavy lock of gold hair that had fallen over his forehead. Or touching the muscle that ticked in his jaw.

Biting the inside of her lip, she washed her hands, then started rinsing the exorbitantly expensive head of lettuce she'd purchased.

"Maggie doin' all right?"

Jaimie looked over her shoulder, then hastily turned her attention back to the lettuce. She really did wish that she had his apparent ability to turn his emotions on and off. "Yes."

She heard the scrape of a chair and knew he'd sat down again. Her nerves tightened even more.

"She's probably going stir crazy."

"Mmm-hmm." She turned off the water and set the lettuce aside while she peeled several cucumbers. "Emily's appointment went well. She said everything's going right on schedule."

"Good thing. Jefferson would be a basket case if it weren't."

Jaimie deftly sliced the cukes and started on the tomatoes.

"You like cooking, don't you?"

She looked over her shoulder at him. He was watching her, his eyes inscrutable as usual. "Yes." She turned back to the salad she was building. "I've worked in several restaurants.'' Her shoulder lifted. ''I'm no chef. But you pick up a few things.''

''You know how to cook, clean, sew, deal cards, drive cabs and soothe scared little kids. What else?''

She rinsed her knife and tossed the salad with her bare hands, then dried them on a paper towel. She turned to face him, crossing her arms across her tomato red turtleneck sweater. Her expression was still. ''You sure are interested in my job history lately. Are you wanting to check my references now? It's a little late, don't you think?''

''Just trying to carry on a conversation,'' he said mildly. ''Got a problem with that?''

Her head tilted and her bangs slid over her forehead. ''Well, let's see,'' she said. ''Bookkeeping, word processing and data entry, child care,'' she nodded at him, ''housekeeper, cab driver, waitressing, cocktail waitressing, teaching at a children's activity center, teacher's aid at a private school in Nevada, retail sales in a couple different places… shall I go on?''

''Why so many?''

Her lips twisted. ''Maybe I don't have any staying power.''

Matthew fell silent for a moment. Her eyes, steady on his, didn't sparkle as they usually did. ''Who was he?''

''Who?''

''The man who convinced you that you don't have any *staying power.*''

''Who says it was a man? Who says it was anybody at all?''

''Who was he?''

She shrugged and carried the salad to the refrigerator. Bending over, her voice was muffled as she reached inside. ''Well, you can take your pick. My father, for starters. Not that he was around all the time, mind you. But when he was, he found fault with everything I did. My grades weren't good enough. My jobs weren't good enough. My friends weren't good enough. Then there's my brother. He never understood why I quit so many different jobs, or about Tony. My fiancé." She straightened and carried several lemons to the sink.

Matthew's attention abruptly went on alert. Fiancé? "What happened?"

Her head tilted back and she sighed. "Is this more conversation making?"

"Call it what you want. You don't have a fiancé waiting for you in Phoenix, do you?" The very idea made him coldly furious, but when Jaimie laughed abruptly, the wind went right out of his sails.

"Lord, no. That was over years ago." With one whack, she sliced a lemon in two. "Tony didn't love me. He loved the person he thought he could make me." Another lemon fell prey to her knife. "When I realized that I wasn't capable of becoming the dutiful, prim and proper corporate wife that he had in mind, I broke it off." She waved her knife. "Oh, he was brokenhearted, of course. He proved that when he turned around and married my roommate two weeks later." Whack. "Turns out that he and Wanda had been doing the bump and grind behind my back for months."

"But you and he didn't—"

"No. He blamed that on me, too. You know. If I hadn't insisted on waiting, then he wouldn't have turned to Wanda." She lifted one shoulder. "Naturally, Joe said I was a fool for passing up the opportunity of marrying Tony. He made it real clear that it was just another example of my...ah...flightiness."

Matthew stood up and grabbed her hand as she went for the last lemon. In his opinion, Joe had no room for criticism. "Your brother was wrong. *Tony* was the fool."

She went still. "That's what Maggie said, too." Her eyes were on the hand he'd wrapped around her wrist. "I was kidding myself, though, in thinking that I loved him. Thinking that I could turn myself into something that I'm not. Trying to fit in where I don't belong.'' She swallowed and pulled out of his loose hold. ''I know better now.'' Whack.

Matthew's gut tightened. God. Even carrying on a simple conversation with her was dangerous ground. He was a bloody idiot for thinking that they could go back to status quo. They could never go back. Not after what they'd shared in Gillette.

Still, he couldn't help thinking that this *Tony* jerk had done him a favor. For if he'd married Jaimie, Matthew had no doubt that she wouldn't be standing here right now, brightening his kitchen with her fiery auburn hair and sassy tongue. And she never would have been in his bed less than a week ago. A place that he knew she fit to perfection.

''Excuse me.''

He stepped out of the way so she could reach the cabinet behind him. Searching for something safe, he focused on the two glass pie pans she'd pulled out and set on the counter. ''What are you making?''

''Lemon meringue pie. Squire told me once that it was his favorite.''

Matthew threaded his thumbs through his belt loops when he realized that he wanted to pull her into his arms. ''Mine, too,'' he said abruptly. Then he escaped for the sanctuary of his office.

Jaimie's hands went still and she watched him stomp out of the kitchen. ''I know,'' she said softly when she heard that familiar slam of the door.

Chapter Thirteen

On Saturday afternoon, Matthew found a discrepancy in yet another bill. If it weren't for the fact that he'd been gathering things up for Emily to do her yearly audit and the taxes, he would probably have never noticed the first discrepancy all those weeks ago at all.

Keeping his temper in check, he called Wayland's, the supplier in question where he was assured that, yes, there must be some error, and they would look into it. The Double-C was one of their best customers, and Matt knew they didn't want to lose his business. But unless they got their billing problems worked out, that was exactly what would happen.

He knew Emily hadn't really had an opportunity yet to look at the file he'd already given her. Not with everything that she and Jefferson had on their plate. So he made some notes on the invoice and added it to the pile he was preparing for her.

Then, temper still simmering beneath the surface, he decided he needed to get outside. He needed to plow the road again. Now seemed as good a time as any. So he shrugged into his coat and gloves. Squire was in the kitchen on the telephone, and Matthew stopped long enough to tell him where he was going.

The chore would have been a lot easier if Joe or Daniel had been around to help. But Daniel was over at Jefferson's again, and Joe was still in Gillette with Maggie. Something which Matthew had been relieved to hear, despite the fact that it made a heck of a lot more work for him and his brother.

He was even thinking of hiring on a few hands early this year. The calves were starting to drop, and with Joe gone...well, he wasn't getting any extra sleep, that was for sure.

His breath puffed in rings around his head as he drove the tractor with its angled snowplow out of the machine shed. A flash of purple caught his eye, and hunched in the seat, he watched from beneath the brim of his hat as Jaimie scurried around the edge of the big house and down the gravel road, a load of firewood in her arms. As usual, Sandy trotted faithfully behind her.

He should have thought about firewood, he realized with disgust. The cottage was adequately heated, but a fire was almost always necessary at night. She shouldn't have to carry her own wood. From this distance, she would never hear him, though. He cut the engine and hopped to the ground. His long legs caught up with her soon enough, and she whirled around when he said her name. "Let me take those."

Her nose and cheeks were pink with cold, her eyes bright jewels against her ivory skin. "I can get it."

"I know you *can*," he said impatiently. "But you don't *need* to. Let me do it."

She looked ready to argue, then abruptly dumped the wood into his outstretched arms. Her boots crunched against the gravel as she continued toward the cottage. She held the door open for him and he went inside, dumping the load in the wrought iron holder. She didn't say a word, just headed into the small kitchen where he could see her working. Sandy curled up in the corner of the living room like she'd been there a hundred times before.

She probably had.

He brought in four more loads before he called it good. The holder was filled and he'd stacked the rest in a neat pile next to it. "That oughta hold you for a while," he said, pulling off his leather work gloves.

She didn't answer, and Matthew glanced in the kitchen. She'd left a teapot on the stove, and it was steaming merrily along. He turned off the burner and went back into the living room. "Jaimie?"

His heart climbed up into his throat when he noticed her long legs, sprawled on the floor in the doorway of the bathroom. His boots turned to cement bricks. Sweat broke out on his forehead. He closed his eyes, wondering if he was having the nightmare again.

Nausea clawed up his throat.

No, screamed silently through his mind.

Then he heard her groan softly. His brain sluggishly clicked into gear, and he dropped his gloves on the couch. Shaking like some green kid, he carefully stepped over her legs and knelt down beside her in the small confines of the bathroom. "Jaimie, come on sweetheart. Don't do this to me."

She made a soft moan and opened her eyes. "I don't feel too great," she said after a moment. "Maybe you should keep your distance."

His heartbeat kick-started and relief rushed through him with dizzying speed. Then he felt like throttling her for being the cause of it at all. But she suddenly moved and lost her lunch over the commode. He shrugged out of his coat and held back her hair.

"Go away," she muttered when she finally fell back.

He rinsed a washcloth and handed it to her. Her face was burning hot. And he realized that the reason her eyes had seemed so vividly bright outside was because she was raging with fever. Okay, fever he could handle. Couldn't he?

"Do you have any aspirin?" He didn't wait for an answer, just leaned over her prone body to look inside the medicine chest above the sink. "Think you can keep it down?"

She shook her head, then winced at the movement. She rested her head on her folded arms. Her legs drew up. "Maybe I picked something up at the hospital," she mumbled. "It's probably just a bug. Go back to the house. I'll be fine."

"I can tell," Matthew muttered. "You need to be in bed."

"I'll go in a minute." Her voice was muffled. "You don't want to catch this."

"Sweetheart, it's a little late for that."

"Then go and just let me die here in peace."

"Nobody's doing any dying," he said sharply. "Come on, Red. Let's get you to bed."

"Promises, promises," she whispered, her lips moving crookedly into a pale version of her usual grin.

Matthew hesitated. He smoothed his hand along her silky hair then pushed to his feet. "Don't go anywhere."

"Mmm."

He went into the second bedroom and pulled back the covers. Then he went back to the bathroom, shooing the dog out of the way. Owing more to strength than technique in the small room, he managed to pick up Jaimie. It wasn't that she weighed much. But her legs were long. And he was big. And the bathroom seemed smaller than he remembered when he and Dan had built the place nearly ten years ago.

"You'll get a hernia," she mumbled against his throat.

"Your faith overwhelms me. I've wrestled cows that weigh a few pounds more 'n you." He smiled faintly when, despite her obvious discomfort, she punched his shoulder. He maneuvered her into the bedroom and set her on the bed before pulling off her boots and socks. Her feet were icy. "Pajamas?"

She drew up her legs and pulled the blankets up to her nose. "I'll be fine," she said again.

"Sure you will. That's why I can hear your teeth chattering." He opened up a few drawers, not letting himself get distracted by the sight of her lacy panties and bras that lay in tumbled disarray inside. He paused only when his searching fingers bumped into something firm and square. He slid away a bra that was so fragile and delicate he was sure it served no useful purpose other than driving a man insane, and stared in surprise at a box of Cracker Jacks. Exactly like the box he'd given her that night in Gillette. Surely it wasn't. Yet he knew it was and something deep inside him twisted. He glanced back at Jaimie, huddled, and quickly continued his search.

Unfortunately, the only nightwear he found was of the type he'd seen advertised in a lingerie catalog that Emily had received once in the mail. Not a stitch of flannel in sight. Only a few pairs of thermal underwear, and quite frankly, Matthew wasn't up to peeling those tight-fitting garments *onto* her. He settled for a dark green T-shirt that looked comfortably loose and a thick pair of socks. "Come on, Jaimie. You can't sleep in your jeans."

"Says who?"

"Me." He sat beside her and tugged her up until she sat. When he reached for the hem of her shamrock-dotted thermal shirt, she pushed his hands away.

"I can do it."

"Then do it."

"Not while you're watching." Her cheeks were really pink, and this time Matthew knew it wasn't entirely fever or chapped skin from the incessant wind. Stifling a smile, he turned his back. Then felt a kick of conscience. It was no time for humor. The girl was sick.

Her thermal shirt hit the floor, followed by a minuscule scrap of lace. Then she snatched the T-shirt off his lap. "Okay," she said a moment later. She leaned over and buried her face in the pillows.

"Now the jeans."

When she didn't answer, he touched her forehead. "Sweetheart—"

"Later," she murmured.

He sat back. She couldn't sleep in her jeans. They'd been damp around the hem from the snow. Besides, she needed socks on those cold feet of hers. He lifted the blankets and reached under the loose T-shirt.

She batted at his hands half-heartedly.

"Don't argue with me." He had her jeans down around her hips before she could summon a response. Then he quickly slipped on the socks and tucked her under the blankets once more. He saw her legs move until she was curled into a ball.

"It's cold in here."

Actually, it was practically roasting. But he went into the living room and nudged the thermostat even higher. Then he started a fire. He had to admit that it was several degrees warmer in the living room than it was in her bedroom. When he went back in, he held his hand against the vent. The heat came through, barely.

Jaimie was curled into an even tighter ball when he checked. The only place warmer than the living room would be over at the big house, and no way could he take her out into the cold afternoon. He returned to the living room where the fire licked furiously at the first log, and he added another, stoking it into a good, solid blaze. Then he pulled the couch around until it faced the fire.

He returned to her bedroom. She looked up at him

through her lashes. Her voice shook with the chatter of her teeth. "Matthew, I'm so cold."

"I know, sweetheart." Scooping her, blankets and all, into his arms, he carried her into the living room, settling her on his lap on the couch. She curled against him like a tuckered-out kitten.

Eventually she fell more soundly asleep, and Matthew slid her around until she wasn't twisted into a corkscrew. With her cheek pillowed on his thigh, he unbuttoned his flannel shirt and shrugged out of it, careful not to dislodge her. But he was still roasting and he peeled out of his own thermal shirt. Finally, he relaxed back into the corner of the couch, breathing deeply. Nothing like a sauna in the dead of winter.

He smoothed her hair away from her pale forehead. She murmured and shifted, catching his hand in hers, then tucked it against her heart.

Jaimie's head felt like it was ready to explode. She opened her eyes, wondering for a moment why she'd fallen asleep on the couch. Then remembrance hit her, and she closed her eyes, stifling a groan. Making a sound would make her head hurt even more.

Honestly, her luck was the pits. Why, oh why, had he come in when he had? It wasn't bad enough that he'd had to tuck her into bed like a child. But he'd had to witness the way she'd lost her cookies like that.

Jaimie hated being sick. It was mortifying to know that Matthew had been right there with her the whole way.

"Here."

She looked up to see Matthew standing in front of her. Then decided she had to be delirious. Why else would Matthew Clay be standing over her without a stitch of clothing covering that magnificent chest?

"Come on, sweetheart, don't flake out on me just yet. It's been hours now. You need something for that fever of yours.'' He bent at the knees and she realized he held two white capsules in his hand, along with a glass of water.

She swallowed the pills and fell back on the couch, practically panting from the exertion. He ran his palm over her forehead, and she caught his hand, holding it against her for a few precious moments. Oh, he was blessedly cool.

''Drink some more water,'' he said, drawing away his cooling touch.

''Do this. Do that,'' she complained softly. But he held the glass for her and she managed to swallow most of it. ''You're such a dictator.''

Still crouched beside her, he brushed her hair away from her eyes and tucked the blankets around her. ''You're such a smarta—leck,'' he murmured, the corner of his lips lifting. But he touched her face again, gently. ''You're still burning up.''

''Mmm.'' Dreamily Jaimie snaked her hand out from beneath her cocoon of blankets. She ran it over his shoulder, then curled it around one side of his neck. ''Mmm.''

Matthew stiffened beneath her delicate touch. She was clearly half-asleep again. He resumed his position on the couch, with her head on his thigh. ''Such a sweet man,'' she whispered, snuggling against him.

He snorted softly. If he were a sweet man, he wouldn't be sitting there, hard as a rock while she was clearly ill. She murmured his name again and he resumed brushing his fingers slowly through her hair. She sighed deeply and grew still.

It was dark and Matthew could hear the wind howling outside when he finally moved Jaimie once more. First of all, Sandy was whining and scratching at the door, so he let her out. He grimaced when blowing snow swirled into the cottage. Sandy did her business right quick, too, dashing back inside and sprawling in between the fireplace and the couch where Jaimie slept soundly.

He had just finished wiping up the snow when the door

shook. He yanked it open, only to find his father standing there.

Beneath the cowboy hat that Squire wore, and above the thick scarf wrapped around his lower face, his father's eyes burned into him with more heat than that which came from the cooking furnace and blazing fireplace.

"What in tarnation are you doing here, boy?"

Matthew pulled his father inside. "Keep your voice down. And what do you mean what *I'm* doing? For God's sake, Squire, you know you shouldn't be out in weather like this. What were you thinking?"

His father unwound his scarf and unbuttoned his coat. "I was thinking that you were s'posed to be out plowing. And that you didn't have the brains to get outta the storm and in where you belonged. So I go looking for you, only to find you nekked over here." Squire shoved off his coat. "It's hot as Hades in here. If you're trying to prove the furnace works, you're right."

"Oh, for God's—I'm *not* naked. And it's hot in here, 'cause Jaimie's freezing." He pointed to the couch. With the back of it to the door the way it was, they couldn't see Jaimie sleeping on it. "She's sick."

"Well now, boy, why didn't you say so?"

Matthew just shook his head. Sometimes there was no reasoning with Squire. "I should have called you," he admitted. Truthfully the last thing on his mind had been his old man.

Squire just waved away the words, walking toward the couch. He peered over the back, then returned to the doorway. "Well, I guess I'll leave you to it, then." He pulled on the outerwear that he'd just shucked. His winter-blue eyes snared his son's. "Don't be misbehaving now, boy."

Matthew felt a slow flush climb his neck. He'd already misbehaved plenty. He definitely didn't need his father pointing it out to him, though. And he didn't figure it was any of Squire's business *what* he did. "Nearly forty is no boy."

His father snorted. "Don't matter how old you get. You're still my boy. And I'm right fond of Jaimie. I don't want to see her get hurt."

"Squire, just leave it, would ya?" Matthew shook his head. "I don't want her to get hurt, either." Fully exasperated, Matthew eyed the back of the couch. "If she's not better tomorrow, I'll drive her in to the doctor."

"Let's hope this snow stops then. Else you won't be driving her anywhere. Makes a body wish we could tempt some doctor to staying in Weaver, don't it?" Squire rewrapped his scarf around his neck. "Well, give a holler if ya need something. Me and Dan'll take care of the chores best we can."

Matthew closed the door after his father departed. Having a doctor permanently located in Weaver was an old wish. Leaning against the door, he couldn't help but think of all the times that the presence of a local doctor might have changed the outcome. Might have saved lives. As it was, the area ranchers contracted with an emergency helicopter service. But there was a lot of land to cover and only one pilot.

He raked back his hair from his sweaty brow and went into the kitchen, pouring himself a tall glass of ice water. Jaimie still slept soundly, and Matthew finally retreated to her cooler bedroom, shaking his head over the irony. Lying back on the coverless mattress, he folded his arms beneath his head, stared at the ceiling and listened to the wind howl outside the snug cottage. He forcibly tried blocking out the memory the sound of that wind raised.

It had been blowing and snowing like this the night his mother died.

He didn't sleep at all that night.

Jaimie's fever hadn't broken by morning. Matthew didn't need a thermometer to tell him that. One touch to her forehead had nearly singed his fingertips. Clamping down hard on the alarm that wanted to rise in him no matter what he did, he pulled the covers off her, fending off her unconscious protests to grab them back. He placed cool cloths over her neck and arms, murmuring softly to her when she moaned and pushed at him.

Finally, she relaxed again and he sat back on his heels. What he wouldn't give for a good healthy dose of her sassiness right now. "Come on, Red," he murmured. But she made no response, and he sat there for a long while, until his toes went numb and his legs cramped, gently brushing her vibrant hair away from her pale, pale face.

Finally, he rose stiffly, went into the small kitchen, stared out at the blanket of white through the window, and called the doctor.

The news wasn't entirely discouraging. Since the mountain of snow that had fallen in the night precluded Matthew's ability to drive her to him, the doctor asked Matthew a couple dozen detailed questions. A couple dozen that had Matthew returning to Jaimie's sleeping form to pull up her twisted T-shirt to look at her torso—that was the doctor's word—for any type of rash.

All Matthew saw was a slender expanse of creamy white skin.

Finally, armed with a list of instructions from the doc, Matthew hung up and returned to his vigil by the couch. Sometime in the afternoon, Squire came by. Then Daniel a while later. But Matthew warned them with the doctor's cautions, and they remained at the door, not coming inside.

Around six in the evening, Jaimie's fever started to break and he sponged her down again, then changed the perspiration-soaked sheet and blankets for fresh. He even managed to get her to drink some water. She'd stared at him as if she were hallucinating, then curled into a ball and fell asleep once more.

But the sleep was more natural. Her breathing easier, and

her color less pasty. Around midnight, too weary to ex-
amine the utter relief he felt, he finally went into her bedroom and sprawled across the narrow mattress, finally
sleeping.

Jaimie wasn't sure what woke her. She bolted upright,
staring at the glowing logs in the fireplace. Her head ached.

There. The sound that had awakened her. Like a
wounded animal. "D.C.?" she whispered past her dry
throat. But the noise hadn't really sounded like the pregnant
cat. She moistened her parched lips and swung her legs
down from the couch. A sport bottle sat on the floor beside
the couch, looking vaguely familiar. She thought maybe
she'd been drinking from it at some point. Moving gingerly,
she reached for the bottle and drank deeply.

Again she heard the sound. Low. Male. Joe?

She set down the bottle and pushed to her feet, waiting
for the wave of dizziness to pass. Then she padded toward
the master bedroom, realizing belatedly that the sound came
from the bedroom she used. She altered course and paused
in the doorway, absently rubbing an itch on her stomach.
Matthew lay flat on his back, one arm bent over his eyes.
"Matthew?"

He just made that low, sad sound again. So sad that it
made her eyes tear. She moved to the bed and sat on the
edge, tentatively reaching for his bare shoulder. "Matthew,
wake up. It's just a dream," she murmured.

He didn't start. Didn't tense. He simply opened his ice-
blue eyes and watched her wordlessly from beneath his arm.

She slowly withdrew her hand. "Are you all right?"

Matthew blinked the remnants of the nightmare from his
mind. "You're the one who's sick," he returned.

Her eyes were green bruises in the whiteness of her face.
And the tumbling waves of her hair accentuated her pale
coloring even more. "Matthew," she chided softly.

"You should be asleep."

"I was."

For someone sick with God knew what, she certainly had enough energy to watch him like she knew exactly what ticked inside him. He jackknifed off the bed and nearly tripped over Sandy when he headed for the living room. "Think you can eat something yet?"

"No. Matthew—"

"I don't want to talk about it."

He could feel the warm weight of her gaze. "Maybe you should," she murmured, slowly following him. She made it as far as the couch while he continued into the kitchen.

"It was just a dream," he muttered.

Jaimie didn't respond, and he looked out to see her watching him.

"A dream," he repeated.

She propped her arm on the couch and rested her head on her hand, as if it weighed too much to hold it up otherwise. "About what?"

Matthew didn't talk about the nightmare. He simply did not. "My mother." The words came out and he couldn't pull 'em back in. He swore to himself and reached for the can of coffee. With any luck at all, Jaimie would fall asleep again. It was nearly three in the morning.

He thought maybe he'd been granted that small wish when she didn't say anything else as he waited for the coffee to brew. But when he carried his mug back into the living room, she scooted her legs out of the way so that he could sit on the couch, too.

"Your mother must have loved you all very much," she said softly.

That wasn't something he'd ever doubted. "Shouldn't you be sleeping?" he asked pointedly.

She smiled faintly, rubbing the tips of her fingers across her stomach. "I feel like I've been sleeping for a day."

"Nearly two."

Her eyebrows rose slightly. "Have you been here all that time?"

He nodded, burying his nose in the coffee mug.

"Oh. Well. Thank you," she murmured faintly.

Matthew looked at her. Caught the hand she was rubbing across her stomach before he knew what he was doing, and tangled her fingers with his. "I'm glad you're startin' to feel better," he said with severe understatement.

Her sleepy eyes softened. And once again she slept.

By morning Jaimie's headache was nearly gone. But her limbs felt like wobbly gelatin. Except for the occasional hiss and pop of the fireplace, the cottage was quiet. And hot.

She didn't want to be disappointed that Matthew was gone, but couldn't help it. She made it over to the thermostat and turned down the heat, then looked out the window. Fresh snow blanketed everything in sight. Talk about March blowing in like a lion.

Another form of nature prompted her to head for the bathroom. When she came out again, she felt marginally better. Brushing her teeth had helped immensely. Unfortunately, her legs felt shaky by the time she returned to her cocoon on the couch. Wrapping a blanket around her shoulders, she stared into the glowing fireplace.

"You're awake."

Startled, she looked over to see Matthew standing in the doorway of the bedroom she ordinarily used. His hair was sleep rumpled, and his jeans were barely fastened over his hips. In fact, she could see...too much. She dragged her eyes upward. But meeting his translucent gaze was even worse. "You're still here," she said, stating the obvious, and flushed.

He leaned against the doorjamb, crossing his bare feet, crossing his arms over his bare chest. Oh, Lord. The man was just too...bare. "How're you feeling this morning?"

"Better. A lot better, actually." Then she hunched her shoulders. "My back itches." She flushed again, miserably self-conscious.

He pushed away from the jamb and in his smooth-limbed way, approached. She nearly jumped out of her skin when he laid his palm on her forehead, then her cheek. "Fever's better. Turn around and let me see."

"I beg your pardon?"

"Come on, Red. I've been swabbing down your body for two days. Let me see your back." When she just looked at him like he was a madman, he leaned over her and tugged up her T-shirt, ignoring her sputtering. "Yup."

"What yup?" Jaimie yanked her T-shirt back into place.

"Chicken pox."

She gaped at him. "What?"

"You've got a few spots on your back. It's what the doctor suspected."

She rose and went right into the bathroom, slamming the door shut. A few minutes later, she opened it again. "Chicken pox. I don't believe this."

"Why not? The doc said there's a near epidemic in town."

"But you've been with me all this time. I've probably exposed everyone!"

"Don't sweat it, Red. We've all had chicken pox. And before you panic about exposing Maggie, Dan checked with her. She's had them, too. 'Course *we* had 'em when we were kids. But you do like to do things in your own individual style, don't you?"

He sat on the arm of the couch beside her, and Jaimie felt her head spin. This time, though, it had nothing to do with being sick.

"How's the stomach?"

The reminder of how he'd been witness to her glorious moments with the porcelain goddess made her blush even harder. "Fine."

"Good. Then it's time you ate something." He left her staring after him. She could hear him rummaging about in the kitchen. "Toast should do for a start. Then I'll put some of that pink stuff on the spots on your back."

Sure enough, within minutes, he'd returned with a plate of lightly browned toast. "I never said I couldn't cook," he said at her astonished look. "Not that toast takes much cooking."

He left her for a few minutes and she heard the beep of the microwave. He returned with a mug of hot tea. "Well, don't just sit there," he said, his voice gruff. "You're letting it all get cold."

He was taking care of her. Still. It was so sweet it made her eyes burn. She'd never had a man take care of her. Her father had usually been gone; only when she'd gotten older had she realized that he'd been out with other women. And Tony…well Tony had turned green if Jaimie had a hangnail, much less something more serious.

She looked down at the toast in her hand. Tony would never have patiently pulled out splinters from her hand, or held back her hair while she lost her stomach. Her eyes noticed the bottle of calamine lotion sitting on the round dining table. Nor would he be prepared with something like that.

Matthew was such a good man.

"What's wrong?"

She shook her head. "Nothing." She touched the toast again. It couldn't have been more precious to her than if he'd handed her a dozen roses.

"Sure?"

She nodded, smiling tremulously, and ate the toast.

Eventually Matthew pulled on his thermal shirt and buttoned up his jeans, much to Jaimie's secret relief. It wasn't that she didn't enjoy looking at his broad shoulders or the rock-hard sculpture of his abdomen. She did. But she couldn't think straight, much less breathe normally, when he displayed all that glorious muscle and bone. He was all briskly business when he asked her to present her back to him and he daubed the soothing lotion over her spots.

"How many are there?"

"About five. Mebbe you won't get covered with them."

She sincerely hoped not. The three on her stomach itched like mad. He capped the bottle and handed it to her before he stomped his feet into his boots and shrugged into his heavy sheepskin coat.

"I'll come back and check on you after I tend to some chores."

Suspecting that he'd already put them off too long, she nodded. As soon as he left, after a stern warning to keep herself quiet, she slid from the couch and skedaddled into the shower. He could warn her all he wanted. She wasn't going to let him come back and check on her when she felt like a dirty dishrag.

Her shaky legs had something to say about her plan, however, and forgoing the quickness of the shower, she ended up taking a bath. Just as well, she decided, as she sank to her chin in the steamy, fragrant water. This was a lot more relaxing and felt like heaven on her itchy spots. She noticed a pink mark appearing on her leg. So far, none had cropped up on her face.

When the water started to cool, she let some out and replenished the tub with more hot. She leisurely washed her hair, blinking away the sluggish sleep that beckoned.

Surprised, Matthew heard the soft splash of water as soon as he entered the small cottage. There he'd raced through the chores, making do with the bare essentials, cramming into just a few hours what it ordinarily took ten, and what does he find when he comes back? That redhead, who didn't have the sense of a goose, taking a bath.

Striding across the room, he shoved his gloves in his pockets and pushed open the half-closed door. "Woman, I thought I told you—"

Standing with one foot in the draining tub and one foot out, her startled eyes turned toward him. She yanked a towel off the rack and clutched it to her, bringing the other foot out of the tub. The towel was too late, though. He'd already seen every glorious, glistening inch of skin that the Man Upstairs had blessed upon her.

He called himself the mangy dog he was when need swept through him with the vicious swiftness of a prairie fire. She was sick, for God's sake! "You were supposed to stay put."

"You ordered me to. It doesn't mean I had to listen." She carefully arranged the towel to cover more leg. But it only reached so far. And as she tugged it down, she gave him a gut-wrenching view of the upper swell of her peach-tipped breasts. *"Do you mind?"*

Yeah, he minded. He minded that he'd been out of his mind with worry for the past few days over her. And now he minded that the towel covered even one inch of her satiny skin. He minded that he'd sworn he wouldn't succumb to her again. He minded that with every soft gurgle of bathwater down the drain, that very promise was dissipating. He closed the distance between them and touched a curl of damp hair that clung to her ivory shoulder. "Lemon," he murmured. "You always smell like lemon."

Her throat worked. Her hand blindly swept behind her, and she pushed a bottle toward him. "Shampoo," she said breathlessly.

He tossed the plastic bottle into the sink and closed his hands over her shoulders, drawing her to him. "You're making me nuts," he complained gruffly.

"I don't mean to."

"I left the snowplow out in a snowstorm, just so I could carry firewood in for you." His thumbs pressed her chin upward. "I think you delight in driving me up the wall." He smoothed his thumb over her lips. Her eyes grew drowsy. "Either you're still sleepy, sweetheart, or you're wanting the same thing I do."

In answer, her tongue snuck out and swirled over his thumb.

"That's what I was afraid of," he muttered. "I sure do wish I knew what to do with you." Before she could voice the sassy answer he saw forming in her eyes, he kissed her. Her slender body arched to his, perfectly and wantonly.

Her fingers clutched his jacket as she kissed him back just as fiercely, just as hotly. When he lifted his reeling head, it was to the sight of their reflections in the bathroom mirror. She was barely covered by her damp white towel and he still wore his hat and coat. Her eyes followed his and he knew the sight struck her as painfully erotic as he found it.

Their eyes met in the mirror, and Matthew's fingers moved to the knot holding her towel in place. With the slightest nudge of his finger it loosened, and the towel tumbled to the floor.

He wasn't sure if she turned first, or if he did. But suddenly she looked straight-on in the large mirror. Like magnets, the tight peaks of her breasts drew his palms and her head fell back against his shoulder, wet hair clinging to his coat. The pupils of her eyes widened, nearly engulfing the glowing emerald.

"You're sick," he rasped.

"I'm a lot better except for the spots." As if to prove it, she reached her arm up and snaked it around his neck, pulling his head toward hers.

Tastes of mint and scents of lemon swirled. His heart thundered, and desire reared uncontrollably. He couldn't get enough of her. Of the slender neck arching back toward him, the narrowness of her waist or the satiny smooth stretch of abdomen. God, was there anything softer on this Earth than her skin?

Then his fingers grazed the juncture of her thighs, and he knew of only one thing that surpassed that softness.

Her chest trembled with the breaths she dragged into her starving lungs, and he turned her to face him, catching her at the waist and lifting her to him. She wrapped her arms around his shoulders, burying her face in his neck as he carried her back to the living room.

Matthew deposited her gently on the couch, and Jaimie was grateful that she didn't have to stand. He barely got off his hat and coat, though, before she was reaching for him, pulling him down to her.

He gave a strained chuckle. "Jaimie, sweetheart—"

"Shhh." She yanked at his shirt and a button went flying. Too desperate to wait, she just shoved his layered shirts up his chest, and he yanked them over his head, coming down to her again, as if he needed the feel of her against his chest as badly as she.

"Hurry," she pleaded.

He ripped his belt free, his fingers brushing against hers as she struggled with his fly. Then he was free, and sinking into her with a savage growl.

Jaimie cried his name, clinging to his strong, solid shoulders as that very first thrust propelled her straight to a shattering, shuddering peak.

He groaned harshly, unrelenting as he drove her again and again. Finally he rolled to the side, taking them to the floor and pulling her over him. His big hands eclipsed her hips, guiding her trembling movements.

Staring into his narrowed eyes as her senses coiled tighter and tighter, she wondered for an insane moment how eyes so icy blue could burn with such heat. Then he stiffened beneath her. That overworked spring within her snapped just as her name, rough on his lips, rasped over her and she hurtled with him toward heaven.

The fire in the fireplace had burned down to a deep glow. Newly swabbed with calamine and propped against the nest of pillows that Matthew had arranged in front of the couch, Jaimie sipped at the fresh tea he'd brought her. He leaned forward with the iron poker and jabbed fresh sparks to life, then added another log before sitting back and picking up his coffee mug.

"Tell me about your mother," Jaimie asked quietly.

He looked at her, then into his coffee. She wasn't sure he'd even answer. But surely, surely, he wouldn't push her away right now. Not when their bodies were still warm from each other.

His shoulders moved, and Jaimie bit back her disappointment. She buried her nose in her teacup.

"She was beautiful," he finally murmured. "She had long blond hair. Shades lighter than mine is now. It nearly reached her waist."

Jaimie knew what Sarah Clay had looked like. She'd dusted the photograph of her that sat in Squire's room often enough. And anyone who'd ever been in the big house couldn't fail to see the beautiful portrait of Squire's wife that hung in the rarely used living room.

He smiled faintly. "She was bitty, too. Even at nine, I was nearly as tall as she was. Sawyer was taller and he wasn't even a teenager. When she stood next to Squire she was dwarfed by him."

"He must have loved her very much," Jaimie ventured. She was acutely aware of every nuance of his breathing.

"They were just teenagers when they married." Matthew shifted. "She was barely older than you are now when she died."

Jaimie knew what he would say before he finished.

"Too young." He shifted again, more restlessly. "You don't want to hear all that."

"Yes, I do," she said steadily. More importantly, Matthew needed to talk about *all that*. "What's the earliest thing you can remember about your parents?"

His coffee mug paused on the way to his lips. He shot her a bemused look and she kissed his bare shoulder. "The earliest thing I remember about my parents," Jaimie said, "was driving. I don't remember where we were going, but it was really late when we arrived. And I had this ratty old blanket that I carried with me everywhere. I can't even remember what Joe was doing, but I remember that blanket. It was faded pink. Anyway, my dad carried me from the car inside to the house. He seemed really tall and the ground a long way away. But he held me real snug, and my mom followed along, keeping that blanket from dragging on the ground." She smiled faintly, surprised despite herself at the warmth that spread through her.

She hadn't thought about that in years. Her memories of her father were generally dominated by the later years. When he'd been so critical during those rare times he'd been around. Then, he'd been gone. Leaving her mother crying in their bedroom at night, thinking that Jaimie was asleep and couldn't hear. Her parents had never separated. Never divorced. And in the end had moved to Florida, still together. Jaimie had never been able to figure out if it was because her mother didn't have the strength to leave her father, or if their love had survived despite their problems.

"What happened to the blanket?"

She blinked. "Oh. You know, I can't remember." She shrugged, smiling slightly. "Now you. What's the earliest thing you remember?"

He gave her an indulgent look. Bending his leg, he propped his wrist on his knee, coffee mug dangling by a finger. His lids lowered in thought. "Jefferson's just a few years behind me…don't remember a time when he wasn't around. But Daniel…I guess I remember when she got pregnant with Daniel. Squire danced her around right there in the middle of the kitchen." The light in his eyes sobered. "I remember her being pregnant, more often than not."

"With five children…that would account for forty-five

months of being pregnant," Jaimie pointed out gently. "That's nearly four years. And you were only nine—"

"When she died," he finished abruptly.

"How did it happen?" She was fairly convinced that he wouldn't say. But again Matthew surprised her.

"She fell and broke her back outside the barn on Christmas Eve," he said neutrally.

She sucked in her breath.

"She hemorrhaged. It was blizzarding and Squire barely got her to the hospital before she died. Whether she was in labor with Tristan and fell because of that, or went into labor because of the fall, we'll never know." He lifted his coffee and drank, his eyes unreadable. "If Squire knew, he certainly never said."

"Maybe it's too painful for him to talk about, too."

Matthew's head tilted in acknowledgment. "He tore that old barn down about two weeks after she died. Didn't have any help. I'm not sure whether he used tools or his bare hands," he murmured, obviously remembering. Then he blinked and lifted his mug once more. But he just looked into the cup. "Anyway," he said after a moment. "Tristan was born. She was gone. And the rest, as they say, is history." He swallowed down the rest of his coffee and stood up.

Jaimie wondered why on earth Matthew's mother had been outside in blizzard conditions, but decided it wouldn't be wise to pose too many questions. Matthew had shared more with her than she'd ever dreamed possible. He reached for her teacup, and she handed it to him, folding her arms across her bent knees, and watched him as he padded, unabashedly nude, into the kitchen.

"Want a sandwich?" he called after a moment. It would be dawn soon.

"No. Go ahead, though." She stretched out her legs, pointing her toes at the fire and resting her head back on the couch. Her eyes fell on his battered cowboy hat, and she lazily drew it over, propping it on her head. It fell right down to her nose.

Smiling faintly, she closed her eyes and listened to Matthew in the kitchen. Before long, she heard his footfalls, then felt his presence beside her. From beneath the hat, she could see as high as his calves.

"Now there's a cowboy's dream," he murmured. "Long legs and silky skin with its nine chicken pox wearing nothing but a cowboy hat. And her lucky bracelet, of course."

It didn't matter that they'd made love less than two hours ago. That need for him hovered under her skin, ready to spring into action at a moment's notice. "I have a thing for your hat. I admit it." She tipped back the hat and looked up at him. She couldn't help the silly smile spreading across her face. "Well. You're certainly not made of clay," she observed softly.

He choked down a half laugh. "Damn straight."

She propped herself up on her elbows, her eyes dancing over him. He was a beautiful male. His shoulders were wide and roped with muscle. Not developed from pressing weights in some weight room, but from the hard physical labor that made up his life. His abdomen rippled down to narrow hips and strong, long legs. His arousal nestled heavily between. "I'll say."

His eyes narrowed as he lowered next to her, his movements sleek and pantherlike. "Kind of sassy, aren't you?"

"So I've been told."

He removed the hat, then drew the brim over her shoulder. Down the valley between her breasts. Grazed over her feminine curls, making her feel faint. His dimple flashed wickedly. "What was that about my hat?"

Jaimie couldn't believe she was already yearning for his lovemaking. Her muscles felt tender and fulfilled. Oh, who was she kidding? She believed it all right. She stretched luxuriously, drawing in a deep breath filled with heady anticipation.

His lips curved appreciatively, "You are something."

"Is that good or bad?"

His eyebrow peaked. "What do you think?"

"Definitely good."

He perched his hat on her head. "What are we going to do now?"

Jaimie pulled him down to the nest of blankets and straddled him, her cheeks feeling on fire. "I'm sure we can come up with something," she promised.

His soft laugh was cut off by a low groan. "No doubt."

Chapter Fourteen

Jaimie hung up the phone. She turned to Matthew and swallowed. Two weeks had passed since she'd come down with the chicken pox. She only had one spot in the middle of her back that wasn't quite healed. Two weeks when Matthew had stopped pushing her away. Had stopped acting as if they could go back to where they started from…the rancher and his housekeeper. And though he'd gone back to the big house at night again, leaving Jaimie alone at Joe and Maggie's place, Jaimie felt closer to him than she'd ever dreamed possible.

"Well?"

"That was Joe," she said. Unnecessarily, since Matthew had been the one to answer the phone in the first place.

She was thrilled for Maggie and Joe. Truly she was. And yet, underlying the happiness and relief she felt that the baby had arrived safely, she couldn't ignore the knowledge that her time at the Double-C was rapidly coming to an end.

Not unless Matthew asked her to stay. And she knew that wouldn't happen, no matter how wondrous the past two weeks had been.

"And?"

She dragged her thoughts under control. "Maggie went into labor again. They couldn't stop it this time. The baby came this morning."

He nudged her chin up with a long finger. *"And?"*

She blinked, managing a smile. "She's fine. It was a girl."

"What's her name?"

Jaimie shook her head. "I don't know. Joe hung up too quickly for me to find out. He did say Maggie would be coming home tomorrow. They want to keep the baby for a while yet. Just in case any problems develop."

"Tomorrow?"

"Yes, well, they don't keep a woman for days anymore. Not if everybody is healthy and all. Oh my…I've got to get that room ready as a nursery. Maggie bought a crib and some furniture a while back, but it's all still in boxes." Jaimie suspected that her sister-in-law hadn't wanted to somehow jinx her pregnancy by setting things up too soon.

"The second bedroom?"

She nodded absently, her mind already busy. She pulled the small notepad off the phone and found a pencil.

"What about you?"

"What about me? I'll try to set it up—"

"I meant, where will you sleep?"

"Oh." She shrugged. "On the couch, I guess. There won't be room in there for the bed with a crib." She felt color heat her cheeks. She had fond memories of that couch. So fond, she wasn't sure she would get a decent night's sleep on it. *Set up crib,* she wrote.

He was silent while she scribbled.

Wash new dia—

"You could stay here."

Her pencil scratched off the edge of the pad. "Oh?" That was good, she thought, about her tone. Just the right touch of casual interest.

"We've got extra bedrooms," he added.

His gruff voice scraped tantalizingly across her nerves. Then she realized. *Extra* bedrooms. With Squire visiting Gloria again, it wasn't as if they would need to protect his sensibilities. Nope. This wasn't exactly a declaration of intent. She set down the pencil. "I see." He sighed and she felt his impatience. "Actually," she added quickly, "I really should stay with Maggie and Joe. She'll need help when she first gets back with the baby." When she dared a glance at him, he nodded, easily accepting her explanation.

What she'd said wasn't untrue. Maggie *would* need help. Jaimie just needed to concentrate on that one fact. Not on the realization that she didn't want to stay in the big house. Not unless it was as Matthew's...*something*. She told herself, yet again, to be realistic.

She tore off the list, and Matthew leaned past her to look at it. "When Daniel gets back from Weaver this afternoon, I'll get him to help me move out the furniture that's in there now," he said. "Then I'll help you set all that up."

Jaimie moistened her lips, nodding. "Thanks."

Matthew eyed her downcast features. He squelched the words that rose in him. Words that would bring her to his bedroom tonight. For all nights. But he couldn't do it. He couldn't let himself draw her that far into his life. No matter how much he found himself wanting her, needing the dash of spice she brought just by walking into a room.

He would help her with the baby furniture. He would help her clean up the dishes after supper as had become their habit over the past several days. He would even lie with her, share the electricity that streaked between them with the quickest of glances. But he wouldn't ask her to stay.

He kissed her, long and more hungrily than he'd intended, then tore away. He had nearly a dozen calves that Daniel had brought in that morning to check. It was like a birthing frenzy these days. Maggie…calves…

He left Jaimie seated at the table, where she'd plopped, sending him a dazed wave. Sandy scrambled out from beneath the table and trotted at his boot heels as he headed to the barn. The snow that had fallen so fiercely when Jaimie was sick had begun melting. Matthew's instincts told him that they'd seen the last storm of the season. Now, they would endure long, muddy weeks until the ground started to dry, then green, then bloom with wildflowers and clover.

In his mind he saw himself laying Jaimie back amongst the lush knee-high grass and flowers that would grow along the road leading to the swimming hole. Then he shook his head sharply. Jaimie would be gone by then.

The calves were fine, and he called to Sandy, setting off for the machine shed. He knew Jasper needed exercise, but this once he'd leave the horse for the snowmobile. In minutes he was zooming across the fields, rapidly, thoroughly checking fence and stock.

Jaimie had loved the speed of the snowmobile, even though she'd been half-frozen the evening he took her to the cabin.

Stop thinking that way. He bounced over a small hill, tilting his head against the cold rush of wind. On foot he checked Dawson's bend, and rousted two stubborn cows out of its treacherous reaches, then aimed the snowmobile toward home.

Later Matthew couldn't have explained how it all happened.

One minute he was zooming along, following the lazy arch of the frozen creek. The sleek black machine flying easily, smoothly, across the snow. The next he was airborne, going one way, and the snowmobile following, almost in slow motion. Everything probably would've been okay, too, if he'd landed just a few feet sooner. He would have hit a solid foot of snow. Cold, sure. But not exactly deadly.

Instead, Matthew saw himself heading straight for the iced surface of the creek, and braced himself. He felt the impact through every bone in his body. Swearing between his gritted teeth, he began to roll, when the ice gave an ominous, groaning creak. He looked up. "Ahhh…hell."

The snowmobile came slamming down on top of him.

Jaimie felt a sudden chill tingle down her spine, and she automatically reached out to push the door to the mudroom closed. Holding the phone to her ear, she punched out Emily's phone number. She had wanted to know when Maggie had the baby.

Jaimie shivered again, waiting. After several rings, their answering machine clicked on, and she ended up leaving a message.

Brushing her hands up and down the goose bumps that had risen on her arms, she went into the mudroom and looked out the storm door. The thermometer that was affixed to the wall outside the door told her that it hadn't *really* gotten any colder.

Shaking her head at her silliness, she pulled on her purple coat and let herself out into the cold, bright morning. She was halfway to Joe and Maggie's place when she heard Sandy bark.

Nothing unusual there. Sandy barked a lot. She barked at the cattle. She barked at D.C. She barked at rabbits and at dust motes in the air. Still…

Jaimie changed course and walked across the gravel road, stopping only when she came up against a fence rail. The sun reflected blindingly off the snow, and she squinted, watching the golden retriever run, low and long, across the horizon.

She felt her mouth grow dry. The urgency inside her

grew. When Sandy finally jumped through the fence rails to circle Jaimie's legs, only one thing hammered through her brain.

"Where's Matthew?" she asked the dog. Sandy sat on her haunches, whining. Jaimie swallowed and stared out over the land.

Suddenly she raced into the horse barn and, cursing the way her hands trembled, managed to get a halter over Daisy's head. She slipped onto the horse, bareback. "Show me where Matthew is," she whispered. Whether a request to Matthew's golden retriever, or a prayer, she didn't know. Probably both.

Jaimie had never been more conscious of the way time flew. By the time she saw the overturned snowmobile, half-submerged in the creek, she figured more than an hour had slipped past.

Sandy bounded through the snow that seemed feet deeper here than it did near the big house. Jaimie sank into it up to her knees as she struggled toward the site.

She felt the cold seep into the legs of her jeans, and snow creep under her coat as she fell flat on her face. She scrambled on her knees toward the rear end of the snowmobile that rested on the edge of the creek. Then she saw Matthew.

One gloved hand clung to one of the bent skis. His hat had skidded across to the other side of the creek, sitting safely atop an intact sheet of ice.

Crying his name, she scurried to the other side of the machine, where she could see him better.

Her breath climbed right back down into her lungs. "Oh, please," she moaned, falling to her knees. His head was barely above the jagged shards of ice. The rest of his body was submerged in the shallow creek...probably pinned down by the weight of the huge snowmobile.

Blood matted the sheepskin lining near his face. If it weren't for the hand that he'd wrapped around the ski, there was no doubt he would have been forced completely under the ice.

"Matthew," she cried, but his eyes remained closed. She prayed he was still breathing. She tried not to think how people could drown in just a few feet of water.

Frustration brought tears to her eyes and she turned to study the snowmobile. She couldn't push it from where she was. It would just slide further down on top of him. She doubted she had the strength to pull Matthew out from under it. It was probably his very size that kept the machine from completely sliding into the creek in the first place.

She stood and looked frantically about. There wasn't a soul in sight. Her eyes fell on Daisy and the reins that trailed in the snow. She dashed over and pulled the horse closer. Her fingers refused to work, and she yanked off her mittens, tossing them aside.

Blessing the knots that she'd learned when she'd worked at the marina in Lake Havasu City, she gently tossed the long rein over the end of the bent ski, above Matthew's glove. If she could shift the snowmobile, just a little, she could drag Matthew out from the other side. If. If. If.

Daisy shook her head, nickering softly. Jaimie rounded the horse and slipped her hand against the rein that pulled tautly behind the horse and the snowmobile. "Come on, girl," she begged. "Just a little." She wrapped her own hand over the length of slender leather. She sank into the snow. Daisy snorted and shuffled her feet.

Jaimie dragged.

And centimeter by agonizing centimeter, the snowmobile started to slide to the left. "Just a little more. Just a little more," Jaimie gasped, adding all her weight to the horse's. The ice cracked sharply and, praying that Daisy didn't move forward, Jaimie darted under the horse's head and the straining leather. She sat down on the bank of the creek. Only an incline of a few feet, it barely qualified as a bank, but she slid down it, feeling the icy cold water penetrate her jeans and seep down into her boots.

The snowmobile began sliding forward. "No!"

She grabbed Matthew by the coat and yanked so hard it felt as if her shoulders popped out of the sockets. "Matthew, please, open your eyes, baby, please." His head lolled back, and she caught him around the neck before his head could hit the ice again. She could feel the pulse in his neck and knew, with nauseous relief, that he was still breathing.

"Open your eyes, open your eyes." Her teeth chattering, she dug her heels into the rocky bottom. She wasn't going to lose him to the water. No way.

His glove was still wrapped around the ski, preventing her progress. She tugged at his arm, then realized that the leather glove was caught on a bent piece of sharp metal. Afraid of what she was tearing in addition to the leather glove, but unable to reach it any other way, she sank her fingers into the sopping wet sleeve of his coat and yanked.

His hand came free; the glove still stuck to the ski. He groaned and his eyelids moved, then he went limp again. Blood smeared across his hand, and Jaimie gritted her teeth. She couldn't afford to cry. Matthew couldn't afford it.

She felt under the water—swearing a blue streak at the pain that engulfed her from the cold—until her fingers were latched inside his belt. Then, huffing and puffing and swearing at him for doing this to her, she managed to pull him free of the ice and onto the edge of the snow.

She called Sandy over, and the dog lay down next to Matthew, her long tongue lapping at his still face. Then Jaimie managed to unfasten the rein. Without that last tether, the snowmobile slid in exaggerated slowness into the creek, breaking through the ice to rest crazily on its nose.

Yanking off her own coat, she wrapped it around Matthew's chest and neck, tying the arms awkwardly across him. "Come on, Matthew. I love you, dammit, but I can't lift you on the horse," she cried. Though she tried. Lord, she tried. But he probably outweighed her by a hundred pounds.

His lips were turning blue, and Jaimie's mind simply shut off. She would get him on that horse, or she would just lie right down next to him and die with him. Because she knew with stark clarity that there wasn't any point in living in a world without him in it.

If she'd thought about it, she would never have done it. Not after she'd had to pull him *out* of the water. But her choices were slim to none. So she led a reluctant Daisy into the water and twisted Matthew around on the snow until his head hung over the bank. Then, climbing into that hideously frigid water again, she maneuvered beneath his chest and pulled his arms over her shoulders.

She decided later that God must have felt inclined to grant a small miracle. Because against gravity and all logic, Jaimie managed to get Matthew sprawled crosswise over Daisy's back. She held him in place, and Daisy lost no time scrambling up the bank. Jaimie was numb when she clambered on behind him. Holding Matthew in place with an arm clamped about his waist, she raced for the cabin. It had to be closer than the big house.

And there was a phone there.

Getting him off the horse proved no easier than getting him on. In the end she simply tugged him down and cushioned his fall with her own body. The interior of the cabin was decidedly cold, but at least they were out of that incessant breeze. He lay on the floor of the single room and she untied her jacket then peeled him out of his sodden coat. She could see the cut along his jaw that had been the source of the blood. Much lower and the cut would have sliced right into his neck.

Swallowing the nausea clawing at her, she stripped him bare, then rolled him inside several blankets that she'd yanked off the bed, before grabbing the phone.

The next hour was a blur to Jaimie. Daniel and Jefferson,

having heard the emergency call, arrived minutes before the helicopter did. Jaimie felt them gently peel the blankets away from where she had wrapped their two bodies together. Jefferson carefully lifted Jaimie off Matthew, though she struggled to stay next to him, and securely wrapped the blanket around her bare body as the helicopter settled on the ground outside the cabin.

Daniel helped lift Matthew on the stretcher, and the emergency medical technician took over. Within minutes both Matthew and Jaimie were enroute to the hospital in Gillette.

So this was hell. Funny, but he couldn't remember doing anything bad enough to deserve this. Except watching his mother die without doing one bloody thing to help her....

God. He was on fire. He could feel the vicious, ferocious appetite of the white-hot flames consuming him. His feet. His hands. He tried to get away...pushed at the hands that held him in those fiery clutches.

He swore and prayed. He growled and fought.

Then collapsed into the pain.

Suddenly she was there. Her rich auburn hair glinted in the sunlight, drifting about her shoulders on the wondrously cool breeze. Every sense within him reached for that soothing coolness.

"We're not gonna lose this one. He's stubborn. Get that drip started."

The voice over his head jolted Matthew, but he dragged his attention back to her peach-tinted skin. *My God, she was beautiful. He wasn't in hell. He'd gone to heaven, after all.*

Her emerald eyes glowed and she smiled, just a little bit crooked, just a lot sexy.

"Nurse! Where's the heat pack?"

Matthew opened his eyes, nearly startling the emergency room nurse out of her starched whites. "Would you all mind not yelling," he asked evenly, his gaze immediately arrowing in on the doctor who'd been barking out orders. "You're gonna scare away my girl."

Then he closed his eyes once more and fell asleep.

They'd brought Jaimie a pair of pale blue scrubs to wear, and she shivered in the lightweight cotton and paper booties, huddling inside a hospital-issue blanket as they awaited news.

Jefferson and Emily sat across the room, his arm stretched around her back protectively. Daniel paced back and forth outside the sliding glass doors. And Squire, who'd arrived by chartered plane barely thirty minutes ago, sat beside Jaimie, his large, warm hand holding hers.

"You saved his life," Squire said after a while.

She had no more tears left. Dry-eyed, she stared at the squares of tile beneath the off-white plastic chairs. The truth was, Matthew had been in that freezing water a long time. And it had taken her ages to get him to help. She really was the city girl he'd accused her of being.

"You did," Squire repeated sharply.

She swallowed and looked at him. Looked at those eyes that could have been Matthew's, they were so similar. "Did I?" Her jaw twisted to the side. She'd never forgive herself for taking so long to get help to Matthew. "Then what's taking them so long? Shouldn't he be conscious by now?"

Squire only sighed heavily and tightened his hand on hers.

Several hours later the doctor came out and told them that Matthew would be all right. Emily started crying at the news, and Jefferson held her tight, his face expressionless, though his deep blue eyes darkened with relief.

Jaimie turned and saw Daniel, leaning back against the wall and raking unsteady fingers through his hair. Several minutes later, he announced he was going to call Tristan and Sawyer to let them know that all was well.

Squire sighed deeply and held Jaimie gently against him. And then she fainted.

"No *we* don't want any tasty gelatin." Matthew glared at the unrelentingly cheery nurse who was trying to foist a tray of unappetizing hospital food on him. "*We* want to get outta here. Where's the doctor?"

The nurse managed to retain her cheerful smile. "He's on rounds. He'll be here within an hour, Mr. Clay, and once all our release papers are signed, we can leave. Now, are you sure we wouldn't like to try a little lunch?"

What *we* wanted to do was wrap *our* hands around some-one's throat. He shoved back the sheet covering him and stood up. He would rather eat that infernal tasty gelatin than tell the nurse… Geez, she couldn't be more than twenty-two…that his abrupt action brought on a serious head rush.

He'd already been in the hospital for two days. Two days too long, as far as he was concerned. He needed to get back to the ranch. No doubt calves were dropping all over the place. Daniel couldn't be expected to keep up with it on his own. What was more important, Matthew had some serious rethinking to do.

The nurse suddenly turned to the door, then threw up her hands. "Maybe *you* can do something with him," she an-nounced as she left.

Jaimie halted in the doorway, her eyebrows peaking even while color rose in her cheeks. "My word, Matthew. You want the nurses to remember you, don't you?"

He glanced down. So he wore only blue silk boxers. "Nothing nurses don't see a hundred times a day," he said. His sharp eyes noted the dark shadows beneath Jaimie's eyes.

She smiled slightly, not meeting his eyes, and closed the door behind her. Color climbed into her cheeks. "I think you're a lot more memorable than you think."

He eyed her. It was the first time since they'd been

brought to the hospital that they were alone together. It had seemed as if every time he'd turned around one of his brothers or his father or Emily or Gloria had been in the way. Even Maggie had escaped the maternity ward long enough to stick her head in his room before her release. They were his family and he loved them. But it was enough to make a man ready to tear down walls. "So are you here to spring me from this place?"

She held up a ring of keys. "As soon as your doctor gives the word."

"Which won't be any too soon," he snorted, then held out his hand. "Come here."

Her eyes danced over his chest, then she leaned back against the door. Her dress of swirling blues and purples clung gently to her curves and drifted around her slender ankles. "Matthew—"

"Come here," he said again. Steadily. "I haven't thanked you yet."

Her hair tumbled around her face when she looked at the keys in her hands.

"Okay," he said. "I'll just come and get you." He did, scooping her against him. He loved the way her eyes widened, the pupils dilating, her lashes falling heavily. "Thank you," he said, serious. "If you hadn't found me...well, let's say I've got stuff on this Earth I still want to do." Most of which concerned this vibrant, tormenting redhead.

"Don't." She slid out of his arms, brushing her hair out of her eyes. "I should have immediately gone to the cabin and called for help. It would've been faster. You'd have been in less danger if I'd—"

"Whoa." He closed his hands over her beautiful face. "You saved my life. You." He kissed her lips gently. "I still don't know how you managed to get me loose. The last thing I remember was getting my hand stuck. I was trying to push the snowmobile off, and then it slid...ahh, sweetheart, don't do that."

"I was so scared," she managed, her breath hitching.

He folded her close, kissing the tears that leaked from her tightly closed eyes. "Scared or not, you did what needed to be done."

She drew in a shuddering breath, shaking her head, and pulled his right hand down. She spread his fingers to show the bandage. "I nearly cut your hand in two."

"Ten stitches was all," he countered.

Her fingers glanced over the dark bruise on his chest. "Your rib."

"Bruised," he dismissed. "You didn't do it. The snow-mobile did." He caught her hand before she could touch the bandage on his jaw. He'd have a doozy of a scar there, it was true. "Better a scar on my face," he added, "than a slit throat."

Her mouth worked soundlessly and she moved away. He watched her stop by the huge bouquet of flowers that stood on the window ledge. Unease climbed down his throat, and he yanked on the jeans that had been lying on the chair beside the bed.

"You've been right all along," she said, fingering a delicate petal.

"About what?"

"City girls."

It was the last thing he'd expected her to say. He slowly finished buttoning his jeans. "What about 'em?"

"That we have no place on the ranch."

He went still for a moment, then picked up the dark blue denim shirt. *What about a place in the heart of a stick-stupid rancher?*

She sighed quickly and turned away from the flowers. "I...um...applied for a job here with the day care center a few weeks ago. The interview was this morning."

Which explained her dress. She was a vision in it, but he preferred those thermal shirts and snug jeans. And he didn't want to think real hard just now on Jaimie finding a job, even if it was right up her alley. He didn't want to think about anything that would take her away from him.

"What about Maggie?"

Jaimie clung to her dwindling control. But it was so terribly difficult with him watching her, his expression unreadable. She'd thought about it for the past two torturous nights. Reliving those awful moments at the creek. Knowing now that she loved him, more than she'd ever realized she was capable of loving anyone. Knowing, too, that no matter how close she and Matthew had become, she was still a city girl. She folded her hands tightly together.

"She's settled back at the Double-C now," she finally managed to say. The baby should be released any day." She turned back to the flowers. "The hospital offered me the job. They'll hold it open for two weeks, so I can help Maggie until then." She swallowed past the knot in her throat, making herself finish. "Gloria said she'd come up and stay for a few more after…after I leave. She can handle meals and…and everything."

Matthew felt gut kicked. If he'd thought it bad when BethAnn had dumped him all those years ago, it was nothing compared to what he felt now. Then he silently swore long and hard at himself for caring. For being soft enough *to* care. He'd known this would happen. He'd counted on it, for crissakes. He'd done everything for Jaimie but pack her bags. "So you're leaving, then," he stated flatly.

She pushed back her hair, avoiding his gaze. "It was the plan," she said unevenly.

He shoved his arms into his shirt and fastened it. Unable to look at her, he pulled on his socks and boots and headed for the door.

The nurse scurried after them, waving a sheaf of papers, when Matthew stalked out of the hospital. Jaimie trailed unhappily after him. He took the keys from her and held her door, then rounded the truck and climbed in.

They drove back to the Double-C in silence.

Chapter Fifteen

Jaimie was so busy over the next few days that she shouldn't have missed Matthew. Yet miss him she did.

It had been Squire who had told Jaimie not to worry about fixing their morning breakfast. He delivered the news as if it would be a great relief to her, since she was so busy helping Maggie get resettled in her home.

But Jaimie knew better. Now that she'd told Matthew about the day care job, he couldn't wait for her to go. If she *didn't* know better, she would have thought the man was acting…hurt. But that was ridiculous, because Matthew all along had made no secret of the fact that she didn't have a permanent place in his heart. Or on the Double-C.

If he felt anything for her at all, other than the mind-blowing chemistry they shared, it was probably some misguided sense of responsibility. She'd been the one to drag him from the creek, after all. And he cared about her as much as he'd let himself care about any woman.

Still, she couldn't quite shake the sense that her plans

had upset him. And since the man had been unrelentingly
scarce since his release from the hospital, Jaimie despaired
of ever finding out for sure.

So she missed him. And she worried about him. He and
Dan and Joe were working nearly round the clock now, and
two new hands would be starting at the end of the week.
Life at the Double-C would only get more and more hectic
as spring grabbed a good foothold.

Staring at the pile of laundry she was folding on the
kitchen counter of the cottage, Jaimie's vision blurred. Oh,
she would miss this place when she left. She would miss
the sights and the sounds and even the smells. She would
miss Maggie and her new little niece. She would miss
Sandy traipsing at her heels everywhere she went, and she
would miss D.C. and the kittens when they came.

But most of all she would miss Matthew. Surviving without living at the Double-C was possible, she knew. But
surviving without seeing Matthew…without being in his
arms…well she wasn't sure how she would do it.

She heard the crunch of tires on the gravel outside the
cottage and folded the last towel, leaving the stack on the
kitchen counter as she went to the door. She threw it wide,
then shivered in the brisk air as she watched Joe circle his
truck and open the door for Maggie.

No matter how much she hurt over leaving Matthew, at
least she could go knowing that Joe and Maggie appeared
to be doing better. Joe was around more, at least. Her
brother helped Maggie out of the truck, then pulled a bag
out of the back while Maggie unfastened the tiny blanket-
wrapped bundle from the car seat.

Maggie's eyes sparkled as she slowly walked up to the
cottage, Joe following her. Jaimie moved out of their way
as they came inside.

Joe took the bag into the newly finished nursery, and
Maggie handed the baby to Jaimie while she removed her
coat and gloves.

Jaimie's finger grazed the downy cheek of her niece. Despite her early arrival, J.D. was perfect. Jaimie had fallen in love with her the very first moment she'd seen her niece through the windows of the hospital nursery. Her little fists and legs had been pumping while she wailed a mighty wail until a nurse collected her and took her to her mama to be fed.

And despite all of Jaimie's own fears and reservations of having a baby after having witnessed all that Maggie went through, she'd known at that moment, that very moment when J.D. wrapped her tiny little starfish hand around Jaimie's little finger, that every single moment of worry and misery and sickness would be worth it, to have a wonderful miracle such as this placed in your safekeeping.

"I've got lunch ready," Jaimie said now, clamping down on the wave of weepiness that threatened to overwhelm her. "I just need to heat up the soup for a few minutes."

Maggie sat down on the couch. She held up her arms for her daughter, and Jaimie handed J.D. to her. Jaimie prepared a tray for Maggie so her sister-in-law could remain on the more comfortable couch and set a place for herself and Joe at the table. Her brother sat down long enough to wolf down the meal, then he crammed his hat on his head and headed out.

By the time Jaimie starting cleaning up after lunch, J.D. was fussing and squirming in her pale yellow blanket. Maggie had just started nursing when someone knocked at the door.

Surprised, Jaimie went to answer it. Emily stood there, her dark hair blowing in the breeze. "Hope you don't mind," she greeted. "But I couldn't wait a second longer to see the baby, again."

Maggie smiled from the couch and invited Emily in. "Afraid you'll have to wait a few minutes to hold her, though," she said. "I think my daughter here has one ferocious appetite."

Emily unwound her bright red knit wrap and laid it over the back of a chair. She leaned back in her chair and rubbed her hands across the swell of her pregnancy. "I can't wait. I mean it. I cannot wait."

Standing by the table, Jaimie looked at the two women. Emily, thoroughly, happily pregnant. Maggie, nursing her newborn daughter.

She swallowed the knot of longing in her throat and finished loading the dishwasher and wiping down the counters. She put away the clean towels and started another load in the machine that had been operating perfectly since Daniel had worked on it. When she joined the other women, Maggie had finished feeding J.D., and Emily held her on what little lap she still possessed.

"I cannot get over how beautiful she is," Emily breathed. She and Maggie shared a smile, then Emily glanced over at Jaimie. "Doesn't it make you want one of your very own, too?"

Jaimie went still. Her smile stayed, but it took an effort. "As often as I've seen the two of you green with morning sickness, I'll have to take it under consideration. For a long while," she managed lightly.

The other two laughed, as she'd expected, then began discussing diaper choices and the absurdity of newborn clothing sizes. Jaimie cared for both women. She loved Maggie like a sister. But she felt like she was stifling in this room. She certainly couldn't tell these two women that she felt like she was suffocating with envy.

She pulled open the door. "I need to take care of some things at the big house," she explained, cringing inside at the huskiness in her voice. "I'll see you later."

Before they could comment, she'd closed the door behind her and hurried along the gravel road. She paused along the way, watching the cattle several hundred yards out. There were dozens of calves now. But as she watched, she felt certain that she recognized that little one that Matthew had saved.

Bittersweet longing settled inside her soul.

Then, as if she'd conjured him out of her thoughts, she turned to find Matthew watching her from the yawning entrance of the horse barn.

Her breath hitched in her throat. She couldn't tear her eyes from him no matter how much she tried. Finally, he settled his hat and started for her. Nerves twisted inside her chest. My God, how she loved this man. This man who was so good and kind and honest...who would love a woman until the earth stopped spinning once he finally decided to give his heart. If only it could be to her. If she could change her "city" roots, she would. If she could be more sensible—tougher—whatever it was that Matthew considered necessary to survive the ranching life. If she could, she would.

But she was still only Jaimie Greene. A city girl whose smart mouth usually landed her in trouble.

His boots crunched across the gravel and he stopped several feet away, propping his hands on his hips. His arctic gaze pinned her in place. Not that she could move, anyway, considering the way her feet seemed to have taken root. Then he shrugged out of the down vest he wore and tossed it at her.

She caught it automatically.

"I don't need you getting sick again," he said curtly. Then he wheeled around and headed back to the barn.

When he was out of sight, she pressed her face against the slick vest. It smelled of him. She pulled it on, hugging the softness to her, not because she was cold, but because she fancied that it still held the warmth of his body.

Her boots carried her to the big house, and she took out the mop to clean the mudroom floor. Not until Daniel came inside more than two hours later and asked if she was cold did she take off Matthew's vest and hang it on the peg inside his office.

Matthew barely touched his dinner that night, and Squire demanded to know what was eating at him. He just stared at his father. "Nothing," he snapped.

Squire snorted. "Then how come that lemon meringue pie is sitting there without a single bite outta it?"

"Back off, Squire. If you want the pie, then eat it yourself."

Unfazed, Squire reached for a second piece. "Think I'll do just that. No point in staring at something you want and not reaching for it when it's right in front of your face."

Matthew dragged his attention in place. "What are you going on about?"

Squire's fork sank through the golden-tinted meringue. He shrugged, then lifted the bite. "Nothing."

His father's eyes met his, but Matthew didn't buy the unconcerned expression for a second. "Spit it out," he finally said. "You've been aching to say something for the past several days. So…say it."

"I don't need to say nothing that you don't already know," Squire said.

Matthew shoved back his untouched plate, impatient. "I don't need this from you right now."

"Well, son, what do you need?"

I need to sleep without dreaming about green eyes and auburn hair trailing over my chest. I need to sleep without seeing my mother bleeding to death before my eyes. "Nothing. Not one damn thing." His chair screeched as he scooted back and stomped from the kitchen.

He unhooked a coat—not his favorite sheepskin one, for it had been ruined beyond repair from his dunking in the creek—and slammed out into the cold, clear night.

He had no destination in mind. He just needed air. And peace from Squire's unsubtle jabs. Shoving his fingers in his front pockets, he strode through the night. Then abruptly stopped, when he realized his steps were carrying him to Maggie and Joe's place. The drapes weren't drawn across the big picture window at the front of the cottage, and he could see easily into the lamp-lit interior. Could see Maggie sitting on the couch, rocking little J.D.

Then Jaimie walked past the window, her hair flowing in luxurious abandon. She paused for a moment and stared straight out the window. He knew she couldn't see him. Not with the way the interior light would be reflecting in the window. It was too dark outside. He stood in complete shadow. She couldn't see him standing out there, watching.

Then she turned and disappeared from his view, and Matthew let out a long breath that he hadn't even realized he'd been holding. Stifling an oath, he turned back in the other direction, walking past the big house. Until the gravel road ended and his boots hit the crunchy, thin layer of snow covering the field. He headed for the stand of trees on the moonlit horizon. But he didn't stop to admire the glistening surface of the swimming hole as it reflected the white moon. He headed around to the other side, then stood looking down at the headstone of his mother's grave.

He didn't need any sunlight or moonlight to read the inscription below her name. Though it had been thirty years since he'd stood at this spot, he remembered it perfectly well without any aid.

"Beloved Wife. Devoted Mother."

He crouched down and touched the cold, hard marble. The breeze kicked up and whispered through the bare branches of the trees behind him. It danced over him, ruffling through his hair like her fingers had once done, and Matthew shook his head at the whimsical notion.

Well, son, what do you need?

He closed his eyes and tilted his head back. A year ago, six months ago even, he could've easily answered that. He needed his ranch. He needed his family. That was all. That was it.

When had it all begun to change?

Again the breeze washed over him, more cold than anything, and he looked down at the headstone once again.

He knew exactly when it had begun to change, but he'd been too stick stupid and stubborn to acknowledge it.

And folks said his brother Jefferson was the stubborn one in the family.

Matthew shook his head and decided that he'd stood out in the cold air long enough. It was freezing his good sense into an ice cube of nonsense. He pushed to his feet, grimacing at the lingering twinges in his chest.

It would be a few more days, still, before Matthew could put the physical effects of his tangle with the snowmobile behind him. He looked down at the headstone. If it hadn't been for Jaimie, his family would've been putting another stone there beside this one.

He still couldn't figure how she'd managed to get him to the cabin. Jefferson had told him how he'd found her, bundled against him, sharing what body heat she had with him. Daniel had told him how it had taken several men to pull the powerful snowmobile from the creek. Yet Jaimie, somehow, had succeeded in getting him out from beneath it.

And he'd been afraid that the life here would be too tough for her. His redhaired city girl might be all soft and sweetly scented on the outside. But inside she had a will of iron. She was as different from BethAnn as night was from day.

He turned his head into the breeze. He really had been standing out in the cold too long. In his head, he'd imagined the scent of lemon on that breeze.

He turned to go, then stopped. Pushing his fingers into his pockets again, he looked at the inscription on the headstone and said the words that he'd never said before.

"Goodbye, Mama. You and BethAnn take care of each other."

When he walked back to the house, his ribs didn't hurt quite so much. And his step was, perhaps, a little lighter.

Jaimie stood in the mudroom, loading the washing machine, when he returned. He stopped at the familiar scene.

She looked at him when he closed the storm door, then turned her attention back to the washer. She busily fed a long blanket evenly into the basket.

"What are you doing?"

Her shoulder lifted. She reached to replace the soap on the shelf above the machines, and the hem of her black sweater rose a few inches, baring the creamy skin above her jeans. "I wanted to get a head start on some of this stuff." She closed the machine lid. "Before I—"

"Go."

She nodded, brushing her palms across her denim-clad thighs.

He shrugged out of the coat and tossed it onto a peg. "How are Maggie and the baby doing?"

"Fine." Her palm moved again across her thigh, distracting him. "What about your—"

"You're still—"

They both broke off, watching each other. Hectic color came and went in her cheeks.

"You first," he said.

The tip of her tongue dashed over her lower lip. "I was just...I wanted...that is...your rib," she finished, flushing even brighter.

He automatically lifted his hand to his side. "Coming along."

She swallowed, nodding. "Good. That's good." The washing machine chugged into action, and she glanced back at it. "You were saying?"

Ashamed as he was to admit it, Matthew lost his nerve. He just shook his head. "Nothing."

"Oh. Well." She stepped toward him, and every nerve in his body went on alert. But she only reached past him for her purple coat and pulled it on, leaving it unfastened. She reached for the door, then pulled her hand back. She looked up at him. "Matthew, I..."

He had to clear his throat. "Yeah?"

She dashed her bangs out of her eyes. "Thank you," she finally said. "For all you've done." She met his eyes, then glanced away, reaching for the door with finality. "There's a fresh pot of coffee on," she said.

He stopped the progress of the door with his hand. "Don't go."

Jaimie saw him nudge the door closed, cutting off her escape. "I don't— Coffee will keep me awake," she said, hoping that the trembling in her limbs didn't sound in her voice. Knowing that they did.

"I'm not asking you to stay for coffee," he said gruffly.

She went still. "Oh." The washing machine chugged again. They both looked at it. "I'll come back and finish the load later."

He leaned back against the storm door. "Getting kind of late."

She shoved her hands in her coat pockets. "I'll be up. I, um, told Maggie I'd stay to help with J.D., so she could get as much sleep as she could."

"You've been a good friend for her."

"She's more than a friend," Jaimie murmured. "She and Joe are the only family I have."

"And now J.D., too."

She nodded.

"About that. You don't have to leave."

Jaimie's heart thudded unevenly at his low, husky voice. "Once Maggie is up to snuff again, I'll just be in the way over there. The house was barely large enough for us adults to begin with. Now with J.D.—"

"That's not what I meant."

Matthew reached over and worked a thick curl loose from the collar of her jacket. She steeled herself against the need to press herself against him. For his hand to curl around her neck in that way he had of doing when he lifted her head for his kiss. Maybe he knew how he was torturing her. Maybe this was just some cat-and-mouse thing for him. "Well, then, what did you mean?" She took refuge in the tartness of her demand.

He smiled faintly. Brushed his thumb down the satiny curve of her cheek. "This place would be entirely too tame without that sass of yours."

Behind them the washing machine clicked and started spinning noisily.

"I don't want you to leave the ranch." His eyes met hers. "Or me."

Jaimie's head was going as crazily in circles as the blankets inside the washing machine. "What are you saying?"

"Don't you know?"

Her heart leaped, but her brain stomped down on it. Hard. "Maybe you'd better…elaborate," she managed.

"Don't go to Gillette. Don't go anywhere." His hands settled on the shoulders of her coat and under his gentle nudge, it slipped off. "Stay with me," he murmured, sliding his hard, warm palm behind her neck.

Her brain was no match for her heart. It jumped clear up into her throat. "Why?"

"Because I care about you."

He didn't stumble once over the words. Not like before. She moistened her lips. "Do you really mean that?"

The muscle in his jaw ticked. "Yeah."

Her knees turned to mush. "Oh, Matthew."

"Oh, Jaimie," he mimicked gently.

She threw her arms around his neck. He laughed softly. Then, taking her by the hand, he quietly led her through the kitchen. At the base of the stairs he lifted her easily into his arms.

She caught her breath. "Put me down. You're not in any shape—"

He swallowed her words with his lips.

"I'm too big—"

He kissed her again. When he lifted his head, Matthew seriously considered just taking her into his office. It was a lot closer.

"You'll hurt yourself," she said in a rush.

With barely a twinge in his midsection, he headed up the stairs. "Where did you get this idea that you're some amazon," he murmured. "You're tall, sure. But that just means I don't have to break my neck bending down to kiss you. And you're slender as a willow." He paused halfway up the stairs. "Until you get rid of your clothes and show off those sweet curves."

She swallowed. "Really?"

His laugh was abrupt and short-lived as he continued up the stairs. "You must be kidding. My fingers can practically circle your waist. Your breasts overflow my hands, and your hips—"

"Shh!" She buried her face in his neck. "Everybody will hear you."

Matthew reached the landing and turned toward his big bedroom. "Who everybody? Daniel's out checking the stock. It'll take him hours yet. Squire's already turned in."

He turned sideways to enter his bedroom and let Jaimie's feet find the floor. The lamp on his nightstand cast a golden glow over the wide bed. "We could make a heck of a lot of noise before Squire would hear us from his bedroom downstairs."

Heat filled her cheeks. Matthew's big bed loomed large and obvious behind her.

"About your hips." His tone lowered.

Her breathing quickened. Matthew stepped toward her. Then right on past into the attached bathroom. Surprised, she followed, seeing him leaning over to turn on the taps. Water gushed into the oversize tub.

He settled on the edge and pulled her to him, his hands molding her hips. "They're perfect. For me."

Her soft moan could barely be heard above the rush of water. But he heard it all the same. "Now, you've seen me *before* a bath. And I've seen you after yours. This time, let's get our timing better."

Jaimie's head lowered over his. Her lemon-scented hair drifted around them. "Our timing has been just fine," she whispered shakily. "But I'm willing to work on it as long as you are."

"I don't know," he pondered slowly. "It might take a long time." His fingers delved up her back beneath the short, loose sweater. They encountered nothing but satiny skin.

"Whatever it takes." She arched like a contented cat. "I'm your girl."

He reached over to shut off the water, then held her steady while she pulled off her boots and socks. His fingers found the snap of her jeans, and unzipping them, he pulled them from those perfect hips. She kicked them off and stood before him, wearing nothing but her tiny, flirty panties and the cropped sweater.

"Matthew." Jaimie's eyes grew heavy when his thumbs brushed across her nipples, urging them to even tighter peaks. "I love you," she breathed.

The deeply blue rim of color surrounding his pale irises seemed to darken to black. "Ah, Jaimie."

He would never have to return the words, she thought fuzzily. As long as he said her name the way he just had.

She stepped back and pulled off the sweater, then tugged him to his feet and began unbuttoning his shirt. "We wouldn't want the water to get cold."

He shrugged out of the blue plaid flannel and tossed it

to the floor. It landed atop her sweater. "No, we wouldn't," he agreed.

The clothes that they'd left littering the floor got a good soaking from the splashing. And the water did grow cold, but they were too absorbed in one another to care.

It was after midnight when Jaimie, wearing a sweatshirt of Matthew's that hung to her knees and a pair of his jeans rolled up and hitched in with a belt, walked back to Joe and Maggie's house. Matthew walked with her.

She turned to him on the steps. "I think you should pinch me," she said faintly.

He raised his eyebrows, and his teeth flashed in the moonlight. "Getting kinky are you?"

She shoved him. He laughed softly and kissed her lightly. "I'll talk to you in the morning," he said. "Well, *later* this morning." She nodded, and he tugged her near. "I wish you could've stayed with me tonight," he murmured.

She wished the very same thing. "Maggie's counting on me."

"I know." He kissed her again, then set her away. "You'd better go in, Red."

"Yes."

Still, he sneaked in two more kisses before Jaimie went inside.

Matthew stared at the darkened house, shaking his head. Then he laughed. When he returned to his bed, he yanked the pillow to his face and fell asleep with her scent filling his head.

Chapter Sixteen

The kitchen was empty when Jaimie walked over to the big house shortly after six that morning. She'd snatched a few hours' sleep between taking turns with Maggie tending to J.D. But she didn't feel tired at all.

It didn't matter that Squire had told her not to worry about breakfasts anymore. She planned to fix the Clay men the best breakfast in the world. She busily began chopping potatoes for Matthew's favorite hash browns.

They were snapping and sizzling in the frying pan when Dan walked in. She grinned at him, not caring that she probably looked like an escapee from the county sanitarium. "Hope you haven't already eaten," she greeted him.

He shook his head and retrieved a coffee mug. "Smells good. Sure looks like you're cooking enough for an army, though."

"Just you guys." Jaimie turned back to the hash browns. "I know it's a little late. But I still hoped to catch you and Matthew before you went out."

Dan poured his coffee. "Well, I'm here," he said. "But Matthew headed out this morning already. You missed him by about thirty minutes. Said to tell you he'd see you as soon as he got back."

"But I saw Jasper grazing..."

"He drove down to Cheyenne," Dan said. His eyes squinted above the steam from the coffee. "You know that prime bull that Matt's had his eye on for the past year? The owner called last night. Told Matt if he wanted to buy him, to get his tail down there today."

"But he never said anything about leaving."

He shrugged. "He didn't get the message until this morning."

She knew how much Matthew wanted that bull. Disappointment still gripped her. "Oh. Well, I hope you and Squire are hungry," she said, turning to the potatoes before they could scorch.

"Squire's gone, too. He left right after Matt. But I'm hungry," he grinned. "Matt'll be back tomorrow morning, probably. Evening at the latest, depending on what kinda hassle he has with the weather and the trailer."

Jaimie would concentrate on that. It wasn't as if she didn't have plenty to do in his absence. She had to call the hospital day care director, for one thing. And caring for J.D. was enough to keep both Maggie and Jaimie busy.

Matthew would be back soon. And he didn't want her to leave. She hugged the knowledge to herself as she finished cooking up breakfast and served Daniel. While he ate, she dashed up to Matthew's bathroom and cleaned it up. Then she changed his sheets and carried wet towels and bundled sheets down to the laundry room.

She pulled out the blankets that she'd put into the dryer before Matthew had walked her back to the cottage last night, and folded them, then started another load.

Even the never-ending laundry couldn't quell the bubble of excitement inside her. In between dashing back and forth to check on Maggie and the baby, Jaimie cleaned the big house from top to bottom. By noon the house gleamed.

She had just added a drop of oil to the squeak in Matthew's office chair when the phone rang. She picked it up. It was Emily looking for Matthew.

"Well, shoot," the other woman muttered when Jaimie told her he was gone. "I need him to give me some check numbers."

"Maybe Dan—"

"No. Don't disturb him," Emily said. "He and Jefferson had plans this afternoon. Listen, would you do me a huge favor?"

Jaimie set aside the bottle of lubricant. "Sure."

Emily walked Jaimie through the production of booting up Matthew's computer and providing the information that Emily needed. "Okay," Emily finally said. "I told the general manager at Wayland's that I'd get this stuff to him this afternoon. Maybe we can find out where the mix-up is with those invoices of Matt's. Thanks a lot, Jaimie."

"Sure."

The two women visited a few moments longer, then Jaimie hung up. She finished with the chair and went to the kitchen to pull a casserole from the freezer. Then it was back to Maggie's, and a brief hunt for D.C., who had been absent long enough to arouse Jaimie's curiosity.

She found the cat in the horse barn, curled in a corner of the tack room atop a saddle blanket that had fallen from the shelf. She had to step over Sandy, who slept in the doorway, to get to them.

"Oh, D.C." Jaimie fell to her knees beside the cat. Four...no five...kittens were wrapped protectively within the circle of the cat's body. Jaimie oohed and aahed over the newborns.

Jaimie brought a bowl of food and water for the cat, then, knowing that she could waste hours with the kittens, made herself go back into the house. Donna called, and Jaimie scrawled a message for Matt, taking it into his office to leave on his desk.

How silly of her to have ever been jealous of Matthew's neighbor.

She set the message on the center of his desk, dropping the stapler over the edge to hold it in place. She absently straightened the edges of several sheets that had come out of the fax machine. Her eyes perked up at the heading. Wayland's.

Well, Matthew would be glad to get some action on that, finally. Then she realized that the fax machine was still printing, but needed paper. She found a stack and added it, waiting until it started printing again. Her eyes caught as the final sheet finished printing. Her brother's name leapt out at her.

"Ohmigod." She plunked down onto the chair. She pulled the letter off the stack and read it through. Then she read it again.

Jaimie found Joe in the barn, washing up after delivering a calf. He looked at her curiously as he dried off. "Something wrong?"

She shoved the sheaf of papers at him. "You tell me."

He glanced at it, then paled beneath his tanned face. "Where did you get this?"

"Does it matter?" Jaimie hugged her arms around herself. "There was no mixup with Matthew's invoices at all. You've been behind it all along. What did you do? Place the orders then sell the stuff on the side after Matthew had already paid for it and pocket the money?"

His jaw tightened, and she realized she'd come close to the truth.

Jaimie swallowed. "Why? Why would you do this to them? You're their foreman. They *trusted* you."

Her brother raked back his thick, auburn hair, so much

like her own. They shared the same hair, the same eyes. But this man who stood before her seemed a stranger.

"Look," he said, suddenly cajoling. "Nobody needs to know. I'll pay it back."

"How? You have money like this just lying around?" She felt nauseous. "What on earth did you need money like that for?"

"I'll pay it back," he insisted. "There's a game in Casper—"

"A *game!* This is about *gambling?*" She yanked her fingers through her hair. "I can't believe this."

"Sis, don't overreact."

"Overreact?" She whirled on him. "You *stole* from people who trusted you. My God, when Matthew learns—"

"Come off it, sis. Matthew's a legend in these parts. He knows his way around a poker table."

"Years ago," Jaimie flared. Matthew had told her why he never gambled anymore. Why his card games now were for chips or matches. Or chocolate Kisses. "And he didn't *steal* to do it!"

"You can't tell him," Joe snapped. "Not unless you want to put Maggie and the kid on the streets."

"You're crazy. If anyone is putting your wife and child on the streets, it's you."

He gave her a pained look. "Sis—"

"No!" Jaimie snatched the papers back from him. "How did you think you could keep this from coming out?"

"I told you, I'll pay it back."

"Even if you did, these invoices still exist. You stole from them, Joe. *Stole,*" she repeated, her voice harsh, trembling. She died a silent death inside. If there had been any hope…any hope at all that she could make something good and lasting with Matthew, her brother's actions had dashed them all. With one toss of the dice. One cut of the deck.

Matthew valued the Double-C above everything. He would never forgive anyone who worked against the well-being of his ranch. Look at that man who'd tried rustling cattle. He'd been a schoolmate of Matthew's.

She folded her arms around her, holding herself together desperately, when she feared she'd just start falling into a million pieces if she weren't careful.

Joe was watching her, his eyes calculating. "I'm telling you, sis. It's a high-stakes game. I've played with these guys before. I can beat 'em. I know I can."

"And if you don't?" She shook the papers in his face. "You think you'll be able to solve it by defrauding the Double-C for a few more thousand? A hundred thousand? When does it stop? Maybe you've been finagling more invoices than just Wayland's!"

"I haven't. Besides that money is a drop in the bucket to the wealth the Clays have," Joe said. "They'll never miss it."

She stared at him, more appalled than ever, if that was possible. "So that's supposed to absolve you of your actions? You *stole* from them. You abused their trust in you. I don't care if it's forty thousand dollars or a box of pens. You. Stole."

"I can make it right," he insisted. "You just can't tell Matt. You can't tell any of 'em."

"And if I don't? What will you do?"

"I won't play another game," he swore. "No cards…no ponies. Nothing."

"I don't think you can help yourself."

"I can stop any time I want!"

"Prove it," she challenged. "Find a Gamblers Anonymous group or something. Tell your *wife!*"

"Fine, fine," he said impatiently. "But you can't tell the Clays. I'll get the money together after this game and everything'll be fine."

She stared at him. "You just said you wouldn't play another game."

"I won't," he promised. "Not after this one."

It was like a drug to him, this gambling, she realized. And she knew instinctively that he was addicted to it as surely as if it were some terrible substance he ingested. Otherwise he would have never stooped to such a level. "No more games, Joe. Not one. You've obviously got a problem. With gambling. And it won't stop even if you win and do pay back the money you stole."

"Fine then," he growled. "Tell your precious Matthew. And while you're at it, say goodbye to Maggie and the kid. 'Cause once Matt knows the truth, we'll be out of here on our cans."

"No! Don't you *dare* put this on my shoulders!" She wheeled around and stood in the yawning entrance of the barn.

"All right, so what are you going to do?"

"I don't know," she whispered, a hard sharp pain driving through her soul.

Maggie walked along the gravel road, J.D. cuddled high on her shoulder as she pointed out the sights of the ranch she so loved to her tiny daughter.

Maggie, who had been Jaimie's friend for ten years, who had always supported her whenever, wherever. And Jaimie acknowledged sadly that it was Maggie who'd encouraged her to find her niche in life. Not Joe. He'd been too busy telling her what a fool she was. Foolish to let Tony get away. Foolish to go through jobs like most men went through shirts.

Feeling dead inside, she turned back to her brother. "The gambling stops," she said with such finality that Joe actually paled. "I promise you, Joe, that if you slip even once, I'll turn you over to the sheriff myself."

"Then you're not going to tell him."

"Matthew will find out," Jaimie assured. "It's a matter of time." She curled the fax into a tube, her hands shaking.

"What about…you know…the money?"

How strange that he was the elder sibling, she thought

absently. Crazily. Well, she was crazy from the knowledge that Matthew, in a million lifetimes, would never forgive an abuse of his trust. ''I'll take care of it.''

Joe's eyebrows rose with disbelief. Then he must have seen something in Jaimie's expression that convinced him to remain silent, and he nodded and left the barn. Jaimie watched her brother walk away. Maybe someday she could forgive him for what he'd done to all of them. Maybe someday Matthew would forgive her, too.

''And maybe someday the cow will jump over the moon,'' she whispered.

She walked back to the big house and sat at Matthew's desk in his office for a long while. Then, when the numbness surrounding her heart started to wear thin again, she stood and left. She had a lot to do before Matthew came home.

Matthew whistled tunelessly as he checked the trailer hitch. Satisfied, he climbed up into the truck and turned the big rig toward home.

Toward Jaimie.

He patted the pocket in his shirt, feeling the small, cubical outline of the tiny velvet box.

Marriage.

It boggled the mind. He was going to make Jaimie Greene, queen of the construction paper cutouts, champion of sass, his wife.

His trip to Cheyenne had taken a little longer than he'd anticipated. Not because of any problem purchasing the bull he'd been salivating over for the past year. That had gone off smooth as glass. But he'd searched through half a dozen jewelry stores before he'd found the perfect ring.

So now, it would be nearly dawn before he arrived back at the ranch. The only thing that would've made it more perfect, would've been to know that she would be sleeping in his bed when he got there. But Jaimie couldn't very well help Maggie with the baby when she wasn't even under the same roof with them.

His powerful headlights cut a wide swath through the night on the empty highway, and he tapped out a rhythm on the steering wheel as he drove on through the night.

It was dawn when his tires finally rattled across the cattle guard of his ranch. He unloaded the cantankerous bull and unhitched the trailer. Pausing on the back steps of the big house, he looked down the road toward the foreman's place.

He ran his palm over his bristly jaw. He would see Jaimie soon enough. He oughta clean himself up a bit before he set about proposing to her.

He didn't know exactly why he didn't head right on up to his bedroom and the shower. But he turned to his office first. He flipped on the lamp and sat down at the desk, absently noticing that the chair no longer squeaked.

Then he saw the long white envelope neatly situated on the center of his desk, held down by the edge of his stapler, his name printed on it. He recognized Jaimie's writing.

Her usual style would have been to decorate the envelope with hearts or flowers. Easter bunnies, even. But only his name was marked on the front of the envelope. He picked it up and, leaning back in his now-quiet chair, slowly peeled it open.

He drew out the letter, and several copies came with it. He glanced at them, his frown growing, when he recognized the items as a fax from Wayland's. He turned his attention to the letter.

Matthew, as you will see from the enclosed, your difficulties with Wayland's wasn't a clerical mix-up. If only it had been. I pray that you'll be lenient with Joe, if only for Maggie's and J.D.'s sake. They are innocent victims in this whole, awful mess. As for the money that is due you, I hope that you'll accept the enclosed

check as partial retribution for the wrong that has been
done to you and the Double-C.

Matthew tossed the fax copies onto the desk. A personal
check fell out. Pink and blue kittens made up the back-
ground on the check. His jaw locked, and he picked it up.
He swore low and harsh when he saw the amount.

Crumpling it tightly in his fist, he finished reading the
letter.

Somehow, I will get you the balance. It will take me
a while. I realize that Joe's dishonesty may not have
been limited to Wayland's, though he claims it was.
What's happened is unforgivable, I understand that. I
only hope, in time, that you'll find some understanding
in your heart and remember me without hatred.

The ink was smudged there. As if water had dropped on
the paper.

Or tears.

He shifted in the chair and made himself finish reading.
There wasn't much left:

You are the most kind and decent man I've ever
known. I will never regret having known you.

He sucked in a harsh breath. She'd signed it, simply,
"Jaimie."

His hands shook as he roughly spread the fax across his
desk. "Bloody hell."

Her letter in hand, he shoved back from his desk. The
chair slammed into the wall behind him and tipped onto its
side, but his steps didn't falter. In minutes he was pounding
on the door to Joe's place.

Maggie opened it, her tired, red-rimmed eyes wide.
"Matthew."

"Where is she?"

"I...Jaimie? I don't know. What's wrong?"

Matthew pushed into the house, then felt like an ogre at the way Maggie scurried out of his way. Jaimie was right. Maggie was an innocent victim in all this. He dragged his careening emotions in with an iron grip. He lifted his hand, gently. "It's all right. I just need to know where she's gone. How long ago she left."

Maggie pushed her hand through her hair, reminding him strongly of Jaimie. "I don't know. She was here earlier. But when I woke up with J.D. this morning, she was gone." Maggie's eyes met his. "I thought she'd gone over to be with you," she said softly.

"You've been crying," Matthew said abruptly.

She flushed. "I—"

"If it's not about Jaimie, then why?"

She hesitated. Tightened the belt of her robe. "Joe. He, um, took off early this morning. I don't know where he is." Her throat worked. "Some of his clothes are missing."

I'll bet. Jaimie takes care of Joe's mess and he gets while the going's good. Matthew kept the thought to himself. If he'd opened his eyes to his foreman's behavior a long time ago, perhaps none of this would now be happening. He tugged Maggie over to the couch. "Sit down," he said as gently as he could. "Is J.D. sleeping?"

She nodded. Her slender fingers worked the edge of her thick terry robe. "Why are you looking for Jaimie?"

If Joe really had split, then who would tell Maggie the truth? He'd left his sister to clean up the mess he'd created with Wayland's. Had he deserted his wife and newborn daughter as well? He stifled an oath and sat down beside Maggie. For the life of him, he didn't know what to say to her.

A soft snuffle heralded J.D.'s morning awakening. Maggie hopped up and went into the second bedroom. The bedroom that Jaimie had used. When she returned, she held the baby cradled to her shoulder. "Matthew," she said, her voice small but steady. "All of Jaimie's things are gone."

This time he didn't stifle his oath. "I'm sorry," he muttered when he shoved to his feet.

She just stared at him. "I don't understand any of this. Why would they leave? I mean, Joe——" She broke off, clearing her throat. "Jaimie said…well I thought you two…"

"I thought so, too," he muttered. The jeweler's box weighed like a stone in his shirt pocket.

"Do you think they're together?" she finally ventured.

"No." Matthew knew it with every bone in his body. J.D. made a soft sound, and Maggie kissed the top of the baby's head. Just as he knew with every bone in his body that he would never turn Maggie and her child away from the Double-C.

Joe, now, was another matter entirely. And something he would handle eventually.

"I have to find Jaimie," he muttered.

Maggie moistened her lips. She sat down in the side chair, situating J.D. in her lap. "That day care job," she murmured. "She doesn't start for at least a week, but maybe she's gone there."

He'd already thought of that. "Does she have any savings?" He knew the answer before Maggie shook her head. "How did she get to Gillette?" He'd noticed all the ranch vehicles when he'd driven up with the trailer. All but his brother's pickup had been parked in their usual places. And where on earth would she come up with enough money to cover a fifteen-thousand-dollar check?

He didn't realize he'd spoken that last thought aloud until Maggie gasped.

"Matthew," she said. "I think you'd better tell me just exactly what's going on. There is no point trying to protect me," she added when he hesitated. "My husband has disappeared. There's not much worse that you can add to that.''

''I'm not so sure about that,'' he said, sitting down again on the couch. He handed her the letter that was crumpled from his tight fist. ''Maybe we oughta just start with that.''

Slowly she took the sheet from him. Her shoulders slumped as she read.

He waited until later that morning before leaving Maggie alone. Not that he didn't think she could handle the bomb that had been dropped in her lap. But he'd been nervous about the color that never returned to her pale cheeks. She was fresh from the hospital, with a newborn daughter to look after. If that meant that Matthew waited a few hours until Emily got free and came over to sit with Maggie, then so be it.

He met his sister-in-law outside of Maggie's house, giving her the sketchiest details that his nerves could provide. She told him that she would stay as long as necessary and had kissed his cheek, thankfully never asking about the Cracker Jack box that he held tightly in his fist.

He'd been plagued all morning with the nightmarish thought of Jaimie hitchhiking her way back to the city. Chances were the only vehicles she'd have run into were local ranchers and truckers. But danger still existed.

He'd even gone so far as to call his neighbors, Colbys and some of the other business owners in Weaver. Bennett Ludlow, even. No one had seen Jaimie, or heard anything about a woman looking for a ride to Gillette. Or anywhere in the state, for that matter.

Matthew had tried to raise Daniel on his mobile phone, to no avail. Chances were that his brother was out tending to the stock, doing the work that Joe—blast his hide—and Matt usually shared with Daniel.

Leaving Maggie in Emily's capable hands, he retrieved his keys and headed his Blazer toward Weaver. He had to start somewhere.

* * *

Two days later Matthew wondered if he would ever find her. He'd been hanging around the hospital in Gillette for so long that a security guard had cornered him.

He knew that Jaimie hadn't called the day care director to say she wouldn't be taking the job. He could have gone back to the Double-C and started untangling the complications Joe had created and bided his time until Jaimie was due to begin working at her new job. But that was assuming that she planned to show up there next week.

Frankly, he couldn't wait that long.

Another day and a half passed before he found her. It was dumb blind luck that he spotted her at all. He'd pulled in at a service station near the hospital to gas up and go back home. He wasn't giving up. Just regrounding himself.

He'd been standing at the gas pump, one arm propped against the side of his truck when he saw a flash of auburn hair reflected in the side window.

He jerked around, splashed gas on the ground and cursed. He shoved the nozzle back on the pump and skirted the island of pickup trucks and one jazzy red sportscar. Standing in the middle of the big parking lot, he looked around, but saw no sight of her.

The woman was driving him crazy. He needed some sleep. He needed to be back at the Double-C, pulling his own weight rather than dumping it all off on Dan and the two new hands. So what was he doing?

Chasing after a crazy female, that's what.

There she was. Crossing the street toward the hospital.

Oblivious of his truck still sitting at the gas pump, Matthew grabbed something from the seat then strode after her, crossing against the traffic and weaving in and out of the cars. Ahead of him she disappeared into the hospital.

An impatient driver tooted his horn at Matthew, but he didn't care. He jogged the rest of the way, stopping just inside the hospital entrance. He saw the tail end of her braid as she entered an elevator. He watched the display impatiently, waiting to see what floor it stopped at. Then he slammed through the door to the stairwell.

Jaimie summoned a smile to her face before pushing through the doors of the day care facility. She needed to start this job earlier than scheduled, or she wasn't going to have a roof over her head by the end of the week. The director had originally wanted her earlier, so she could only hope that it would still be the case.

She didn't feel much like smiling. But the situation seemed to call for it. Besides, she didn't want to scare the kids, who she would hopefully soon be watching, with the grim face she knew she'd been carrying since the moment she'd read that fax in Matthew's office.

Lillian Flowers, the director, looked up from the book she was reading to the circle of preschoolers lying quietly on their mats, when Jaimie's footsteps sounded in the spacious room. Surprise lifted her eyebrows, though she didn't miss a beat of the story. Jaimie managed another smile. Lillian looked toward the small-scale chairs surrounding the trio of tables, and Jaimie nodded, quietly pulling out a chair to sit. She arranged the hem of her dress around her sharply bent knees and listened along with the children while Lillian finished reading.

Then the director was stepping around the resting children and joining Jaimie at the table. "I didn't think we'd see you for another week," she said softly.

"Well, I—"

"I'm glad you did though. There's been a gentleman here for the past several days asking for you."

Jaimie sat up straighter. "What? Who?" Her first thought was Joe. Surely he hadn't gotten into more trouble.

Lillian looked past her shoulder. "Well, him, actually."

Jaimie whirled around and her heart climbed into her throat. "Matthew."

Chapter Seventeen

He stood in the doorway, leaning one shoulder against the jamb, his arms crossed. Despite the hat pulled low over his brow, or perhaps because of it, he looked hard and forbidding.

What was he doing there?

Lillian rose behind her and stepped over to Matthew. "Perhaps my office," she suggested in a tone low enough not to disturb the children. She lifted her arm, indicating the small cubicle immediately to the right of the doorway. He nodded, speared Jaimie with an unreadable look and went into the office.

Swallowing the boulder-sized lump in her throat, Jaimie rose, nervously brushing her damp palms down the sides of her dress and followed. Her unease mounted when he firmly closed the door behind them.

The office was barely large enough for the desk and filing cabinet it contained. With him looming large in front of the only exit, Jaimie felt positively hemmed in.

"You forgot this," he said without expression.

Jaimie's stomach clenched when he set a Cracker Jack box on the desk. She hadn't forgotten it at the Double-C. She'd left it behind, deliberately, because she knew that she'd never be able to put Matthew behind her if she was forever looking at that box. She knotted her fingers together to keep from snatching it to her. "I don't understand."

"That makes two of us."

"You saw the fax."

His hat dipped.

"It was pretty clear," Jaimie managed. ━━━

Again he gave that single nod.

The muscles in her stomach were so tight, she felt like doubling over. This was the man who could put her brother in jail. Deservedly so. Yet the only thing she could think about was how wonderful he looked, even with his sharp jaw shadowed with more than a few days' whiskers and the unsmiling set of his lips. His silence tormented her. "What do you plan to do?"

"That depends on you."

She looked out the window overlooking the Center. The dozen children who lay sweetly, silently, on their mats. "What more can I do, Matthew? I told you in my letter that I'd get you the rest of the money. Somehow. I know it doesn't excuse what he did." Her hands lifted helplessly. "I guess you being here means you aren't satisfied with that." He remained silent. "What will happen to Joe now?"

He shifted. Pushed his fingertips into his front pockets. "He's gone."

"You pressed charges, then."

"No. He was gone before I got back."

She absorbed that. Matthew hadn't gone to the sheriff. "And of course they didn't say where."

"I didn't say *they*. Maggie and the baby are still at the ranch. I haven't heard a word from Joe."

Jaimie's head dropped back and she stared up at the ceiling. She couldn't even pretend to be surprised. "He ran out on them. On top of everything else, how could he do that?" She didn't expect an answer, and she didn't get one. She brushed her hair back. "Well, now what?"

"Like I said, Red. That depends on you."

Pain washed over her. *Red.* "I swear to you, Matthew, I had no idea what he was doing. If you don't believe anything else, believe that." He lifted his hat, and his eyes met hers. Regret flooded through her. Regret that she hadn't known about Joe's activities earlier. That she hadn't been able to prevent any of it from occurring. That she hadn't been able to help Maggie after all.

Regret, most of all, for what she could never have with Matthew. "I'm so sorry."

"You should be."

The knot in her throat tightened. She hugged her arms to her midriff. "I left as much money as I could." She'd had to borrow one of Matthew's trucks to make the rushed trip to Casper to sell the bracelet. And she'd been lucky enough to hitch a ride to Gillette with a trucker bound for Canada. She'd thought she'd kept enough cash from the sale to get herself started over again in Gillette. There wouldn't be any way to continue paying Matthew back if she didn't have a roof over her head. Unfortunately she hadn't counted on the cost of a room in town while waiting for her new job to begin, and she was woefully short on funds.

Beneath his dark blue denim shirt, his big shoulders moved impatiently. "I don't care about the money."

"What do you want me to do?" Her voice rose. "I've apologized as much as I know how to. You said Joe's gone. I don't—" She paled. "You think he's with me, don't you?"

"Jaimie—"

"That's why you tracked me down."

"Jaimie—"

"He wouldn't have come with me, Matthew. He—"

"Woman, would you please be quiet for one minute?" Her mouth parted soundlessly. His jaw cocked. "You didn't know what your brother was doing."

"No."

"You weren't responsible for him leaving his wife and baby."

"I threatened to call the sheriff," Jaimie said hoarsely. "On my own brother. You don't think that had anything to do with him skipping out on them? He'd been gambling. He has a problem—"

"I know."

"He…what?"

"I know about the gambling," Matthew admitted grimly. "I have since the day Maggie went to the hospital."

"But—"

"I know because when we located him in Casper, he was losing his shirt in a poker game. Well, he's gone now. Personally, I hope he stays gone. He doesn't deserve your loyalty. He doesn't deserve his wife and daughter. Now could you please stop jabbering about him?"

"But you…why are you here, if not to find him?"

"Don't you know?"

Frustrated tears burned at the backs of her eyes. "No!"

He thumbed back his hat and stepped around the side chair separating them. "I did a good job convincing you that you didn't belong at the Double-C."

"You were right."

His lips pursed. "I was wrong." Her breathing ground to a halt when his warm hand brushed across her cheek. "I asked you to stay."

"That was before." She swallowed. "You have to know why I left."

His eyes narrowed. He took a step closer. "Do you love me?"

His husky voice wrapped around her senses. "Matthew."

"Do you? You said you did. Or have you changed your mind?"

"No." She hauled in a shaky breath. "I think I've always loved you. Right from the first," she admitted. "You were racing after those calves that got out…"

"…when you plowed into the fence…"

"…and you were so angry. Then you managed to get them penned in and you stopped yelling. You looked at me, with sweat and dirt streaking your shirt and your face. And you smiled. Just for a second. Just long enough for me to know that you weren't going to escort me to the county line." She swallowed back the lump of tears thickening her voice. Her eyes touched on the still-angry-looking wound on his jaw. "I just didn't admit it to myself until your accident with the snowmobile."

"But you still left," Matthew said softly.

"You know why." Her jaw ached with the strain of holding it still. "The Double-C is your life. Joe hurt that."

"Yeah, he did," Matthew said steadily. "But you hurt me a darned sight more."

A burning tear leaked out. "I'm sorry."

"So I guess now you'll have to make it up to me."

She dashed her hand across her nose. "What do you think I've been trying to do? I can't just pull that kind of money out of the air!"

"Would you forget about the damned money? I'm not talking about the money! I'm talking about *us!*"

"There is no 'us.' Joe…the Double-C—"

"The Double-C means nothing unless you're there to share it with me." He stared at her, his eyes burning over her. "*That* is what you've done to me. And what do I find when I come back after hunting all over Cheyenne for the perfect ring to match your eyes? Nothing! Because you've disappeared on me, leaving me nothing but that bloody check and a note telling me you'll never regret *knowing* me!"

"But Joe—"

"Forget Joe! His mistakes are gonna catch up with him soon enough. I'll tell you this, though. If *he* is what keeps you from me, then I will track him to the ends of the earth and make him regret the day he set foot on Double-C land. Don't you get it by now? I love you. Not your brother. Not the money. *You!*"

Stunned into silence, Jaimie stared at him as his voice rose until he was shouting. Her heart felt like he'd pried it open and jumped inside with both of his size-twelve boots. *He'd come after her.*

"Come home, Jaimie." His voice was rough. "Come home and cut out your paper Christmas trees and hearts and shamrocks. Spoil my dog and make pets out of the stock. Tell Miz Flowers out there that you've changed your mind about this job and come home."

Jaimie bit her lip, uncaring that she couldn't keep the tears from coming. She didn't even care that a half dozen small, tousled heads were peering into the window. All she cared was that Matthew had come for her. He could talk until the cows came home, but the very fact that he'd come for her spoke to her heart more deeply than any words.

Matthew didn't care that he had no pride left. Pride wouldn't keep him warm on a cold winter night. It wouldn't laugh with him and argue with him. It wouldn't wear snug thermal shirts or smell of lemon, or make angels in the snow. "Come home with me, Jaimie. Wear my ring and have my children. You can even scratch up my trucks if you have to. Just come home. And give me all the rest of your nights."

"Oh, Matthew." Her lips trembled and she closed her hand around the Cracker Jack box to hold it to her heart.

He cocked his head to one side and cleared his throat. "You never did open the box."

No. She'd only treasured it more than she treasured her bracelet.

"Mebbe you oughta," he suggested.

She looked at him. Noticed again the tense set of his lips. Dashing a finger across her damp cheek, she pulled open the box. She stared inside at the scotch-taped paper packet that contained the "prize." Her heart thundered and she lifted the little square out from its bed of caramel popcorn with fingers that shook. As soon as she touched it, the paper parted and she caught her breath when it revealed a ring.

Not a dime store ring. Not a Cracker Jack prize.

She looked up at him. "Oh, Matthew," seemed to be all she could say.

His heart beat like a runaway train. He took the ring from her and slid it in place on her slender, trembling finger. "Is that a yes?"

The beautiful smile that lit her face would fill his dreams for the next hundred years.

At least.

"Yes." She laughed and wound her arms around his neck. "Oh yes, Matthew. Let's go home."

Epilogue

Jaimie looked at her reflection in the long cheval mirror. Voices and laughter drifted on the April breeze that flitted into the room, ruffling the curtains at the window. "You sure this isn't too...too, you know?" She looked over her shoulder at Emily and Maggie who were both sitting on the foot of the bed in the room that had been Emily's when she was growing up.

Emily shook her head, sending a wry glance toward Maggie. "It's perfect," she assured.

Jaimie drew her lip between her teeth and turned back to her reflection. The ivory lace clung to her shoulders and arms, skimmed demurely along her slender hips and fell in a swirl around her ankles.

"I think the boots have to go, though," Maggie finally said.

Jaimie looked at the cowboy boots covering her feet and calves. "Really? I thought they provided a real fashion statement.'' She grinned and walked over to Maggie. ''Here. Undo me.''

Maggie deftly opened the row of buttons down the back and Jaimie stepped out of the dress, carefully hanging it on the padded hanger. Then she pulled on the denim dress she'd been wearing earlier. The long hem fell to her ankles and looked entirely suitable with her boots. She rather liked the way the white eyelet underskirt ruffled against the soft gray suede boots that Matthew had given her just the other day.

She ran her fingers through her hair. Finally, she was satisfied with her appearance, and she looked at the other women. ''We ready?''

Emily nodded, then groaned when she pushed herself to her feet. ''This baby better come soon,'' she complained lightly. ''Every time I move I have to head toward the bathroom. I'll be lucky if I can make it all the way through your wedding tomorrow.''

Jaimie couldn't help but notice the pensive smile on Maggie's face as the trio trooped out of the bedroom and headed for the stairs. ''You okay?''

Maggie nodded, her expression clearing. ''I'm fine. We'd better get down there, or Matthew's liable to come looking for you. Whenever he does that, you guys disappear for *hours.*''

Jaimie flushed, but grinned. ''I'll be glad when all this hoo-ha is over with. I can't believe Squire insisted on having most of the state's population come for this barbecue. We'll have a gazillion people tromping all over the place during the wedding tomorrow. Matthew and I thought we'd just have our friends and family.''

Emily stopped at the foot of the stairs, looking back at Jaimie. ''Honey, if Matthew had been determined to stop Squire, he would have. He's enjoying showing you off, just as much as Squire is. Get used to it. Once a Clay decides to make you his, he has to let the whole world know it.''

The three trooped through the bustling living room and out onto the front porch. A huge barbecue had been set up across the circular gravel drive on the spring green grass. Jaimie inhaled the delectable scent of the barbecue and spied Matthew and Jefferson standing by Squire. All three men were squabbling over the best method of cooking the mountain of steak. Sandy and D.C. and her brood of kittens sat only a few feet away, obviously interested in the fate of the meat.

Donna Blanchard came up, and she and Maggie headed for the playpen where J.D. slept beneath the shade of the porch. Emily headed for one of the lawn chairs scattered around, and Jaimie stood on the step, propping her shoulder against a pillar as she eyed the men. How she loved them.

Her smile grew when a strikingly handsome man jogged toward the group huddled around the huge barbecue. Blond and sinfully good-looking, he was a towering hulk of a man. Tristan. He'd come home to see his brother finally get hitched. Tristan, who was as playful as a pup and who had even managed to coax a smile or two out of Maggie.

Then Sawyer joined the group, and Jaimie heard Emily's snicker. The two women exchanged a look. In minutes, Squire was swearing, testy as an old bear. The only Clay missing from the delightful scene was Daniel. He'd announced, much to Matthew's shock, that he'd taken a job with an outfit in Montana, and he'd packed up his gear and headed out several days ago. Matthew had already hired on two more hands to replace the load that Daniel had carried.

She'd asked Matthew last night if Daniel's absence bothered him. Matthew had shrugged, only saying that Daniel needed time away for now. And he would come home when he was ready. Personally Jaimie hoped that would be sooner rather than later.

The argument over by the barbecue grew louder and louder, and Jaimie crossed over to the men. She stepped between them and whisked the barbecue tongs out of Squire's hand, turning to study the sizzling meat.

"Guys, guys," she clucked, turning a steak that was rapidly charring. "Don't you know how to keep the meat from burning? I had this job once. The Chuck House. Now, we specialized in charbroiling steaks. And let me tell you—"

Matthew scooped her off her feet just as Tristan grabbed the tongs. "Listen, Red," Matthew said in her ear. "Barbecuing is a man's job." Safely several feet from the barbecue, he set her on the ground.

"*Man's* job?" Jaimie's tart response died a hasty death under Matthew's lips.

Jefferson and the rest cackled as they turned back to their bickering. "They're at it again," he said, dismissing the couple.

"As usual," Squire added. "Can't turn a corner these days without running into the two of 'em making moon eyes at each other."

Tristan elbowed Jefferson. "You'd be moon eyeing Emily if she weren't about to pop with that baby."

Jefferson shoved Tristan out of the way and snatched the barbecue tongs. "Shut up, kid."

Matthew and Jaimie grinned and he led her away from the crowd of people. Jaimie had been introduced to them all, but she couldn't remember most of their names. "What a circus," she whispered.

He drew her behind a tree. "It'll be over soon."

Jaimie smiled happily. "Tomorrow afternoon, we'll say our piece, sign the license, cut the wedding cake that Gloria arranged, and hotfoot it out of here for two whole weeks. We'll be lazing on the beach in Jamaica, and these guys can party on without us."

He snorted. "Can't believe I let you talk me into taking you to Jamaica."

"You just want to see what I look like wearing that teenie weenie little polka-dot bikini and nothing else."

"Well there's something else you're gonna wear."

"Yeah. Your wedding ring." She kissed his jaw. "I can't wait." She'd been wearing the beautiful emerald and diamond ring since she'd found it in the Cracker Jack box that he'd doctored. It was a beautiful ring. But the one he would place on her finger tomorrow was the one that really mattered.

"There's something else you'll be wearing," he said, and pulled a velvet-wrapped bundle from his pocket. "Here."

Surprised, Jaimie took the bundle. "What is it?"

"Open it and see."

"You're spoiling me," she murmured, eyeing him.

"Indulge me."

Her breath caught at the glimmer in his eyes. If she lived to be three hundred, she'd get butterflies in her stomach at that particular glint.

"Open it," he prompted with a faint smile. The man knew *exactly* what effect he had on her.

She dragged her eyes from his and opened the velvet. "Oh, Matthew." A familiar strand of gold and diamonds twinkled in the sunlight, stealing her breath. "But, how did you—I never told you where I sold it." She blinked against the tears that welled in her eyes. "And the cost..."

"I told you before, the money wasn't important."

"But—"

"You matter more to me than anything. So I found the bracelet and bought it back. I want you to pass that bracelet on to our own daughter someday."

"Oh, Matthew."

"Oh, Jaimie," he returned softly. He took the bracelet and fastened it around her wrist. "There. That's better."

They were kissing again when Squire hollered for them. Matthew and Jaimie shared a soft smile.

"Tomorrow," he murmured, "we'll put this folderol behind us and get on with our life."

The ceremony scheduled for tomorrow would be held

right on the beautiful patch of grass in front of the house that had become her home. She would wear the delicate lace dress that had belonged to Matthew's mother. It had taken careful alteration to retain the style, yet adjust it to Jaimie's height.

If her prayers were answered any more fully, it would be to tell him very soon that the children he'd asked for might already be on the way.

"Tomorrow," she agreed, her heart in her eyes.

Matthew touched her cheek intently. A sharp peal of laughter startled them both, and he muttered a heartfelt oath, moving his hand instead to her shoulder. There were too many people around. "Tomorrow," he repeated meaningfully.

Jaimie's bones softened at his look. Not "The Look." This one was far better. And the only one she received from him now. She leaned against him and lifted her lips for his kiss.

Squire bellowed again. Matthew heaved a huge breath and dropped a light kiss on her lips. They shared another smile. Then he folded her arm in his and held her close as they strolled back to join their family.

* * * * *

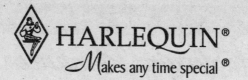
HARLEQUIN®
Makes any time special ®

HARLEQUIN®
AMERICAN *Romance*

Upbeat, All-American Romances

HARLEQUIN®
Duets™

Romantic Comedy

Harlequin®
Historical

Historical, Romantic Adventure

HARLEQUIN®
INTRIGUE

Romantic Suspense

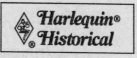
Harlequin Romance®

Capturing the World You Dream Of

HARLEQUIN®
Presents

Seduction and passion guaranteed

HARLEQUIN® *Super* ROMANCE®

Emotional, Exciting, Unexpected

HARLEQUIN®
Temptation.

Sassy, Sexy, Seductive!

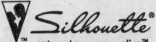

Where love comes alive™